Marry
OR Burn

• ALSO BY VALERIE TRUEBLOOD •

Seven Loves: A Novel

VALERIE TRUEBLOOD

Marry
OR Burn

• stories •

COUNTERPOINT | BERKELEY

The passage about trees read aloud by Diana in "Beloved, You Looked into Space" is from Donald Culross Peattie's *A Natural History of North American Trees*, Vol. 2 (Boston: Houghton Mifflin, 1953).

Library of Congress Cataloging-in-Publication Data

Trueblood, Valerie.
Marry or burn : stories / by Valerie Trueblood.
p. cm.
ISBN-10: 1-58243-598-7
ISBN-13: 978-1-58243-598-5
1. Marriage—Fiction. 2. Man-woman relationships—Fiction. 3. Love-hate relationships—Fiction. 4. Desire—Fiction. 5. Loss (Psychology)—Fiction. 6. Love stories, American. 7. Domestic fiction, American. I. Title.

PS3620.R84M37 2010
813'.6—dc22
2010017803

Cover design by Domini Dragoone
Interior Design by Neuwirth & Associates, Inc.

Printed in the United States of America

COUNTERPOINT
1919 Fifth Street
Berkeley, CA 94710

www.counterpointpress.com
Distributed by Publishers Group West

10 9 8 7 6 5 4 3 2 1

Marriage is the second music, and thereof
we hear what we can bear. . . .

—John Berryman, "Canto Amor"

Contents

Amends

· · ·

WHEN SHE WAS twenty, Francie Madden shot and killed her husband Gary. He had joined the Seattle police force six months before, and she shot him with his service revolver. She aimed at his shoulder as he had shown her with the human silhouette at target practice, but she hit his neck and blew out an inch of the carotid artery.

Gary had roughed her up in the two years of their marriage, but this was not unusual in either of their families in 1975, or in fact around the south city limits where they had grown up. He had been a popular football player, known for the fights he got into after a few too many, as well as his liking for the upper hand with his girlfriends. At Francie's trial his own mother Sharla testified that when his dad left, Gary took over the TV, the car keys, and the correction of his little brothers.

In spite of that, a picture of Francie emerged that was worse. All her life she had had a violent temper, and the prosecutor saw to it that that came out: how she had pounded the head off a doll, how as a little thing she would shout at her brother during Mass. How they had to lock her in the basement when she got going, how in middle school she had chased her two-timing boyfriend (the one before Gary) off a dock, and the poor kid, in front of his friends, had cannonballed into the lake fully dressed rather than let her catch him. These things were said by people with no particular grudge against Francie, said even in her defense. She wasn't mean; she was hotheaded. She came from a line of hotheads. Her father had been in the county jail for shooting out a picture window when the neighbors crossed him.

And she did not shoot in self-defense while Gary was wading over the furniture and sending the cat flying, or when he had her down. She got away. She grabbed his gun out of the closet and ran back to the room where he was picking a lamp up off the floor.

She went to prison for twenty years. Her lawyer said she had killed a cop and she could forget about parole, and that proved to be true.

The first year she spent reading. The library took up one wall of the lounge, a long room with a TV, orange chairs, and a world map from the donated stacks of *National Geographic*. Newcomers were surprised to hear the girl slumped there was the one who had killed her husband in a fury. That served as a kind of insurance; nobody called her a snitch or threw used tampons into her cell or said she was the cause of an inspection. She read through all the magazines, new and old, including the recipes and the ads for things she and Gary had been saving to buy—recliners and speakers and the new gas barbecues. Then in a trance of boredom she read books. She read the lives of female scientists. She read books about selling crafts from the home, books about beating alcohol and drugs, horror novels, historical novels mostly set in England, and books of poetry from a Christian press. From time to time new ones arrived in batches and she read those. She turned the pages of the law books, volumes decades old with sections torn out of them.

After the reading phase she went to work in the new wood-shop, making the tiered bases of sports trophies. She watched TV. They argued over the TV but they all agreed on things like the Olympics, and soap operas. They all objected as the soap operas veered into crime, the mob, even the occult. They laughed at young women in expensive outfits being drugged and held in underground suites and made to have amnesia. Eventually a VCR came in and you could earn movie time, but by then Francie was out of step with what showed up on the screen. She had lost interest in how people her age were talking and acting, and in how things panned out for them or anybody. In reality, time brought nothing to a noticeable close. Nothing drew its edges together or untangled itself. The real nature of a day, of time, was plainer than it would have been outside. It was not a road heading somewhere but a space that filled up, like a vacuum cleaner bag.

Most of the donated videos, and all of the popular ones, were comedies. Disputes went on as to what was and was not funny. They sat on the small orange chairs until the moment came for somebody to snap on the overhead lights as the tape jolted, reversed itself, and rewound with a dry rustle. There would be years of this. When it was Francie's turn she picked National Geographic tapes—hurricanes and tornados. She liked disasters. She thought there might be something she could do in a disaster setting, someday.

She did not remember the occasion of her crime with any exactness. A lot of them said the same thing: "Can't remember that shit. They said I did that shit." A good number were in there for drugs anyway—that or accessory—and had been messed up at the time.

Among women who cursed, threatened, and fought, she didn't find anything to rile her. Where was her temper when somebody decided to tease her as she stood in the shower line before dawn with her towel, stiff in the legs and unspeaking?

She was not homesick. If she missed anyone, it was Sharla, Gary's mother. At the beginning she wrote to Sharla, but she didn't hear back. She could see that. Sharla had let herself be called by the defense, and right after the trial with its publicity she had reported a prowler and the cops had not responded. She had two more boys coming along; she wouldn't want to be on the bad side of the PD. She would want all that behind her. Who could blame her for that?

All through high school Francie had half lived at Sharla's. Her yearbook photo hung with Gary's on the wall of the cubicle where Sharla cut her hair for free. They talked to each other in the mirror. "If you were my daughter, I'd get that tooth fixed." Francie had a BB scar on her bottom lip and a bluish tooth behind it. "A beautiful girl like you. Those great big eyes, that hair."

Sharla had sewed her wedding dress and veil, pumping away at the treadle as the needle pounded and jammed. "Look at this old thing. Never did get to sew on it like I would have."

Somewhere in between Gary and his little brothers, Sharla had lost a little girl. "The ambulance got her to the hospital but it was meningitis and they couldn't do a thing," she explained every so often, as if Francie might speak up and defend the daughter's right to have received something more. But Francie didn't argue, because she was in high school and at that time a person's life seemed cut and dried to her. Whatever happened was halfway done with before it even got started. No point in contradicting yourself, as Sharla did as often as she told the story, by adding, What if she had been able to talk, and tell me? The daughter had come only so far as standing up on her fat baby legs. Here, Gary would get to his feet. "OK, Mom, that's fine, we gotta go." He was tired of those legs. So Francie was too. And she couldn't sit there too much longer, or Gary would pick her up off the couch and carry her out of the room. He liked to do that. She would just stay a minute while Sharla wound up the story. That seemed to be enough for Sharla.

She had stories of her own for Sharla, when they were off by themselves. Her father still took a belt to her brother and to her too. Sometimes he cut switches from the neighbor's willow tree. This had brought on the row in which he shot out the window. Sharla said not to let her father get her mad, even though with her shrieks, her clawing, she was his match when she was mad.

No sense trying to get back at him. That was Sharla's view. He wasn't the worst.

Smoking on the steps of the beauty shop with tape on her bangs, smiling in her bright makeup that was somehow beyond the matter of looks altogether: Sharla was easier to picture than Gary. Gary's big-armed, hot-skinned body was beginning to lose its outlines; Francie had a hard time assembling his features around the grin. His voice, high for a man, like the voice Neil Young sang in, no longer rebounded from some stairwell as it had done more than once when she first got there, setting off that flash of relief: "Gary! Where has he been? Gary's coming!"

AFTER FIVE OR six years a woman named Dale Bowie started in running a weekly group called Gather in the Spirit. She was not exactly a chaplain because nobody had ordained her; she came from one of the new programs in the Catholic university that allowed people to go back to school in middle age.

Dale wore rubber-soled shoes—"so's she can run if we gang up on her," said Maxine, who had been there the longest—and her shirts were always blue, or a print with blue in it, as if she were harking back to some constant. "The Nun," they called her, but she was not a nun and never had been. She had on a wedding ring; it took her a while to say she was married to a priest. An ex-priest. A priest was what she had wanted to be. She had considered the convent, but convents were deserted now, or they were serving as retreats for guests with a week to spend in a mirrorless dormitory. So these guests had time, they had money to pay for sharing a bathroom and being hushed if they spoke out in the halls. Dale had nothing against that kind of person but she wanted to be in the world.

Francie raised her hand. "This is the world?" she said. This was a period when she had come out of her daze and had a reputation as a smart-mouth, though she got along with everybody.

Dale began on one of her long answers. She interrupted herself to ask Francie, "How old are you?"

"Twenty-four," Francie said. "Or no, that would be twenty-five." Because of a particular guard, Paloma, they were all in the habit of talking that way that year. "Where would you be going?" "Who in here would be the Miss Clean took all the soap?" Before Paloma came, none of them had liked anybody thin, the exceptions being those who were sick or who couldn't help it and ate everything without gaining weight. But they all liked the bony Paloma, who pretended to threaten them and had a flat way of talking out of the side of her mouth that would have been sarcastic if she had had any meanness. Paloma had a baby boy, Rafael. She was Mexican as well as black, but she couldn't understand the Spanish-speakers because her black grandmother had raised her. She had a girlfriend, and never spoke of how Rafael, whose pictures she showed around, had come to be.

The rumor was that Paloma had been a hooker. How could that be—a prison guard? But the rumor that she had been on the street, the vague word of that, put to rest but always resurfacing, enhanced their liking.

"So, what would you be doing in there?" she would call into the cell.

"I would be braiding my sheet to make a rope. How the hell do they do that anyway?"

Paloma attended Gather in the Spirit, though a guard was not required there. She didn't say anything when Dale broke the rules. Dale liked a table in the middle of the circle with a candle burning, but the aluminum tray tables had been taken out when somebody stomped one of them, and candles were not allowed. She lit one anyway and set it on the floor.

Dale had come around behind Francie.

"Twenty-five years old," she said in a marveling voice.

"Francie a baby," somebody said.

"Not your baby," somebody else said.

During prayers Dale liked to move around and do her deep breathing. She was walking behind the circle of chairs now, with a smile you could hear in her voice even if you had your eyes closed, as if she might be getting some answer in an earphone. She wasn't supposed to touch them but she would lay her hand lightly on the shoulder of one or another of them.

"Man, this is like that game," Maxine said. "That game we played. What did they call that? Where they would drop the Kleenex behind you. They was It. You would run. If you'd catch them, you was It."

"Flying Dutchman," somebody said.

"You mighta called it that, that's not what *we* called it," Maxine said.

This was what Dale wanted, to hear what they said, to accompany them on the journey they were on, of making amends. The adventure. That was not the best choice of words. It took them a while to get past saying "the adventure of laundry duty," or "the adventure of taking a shit in the new john." Dale put up with that. She said she wasn't there to find fault with them but neither was she there to provide forgiveness. She didn't bring the Eucharist in a gold compact the way the other volunteer, Ellen, did every week. As a Catholic Francie was allowed to receive the sacrament from Ellen, and she did it as a time thing, time out of the cell. "What's that new group?" she had asked Ellen.

"Dale Bowie," Ellen said. "Goodness—the Bowies. Dale and Father Patrick. They're not charismatics but they're close. If that kind of thing interests you, well, by all means."

One day when she had been in Dale's group for a while Francie raised her hand—sooner or later, they all took a turn—and said, "So tell me this. You just did it. Your crime. What got you in that room where you did it? Not what made you do it. I mean were you going to get in that room from the day you were born?"

"What do you think?" Dale asked the group.

"You done it, you done wrong," said Maxine, with a down-turned mouth like someone wiping up after a child. Nobody objected that that was not an answer to the question. Thirty years before, Maxine had come up behind a man in her building and pushed him down a flight of cement steps. Everyone mentioned the cement, though no word was ever said about how or why this happened. Her lawyer wanted manslaughter. Slaughter of a man. You'd think a crime with *slaughter* in it would be the worst. But murder was worse, and that's what she got. First degree murder, because it had been in Maxine's mind long before she did it. How did the lawyers know that? She told them. She and Francie were the only ones there, at that time, who had killed anybody on purpose. "Done wrong, you say I'm sorry, you take your punishment, and you get on with it."

"With what?" said Francie.

"With life."

"So what is life?" said Francie. "Is this it?"

"That's a very good question," said Dale. "What is life?" When nobody answered she said, in the way she had of salting prayers into the talk, "Lord, that you would help us see that life we can lead. Each of us. That life that is out there for each one of us. We pray to the Lord."

To differentiate their group from others that were in the prisons by then, encounter groups, the Catholics were encouraged to reply, "Lord, hear our prayer." Francie had grown up with that but she didn't say it.

"And why don't we visualize that life right here and now," said Dale. "Let's close our eyes." Francie never did that either. "Simone," Dale said. Simone was from Barbados and she was shy, despite being down for accessory to an ATM robbery in which a man had been run over and dragged half a block. "What do you see?"

"Oh mon, I see a big house, got carpet, sofas. Big pen of chickens."

"There's a big house all right and this is it," said Maxine.

"Now close your eyes, Maxine," said Dale.

"I gotta get home," said Rhonda, who was new. "I got a boy at home, slow. They don't know how to watch him. Let him play with the scissors. Let him go and cut the ear off the cat."

A silence followed while a weight came down on them like the mangle in the laundry.

"Home is our first thought," said Dale. "Lord, that you would be with Rhonda's son. Her family." She let them sit there a minute in the cold state to which she gave the name silent prayer. "What we imagine, really imagine for ourselves becomes real. That each one here today would have that experience. We pray to the Lord."

"Lord, hear our prayer."

"So can you think about the sun and look straight at the thought of it and go blind?" said Francie. She looked around. "Hey, I can ask a question. I mean isn't that what she said?"

"You hush," said Maxine. "Talking about pray to the *Lord*. Girl, you got a lot to learn."

ONE DAY DALE had a rubber band around her wrist. "What's that?" Francie asked her.

"That's to remind me to pick up my son's immunization records today. He's starting first grade."

Dale had a son in first grade? Dale, whose ironed blue shirt hid a body like an ironing board? Whose perm had gray in it? Who almost never referred to a husband? What was this, now that they had fallen into the habit of opening up their lives to Dale's examination every week like laundry bags? Where had this child been hiding?

Thomas. Dale drew one of her deep breaths. Thomas was six years old. He was an independent child. You could tell that she meant something else by independent. Something better, not worse. At five, instead of going to kindergarten, Thomas had made the choice to go with Patrick in his truck to projects in the parish. Patrick did this work because although he had left the priesthood and married, he had been partially received back, encouraged to offer his skills to the archdiocese. Before applying to seminary he had been a builder. So while Dale was in her program and Patrick worked on the renovation of church kitchens and tore out old confessionals, Thomas sat in the sawdust building things out of Legos.

Thomas, it had turned out, was exceptional. At four he could read the Lego instructions, by five he had discarded them. His castle won a prize at the state fair and remained on exhibit in the center court of a mall.

When he was little more than a baby, fifteen months to be exact, Thomas had begun to ask questions. "Where moon?" "What him?"—pointing at the crucifix Dale wore. Other than that, there was no mention of God in this life of Thomas. Dale did not call on God to approve her account of her son, which she seemed in fairness to recognize was bragging.

That a fifteen-month-old might have an idea of the word *where* did not seem like a miracle to Francie. How was one word any different from another? *Who, what, when, where, why.* She had written them down, sitting behind her boyfriend, the one who was going to jump into the lake. It was a remedial class because they had both skipped so much school.

The story went on. Thomas had a particular liking for buildings— already he had gone beyond Legos to wood and nails—but he didn't like the ones he was told were schools. Why did people have to go to school if they didn't want to? "I had to say I honestly don't know," Dale said. It didn't matter; in a year Thomas had made the decision on his own that he would, after all, go to school.

Francie looked at the other faces in disbelief. Nobody was sneering at the thought of Dale's show-off kid. "Paloma?" said Dale. By the door where she lurked, Paloma had raised her hand. She said Child Protection had taken her baby Rafael away because of her girlfriend. She had him back now, but she had to live by herself.

Nobody said, "What does that have to do with it?" This was one of the things that had come gradually to Francie's notice. Nobody ever worried about what the subject was, they all went with whatever you put in front of them.

Everyone comforted Paloma. More than half of them had children. *"My kids."* They said that all the time. *"My kids."* For years Francie had been hearing about, even seeing, their children. If you woke up at night after a visiting day, you heard the moans and sobs, the aftermath.

HER MOTHER WENT into the hospital. She went by ambulance to the county hospital, the same one where they had taken Sharla's little girl, and there she too died. Francie did not learn of this for three days, until her brother, who had joined the army, made a sobbing phone call from the base. No use in trying to get a pass because there wasn't going to be a funeral. Their father had seen to that. She was already in the ground.

"I don't know, I don't know, Francie," her brother kept saying after he broke the news. He kept covering the phone with his hand because his buddies were talking to him, trying to settle him down. "He never said she was sick. He never said."

"Never told me neither," Francie said. She had not heard her father's voice in eight years. "But I figured she might be."

Around then the warden had her see the counselor. Not because she kept having the same dream; the warden didn't know that. She sent her because of fainting, from holding her breath in the cell. The warden said that was what she was up to.

The dream would wake her in the flicker of the tube lights that stayed on, a dream of a baby—or a kind of abbreviated baby, the weight of a cat in her arms. But it had a flat-out helplessness a cat would never give off. It had to be hidden, in a curved hollow not unlike the eggshell ornaments her mother had made for the nurses' tree when she was a transporter at the hospital. Francie had to be in the hollow with it, where despite its lack of any muscles, gradually it would begin to thrash like a maggot until she couldn't hold on to it. Things would go on from there.

Francie didn't believe in broadcasting what showed up in your dreams or visited your mind in a cell, but the counselor got the story out of her by asking for two positive memories. Her first thought was of Sharla—in the mirror, with her black bangs and her mascara, her smiling cheeks in a coat of her special foundation. Francie could almost smell the ammonia as the plump fingers snapped the roller. She had to shut her mind against those fingers, some with Band-Aids on them for a rash, dabbing to get an endpaper off the stack. She got away from that and told about Sharla's refusal to testify for the prosecution. Then, because the counselor just sat there waiting for the second positive memory, she came up with the egg ornaments.

First you edged half a shell with rickrack, and then—Francie was eight and did this part—you glued in green felt, and onto that a plastic lamb, or a donkey, or a baby. Between them she and her mother had ruined a lot of eggs. It was a day when nothing they did had any consequences. Her father was doing a week in the county jail. Her mother could drink a bottle of Almadén and open the next one, they could smash so many eggs they had to go out and buy more, they could laugh so hard at the kitchen table, with the cat sitting on the green felt, that her mother tipped over in the chair and didn't hurt herself. The day had a soundtrack of her mother's high wandering laugh and her voice saying, "OK don't get mad at me, Francie"—because when her mother was drunk Francie could get just as mad at her as her father did—"but there went another one!"

The counselor had a lot of questions about Francie's mother. She explained that the enclosure where Francie saw herself holding her "baby" in the dream was not a tree ornament but a jail cell.

"Of course you know, Frances, that you could not keep a baby with you for very long, here," she warned Francie, who rarely had a visitor, let alone somebody she could have had sex with during a supervised encounter.

"It's not Frances," Francie said.

Sometimes the baby was even smaller than a cat. Awake, she wondered what was normal. Exactly how heavy was a baby? Better not to stir up anybody on that subject. Sometimes the dream took a turn in which, to her horror, she had left the baby somewhere and time ticked away while she slogged over footbridges or through sewage.

This was a common dream. Among new mothers, the counselor told her, practically a universal.

Francie didn't argue that she was not a mother and that every day she was leaving the chance of that behind. She didn't come out with any of her usual remarks.

Dale had a different attitude. No commenting in a disrespectful way on what anybody saw fit to bring up, no matter how stupid, boring, or plainly untrue. *Just what you'd expect*, Francie thought. Dale didn't laugh. She smiled. A smile could be the opposite of a sense of humor. No room for humor, in Dale's job of praying over their problems—which didn't have to solve anything, because if you received a solution you wouldn't need to pray any more. But on the other hand neither would Dale say "practically a universal."

Where dreams were concerned, the ones who had a problem—Francie had noticed this—were women from an island, just about any island on the map in the lounge, from Samoa to Haiti. They were the ones who wrestled with headless animals, ghosts with knives, man-birds that sucked out your intestines. Simone, for one, had a recurring dream in which the doorknobs were human heads. "I turn it, every time, the neck crack," Simone said in her soft accent.

"What do you think it means?" said Dale, as Francie was thinking of what size the heads would have to be to be grasped with a hand.

"Maybe some neck she'd like to break," Francie said.

Dale gave her a look. "Lord," Dale said, taking Simone's hands and folding the pink palms together inside her own, "we don't know why we do harm, but we do. Even in our sleep. That you would keep Simone in your care. We pray to the Lord."

As soon as her brother said the word *Safeway*, Francie knew who it was. A bucktoothed woman, wrapping meat. Blond hair in a French twist, with a net over it.

She could hear Sharla. "I've cut that hair and that's naturally blond hair. And it's long, down her back. What I'd give for that hair." Sharla put a good amount of time into dyeing her own and teasing it to the height it was. Francie said, "What if you had to look like that to get it?"

"Hey," said Sharla. She had Francie working on her temper and her tongue.

That was the woman. She had been in the Safeway meat department for years.

Their father had the house up for sale, her brother said, and he had moved in with her. When she went to kick him out, he turned around and married her. Quit drinking to do it. "All— those—years," her brother said in a drunk voice. "Got my mom started drinking and here he goes and gets married and *quits*." *My mom*. Francie didn't call him on it. She didn't say, "Hey, mine too." He still called her, this decent brother. He would put a call in to her on his own birthday. But he had forgotten hers, he had forgotten her.

• • •

By bus it was going to take Francie an hour and a half each way, but she had it figured out so she could get back in time for the party. Or maybe she would let them see how they liked it if she wasn't there. All of them.

"I don't know that I'd do that," Patrick said when Francie said she was going to see Sharla in the home. She was living with Patrick and Dale, in the halfway house they managed. In recent months it had become three houses, the second and third a run-down duplex next door that they were rehabbing so that they could house six more.

"Why not?"

"Well, this is somebody you haven't seen in twenty years. You know Dale went and saw her that once. Even that was what, six, eight years ago. Quite some time. Before her stroke."

"Yeah. So?"

"Well, Dale thinks it's fine, it's right, for you to go if you want to. But I don't know if it will do you that much good."

"I want to."

"She's been up there a couple of years, in the home. I don't think she's herself. But it's up to you, of course."

"I'm going."

"Be sure you get back for the party." They were celebrating the completion of the duplex.

Dale and Patrick had let her set aside her tasks in the house, and her job hunt, to work on the remodeling. It turned out she was a natural. Their son Tom had gone to them and asked for her full time. He was the foreman. With his two best friends he had put together a construction business. While he finished up the duplex with his dad, his partners were getting a start on the first contract they had landed. One of the partners was a musician, Tom told Francie, and that was a problem. Chip, his friend since grade school, practiced late with his band, so he got up late, and when he got to work he turned on loud music, rap, disturbing the tenants who were already mad because it was a condo conversion and they had had to buy their own apartments. So Tom had to look in every couple of days to be sure Chip was on the job and make him turn the sound down. His work, however, did not have to be checked. Even hung over, he was good at what he did. The best at finish and trim.

"As good as you?" Francie said.

"Way ahead of me. Almost as good as Dad." That was the way Tom was.

Both Tom and Chip had learned most of what they knew from Patrick, who had gone down to Mexico to build houses every summer with a crew of kids from the parish. They did it in a particular village because Pentecostal missionaries had arrived in the area, in such numbers that the villagers hung little painted signs on their doors—Tom showed Francie one—saying ESTE HOGAR ES CATÓLICO. NO ACEPTAMOS PROPAGANDA PROTESTANTE. He let her figure out the Spanish. She didn't know whether to laugh when the topic was religion, but Tom released her by laughing himself.

Tom had his own ideas. He didn't go in for all the disciplined refusals and dreamy hopes of his parents. He liked to sit on the floor, stretch out his long legs, and drink a beer with Francie at the end of the day. He worked hard but he liked his hours off. At those times he disappeared. If he had half a day off, she knew he biked to the condo or all the way to the university, which was how he got the leg muscles he had. He sat in on lectures if he felt like it. This worried Dale because it wasn't honest and he could have been admitted as a paying student, but Francie knew a college boy was the last thing Tom wanted to be. She knew him. She could have reminded Dale, but she didn't, about how they had raised him to do whatever he wanted.

He had brown eyes with yellow in them and brown wavy

hair—light golden brown, Sharla would have said, holding up one of her numbered swatches—in the short messy cut men were wearing. Young men. Not long, the way they had worn it in the '70s when Francie had hers down her back and parted in the middle. Though not Gary; Gary made fun of long hair on a man.

Women looked at Tom. Francie had seen one glance back and trip on the sidewalk.

But Tom's mind wasn't on the attention of women. He was thinking. He was reading. At the duplex there were always paperbacks lying in the sawdust, with pencils stuck in them for writing in the margins at lunchtime. *Modern Man in Search of a Soul. Tolstoy or Dostoyevsky.* Francie had opened these books. *The Histories. Amerika.*

He taught her how to pull down a wall and how to pull up a floor. He taught her how to frame in a door and a window. The door was harder, but she mortised in the hinges and got them right. When she had finished her first one, his father came in and stroked the frame. "Would you look at this, Dale. Look what we've got here."

Francie liked Patrick. Everybody did. He was at least ten years older than Dale and maybe more; he could be pushing eighty. He went around in his plaid shirt and his hanging tool-belt, slowly unscrewing electrical plates and fiddling inside and putting them back on, humming to himself. Dale did all the back-and-forth with the jails and the going after funds, but Patrick grew zucchini in the back yard, made the soups, sat down with whoever wanted to spill out to him everything she had ever done. When one of the women went off her Prozac and tore up her room, he would propose some general agreement in the house that had nothing to do with the door slamming and shouting going on. And he had begun to skip the roundtables at which they said what they expected of each other and visualized their futures. His own expectation was for some of them to be more help than they were. Work. Take Tom as their example. His son he regarded as an angel who had briefly descended to be his on Earth.

Because of this humility of his, Francie didn't listen to Patrick. With Dale, you never knew if she might let you have it. Not meanly, not, sometimes, even in words, but so you knew she noticed, knew she waited for you to be disappointed in yourself.

Their son was somewhere in between. He would watch you. He wasn't going to judge you, but he was right there, paying attention to how you did a thing. Even, Francie thought, to how you looked as you did it.

He taught her to use a chop saw and a router and how to glue boards and clamp them; he said she was about ready to take over the kitchen counters and then go on to the cupboards and drawers.

Pretty soon they had traded enough information that they could laugh at what Dale had led them to expect about each other. "You know, when we first heard about you," Francie said loudly, when their ears were ringing from the scream of the table saw, "I thought, that has gotta be a creepy kid. I'm sorry! Because I mean—good grief." Around Tom she didn't swear. "Because wait a minute"—he was laughing his collapsing, boy's laugh, his take-off-the-goggles laugh—"you have to see it, somebody telling us about this little kid, in that *circle* we sat in, in *jail*." She put on a mincing voice. "'*He's only thirteen and he's in high school!*' And then, '*Guess what, he quit high school!*' How would *we* know you were normal? We would never know it was—this kid, you, she was referring to. We would see some kinda . . ." She stopped laughing. No way to say what she was thinking. *Wait a minute, what about her? Do you ever think about how the person she found to marry was a* priest? *About what went on? With a priest? Do you think she was always good? Think you can just make amends and then you're good?*

One afternoon she came up behind Tom at the drafting table and put an arm loosely on his shoulders. She had done something like that before, laid her hand on his back when they were bending over his scale drawings. When he reached for the straightedge, muscle slid over the ribs. In twenty years you could forget the shape of a back, the thrust of it under cloth.

After a while he said, "Is that a hello, or is that something else?" She didn't answer. He turned around with a kind of tiredness. "Francie," he said. He would never start talking like somebody else would, just to have spoken. He was close enough that she could put her arms around him and she was almost going to do it, and then she did it. Did a second pass before he took her by the shoulders and stood her away from him? And then they both laughed. Thank God they did, at that moment, or she might have—what might she have done, with the fire to surround him in her, in her legs and arms?

THE AIDE TOOK her down a hall with a smell she had to shut out, not because it was strong but because it was familiar. A group smell. The smell of a house where activity divided itself between bedroom and bathroom. On either side of the door to each double room were framed photographs of the residents at an earlier time in their lives. It was midmorning and many of the doors were open. Sharla's was shut. There was her picture, with a lettered card: SHARLA MADDEN AND FAMILY.

It was the picture from the mantel in her living room, with a backdrop of rail fence and red and yellow maple trees. There was Sharla: black bangs, red nails. Band-Aid. Wedding ring she couldn't get off. She sat on a bench at the fence, with her knees to one side and her hair teased, the smaller boys on either side of her. Behind them in his football uniform, with a hand on her shoulder and his helmet under his arm, stood Gary.

Francie raised her eyes to his. It was before the school changed the uniforms, so he was a junior. She was in the ninth grade. Already she waited through football practice every day. Already they were planning to get married, already down in the back seat of Sharla's car.

Why did she never get pregnant? And now—impossible now? A quick pain ran through her head behind the eyes. She got these. The prison nurse had said to stay away from cheese.

To the right of the door the picture was of a fat cheerful couple standing beside a truck. The aide pointed her back. "There she is. That's Sharla," in a warning tone, as though Francie might not know which woman was which. "Sharla? Muriel?" The aide turned the knob and Francie stepped in.

On the bed sat a woman who, if she was Sharla, had had the innards sucked out of her and a formation of dry black hair set on her like a drink umbrella. On the other bed lay the fat woman from the other picture, fast asleep on top of the covers.

"Get me out."

The aide was gone. Francie wasn't worried; she could help somebody out of bed. She knew how from times with her mother, getting her up off the couch or the floor. This woman didn't weigh anything. Nevertheless it took effort to get her into the wheelchair by the bed, checking the brake first so it wouldn't slide out from under them. Her mother had had this happen, and this had lost her the job of transporter at the hospital.

"Sharla," Francie said, kneeling beside her. "It's Francie." She spoke softly so as not to wake the other woman.

With chewing motions, the woman adjusted her cracked, shiny mouth. She rolled her tongue several times as if she had a hair in her mouth. "Juice." She had a tube of lip balm in her hand, which she pointed with. Francie could just make out the words. "That's juice, I said Coke."

"I'll get you some Coke," Francie said, jumping up. There was a kitchenette at the end of the hall, with paper cups. Were they pill cups? Who would want a drink that small? In the refrigerator, apple juice. She poured it.

"This is only thing I can find out there, apple juice," she said. "I'm sorry, I'll ask. I'll find somebody to ask." But Sharla reached for the juice, whereupon the thin cup gave and spilled. "Wet, wet!" Sharla slapped at Francie's hand.

She found Kleenex; she wiped the sleeves of Sharla's robe. She sat down carefully on the edge of the bed. "I've been back a while," she began. "I'm not sure if you heard that. I've been wanting to come. I don't have a car yet. Forty-one and no license!" She laughed but found she was close to tears. "So, I just took the bus. I'm down by the airport. Oh, Sharla. I've been wanting . . ."

Sharla made no reply. She rummaged in her lap for the lip balm. What was she doing? She wanted more tissues; she was pointing at the box, exasperated. She thought Francie worked there. She didn't know her. She thought she was an aide.

Francie passed her the box. "Well, it's good, it's good to see you again." She would go a little way into what she had planned to say, she decided. Just to have it said, whether Sharla made any sense of it or not. "Because you mean a lot to me." What kind of a half-assed thing was that to say? Was that what she had been preparing all these weeks? "You always have. Sharla, I know I was . . . you know I—I was . . ."

Sharla was chewing her lips on the inside and staring at a flagpole out the window.

Francie kept still for a while and then she sighed. "Well, I'll come another time." She got off the bed. "Is that all right? I will, I'll come again, if it's all right."

What was that sound? Did Sharla sigh too? She had reached out and taken Francie's wrist. She held it lightly, in fingers from which the plumpness, the flesh itself, was gone. To Francie it was like having her wrist taken in chopsticks. But the hand gently pulled her. Relief flooded Francie and she bent close, to lay her cheek on Sharla's.

"Killer," Sharla whispered.

ALL THE WAY home on the bus she had a pain over her eye. Back in the kitchen, with the pain still making her half sick, she talked to Rafael. He said he had friends coming over and he didn't know why he was the one who always had to make the cake. He meant his girlfriend Tonya was coming, but Francie didn't argue; she kept it short so he wouldn't look at her hands shaking.

Twenty people were coming—everybody from the house, the neighbors, Tom's partners—to *process,* as Dale put it, through the duplex and bless it. This was Dale's plan. She got the idea from Georgette, who was newly out of the penitentiary and said she was a Chinook. Dale had candles and feathers, she had a smudge pot, a big bowl of sage leaves to be burnt as Patrick and Georgette performed the blessing.

Dale and Patrick were going to break their rule and give everybody except the ones in AA a glass of champagne, including Rafael. Francie happened to know that alcohol was nothing new to Rafael. He was only fifteen but he was living by himself over the garage, where he had taken care of his mother Paloma after she got too sick for her job at the prison and then too sick to work in the halfway house. "Look in the trash," Paloma had whispered to Francie. "Beer cans."

Kids drank beer. Francie knew that; it was Dale and Patrick who didn't know it. They always said Rafael was Paloma all over again, but lately Francie could see that more than just his mother's nature had gone to make up his. Until recently, tall as he was, he had been a little boy. In Francie's brief time there he had gone from a stick-limbed kid she could boss around and buy T-shirts for and even bundle into her lap with his feet dangling to the possessor of a place on the basketball team and a girlfriend two years ahead of him in school. He had grown another three inches. He would roll his eyes if you talked to him. Tom told him where to put the extension ladder and he slammed it down somewhere else. He bounced the ball so hard on the siding it left scuff marks. He screamed at the refs on TV.

Francie had made promises to Paloma: that she would watch over Rafael, be the next best thing to a mother to him. Make sure he graduated. Make sure he kept up his art. Keep an eye on his girlfriend.

Tonya came over every day. Dale and Patrick didn't know what you could be up to at that age.

As she was getting the cake out of the oven, Dale came in. Francie had been moving fast and there was batter all over the counter and a mess in the sink. She wasn't crying, but Dale's glance made her feel as if she had been. "I was just over putting up some streamers for tonight. Oh, it's amazing what you've done, you and Tom," Dale said. She began to pace the kitchen without picking up any of the mess. She had the look she got when she was going to pray. "Francie, we've had some bad news."

Francie turned away. She didn't want any of the sadness Dale tried to coax from them. The only thing worse was when she put effort into cheering them up.

"Maxine passed away. We got a call this afternoon, from the infirmary." Dale never said *prison*. "She had such bad diabetes, you know. I'm sorry. I know you loved her."

Loved her? Dale was always telling them they loved this person and that person and each other, as if that would make them do it. Maxine. Francie wiped her eyes.

Dale wiped hers too. "So many changes. You know, Francie, you've added so much to our lives here." Francie got behind the butcher block island Tom had built. Dale came around the island and took up a position in front of her as if she might shake her hand. "And I must say we've relied on you. But lately I think—and maybe you think so too—that it might be you don't need us as much anymore."

Francie didn't say, But I do. I need one of you. Not you.

"What I think is that you're pretty much ready for your own place. You're not on parole like Rhonda or Georgette. You can do whatever you want. You can get started in your own place. I think before you know it we'll be blessing your apartment."

"You mean," Francie said, pressing her eye to relieve it, "leave your son alone."

This did not seem to surprise Dale. But nothing surprised her; she was like one of those blocking sleds they had at football practice, that couldn't be knocked over. "No, dear," Dale said. "No, I mean find your life."

"My life. How about if we picture it." It didn't matter what she said, Dale was going to hug her. When they finished hugging, she gave Dale a thumbs-up. She didn't say, I won't leave, I can't, not yet, I love him.

• • •

IT WASN'T THAT she fell. She simply slid down the steps, six or eight of them. She had climbed the rickety outside stairs to Rafael's room. When he didn't answer her knock she yelled that the cake was made and he had said he would ice it.

She heard Tonya's voice, muffled, asking a question. Then Rafael's, louder. "Bitch is up in my business, that's how come."

Francie's sight grayed over and that was when she grabbed the railing, which buckled and came with her. By the time they got to the door she was halfway down. She must have made a racket getting there.

Broken posts rolled down the steps as she tried to think of the word Tom had taught her for them. "Whoa momma," said Tonya's voice. "But she's OK, aren't ya." Francie had slid on her back; nothing was hurt except her tailbone. Tonya bent over her. "Not gonna talk."

"You'd talk, if it was you," Rafael said to Tonya.

Tonya slapped his arm. "I would, you be running out here to save me like that."

Rafael squatted down beside Francie. He said, "Would you look at that. Dry rot. How you doing?" Francie could tell by his voice that he was scared and sorry. He closed his hand around her wrist, to show her.

"You took a tumble." Tonya bent over them, showed the sweat between her breasts. "Well, help her up why doncha?"

Rafael pulled Francie to her feet. "I slipped," she said, dusting off her hands.

"Better watch that," he said, in his old way.

"Here." Tonya got her arm around Francie, up against her ribs, and made a show of bearing her weight and lowering her step by step to the bottom.

Tonya wasn't pretty, but she didn't have to be, she had the confidence without it. She did have pretty teeth, which she uncovered in a cold smile at Francie. The advantage was hers. She had Rafael. She knew how to comfort somebody who had a dead mother. She knew how to take him away from everybody else who had a claim on him, and how to make him hers.

THEY HAD FINISHED Patrick's chili and gone on to Francie's cake, on which at the last minute Rafael had drawn a house in red icing, with the chimney coming out of the roof sideways.

"You poor thing," Dale said for the third time. "Those stairs are terrible."

"Rafael's going to fix that," said Tonya, as if she were as much a part of what went on as any of them. They had fanned sage smoke into every closet, Georgette had chanted in her language, they had toasted Melanie because she had finished her thesis.

Melanie. Melanie was the other partner. Tom's other partner.

Melanie had long black hair twisted up with a comb. Francie guessed her weight at no more than a hundred pounds. She was some kind of Oriental and she was beautiful, wearing overalls because she had come straight from work at the condo and a tank top that showed the perfection of her slimness.

Chip sat with Tom on the floor putting CDs into the player. "I was going to bring Tupac," Chip told him. "You may not know this because you're not a fan. Tupac *died*. He died yesterday. It looked like he was going to make it after they shot him, but he died." At the word *shot*, Tom shook his head warningly. "Don't worry, man, I didn't," Chip said. "I didn't bring it."

Francie wasn't listening when Patrick started to speak. She was looking at Tom, thinking about his concern for her, and about music, how she couldn't get used to music as it was now.

When Patrick said, "And now for the final toast, the big one. Are we ready?" a hush fell. He was holding the bottle high. "To Tom and Melanie!"

Everybody cheered. The two of them, Tom and Melanie, came forward from opposite sides of the room. They met under Dale's streamers; they took each other's hands. "Tom and Melanie!" The noise made everything seem to be proceeding slowly. Patrick took their joined hands and raised them high, as if they were at the Olympics.

Uganda. They were going to Uganda. They had come up with an idea for modular dwellings that could go up fast and hold more than one family. They had done this together. Once they had the design everything had fallen into place in a matter of days. "Oh, it is a disaster there," Melanie said sorrowfully. They had their sponsor and they were going to build the first models in a refugee camp. They had their passports and they were leaving in a week.

Before that, in five days and in this very room, they were getting married.

That was better than waiting until they got back. Tom said, "We'll be back in a month. We'll be back before Chip can sell off the tools." Everybody cheered again. Francie sat still, on the cleaned-off bench where she and Tom had kept rulers and levels and stashed their books.

"So, a week from today," Tom said. "And meanwhile, all she has to do is defend her thesis."

Into the clapping Francie said, "What's it on? Your thesis."

"Oh, it is on buildings," said Melanie. People had quieted down and she turned to Tom in embarrassment, lowering her smooth lids. "Actually, on buildings in . . . in literature. Because, my program is comparative literature."

"Buildings in literature," said Francie stubbornly. "What literature?"

"A French novelist," Melanie said, looking up with a soft smile, as if Francie might be a friend to her. "And an Egyptian and an Israeli. And"—she hurried on—"*Crime and Punishment.* Because you know, those rooms, they are so important. And of course Kafka."

"Of course," said Francie. She knew who Kafka was. She had picked up *The Castle* from the bench. "Would I like this?" She always asked Tom that.

"You might."

"But it's not my kind of book, right? It's not *Pet Sematary.*" She brought books with her and put them down and Tom looked at her books too.

"It's a painful book to read."

"Oh, dear, no, I don't go in for that kind of material. Pain."

He laughed. He always joined in if she was in a good mood, stayed quiet on a day when she was down, always.

"Melanie was our woodworking teacher," Tom said. He was explaining to Francie and no one else. "Chip and me."

"Your teacher, no kidding. Is she older than you?"

"I am twenty-five," said Melanie, with a sad smile. "I am older than he is."

Tom, who never bragged, said, "The students thought she was fifteen." She looked fifteen.

"So . . . how many years have you been doing this stuff?"

"In Korea, I started when I was a child, with my father. Like Tom. My father was a builder of shrines."

"Korea. Did you have a name in your language?"

"I have the name Young. But it does not mean *young.*" Melanie laughed, a laugh of such sweet apologetic lightness that it dug a splinter into Francie.

When no guesses came to her, even mean ones, Francie said, like a lawyer pressing forward, "What does it mean?"

"Oh, you will laugh, it means *eternal*," said Melanie.

"Why would I laugh?"

"I've told Melanie about your sense of humor," Tom said.

"Yeah," Francie said. "If something's funny." She heard the mean sound in her voice.

"Are you doing all right?" Dale asked, sitting close to her on the bench.

"I'm fine." She was near the wall, the drywall she and Tom had just finished sanding. Let the others mill around admiring the work of months, the pine sills, the flush baseboards.

Patrick was clearing away the chili bowls. Dale patted Francie's leg and got up to join the circle the women were forming around Tom and Melanie so Georgette could bless them too. They had lit more sage and the smell bloomed up again in the room, like the pulse off the table saw when the wood fell in two.

After a while Francie got up dizzily. Chip was still on the floor, sorting through his CDs. He hadn't crowded in like the others to hug Tom and Melanie. Maybe he had wanted Melanie for himself. Or maybe he knew something about her. Something he couldn't warn Tom about because they were all friends. He worked with Melanie every day. You knew everything about a person you worked with. Almost everything.

"I'm sorry about Tupac," she said to him.

"Yeah." He looked up at her like a kid. "Why did they do it?"

What a shock to Tupac. How much did you see, in that second? How much did you know? Did you know your life was over? Did you know in that second that others were going to go on just as they were, but you were dead? "I'm sorry," she said again. She thought of the day she had killed Gary. After he hurt her. Was it that? Was that all? And then, yes. She got the gun. She shot him. Shot him in the neck. With that neck, his coach used to say, Gary could drag a truck. He would pick Francie up and carry her out of the room. That was when she weighed a hundred pounds herself. They were going to get married in a few years. Nobody warned them not to. A suds of blood and something else pumped out of his neck. And then what? Nothing, after that. For him nothing. For her, this. This life. If she closed her eyes she might see what was going to let her live it.

Suitors

• • •

THESE WERE NOT the captions under the three faces chosen for our daughter by Lali of DataMate. They were our
captions.

The first: a blurred picture taken from some distance away of
a tall blond man standing in front of a tractor:

> *"Love of country!" Mark loves country life. He enjoys his 4X4 and
> his fly rod but wouldn't miss a Valentine's Day dinner, and he'd
> prepare it from A to Z, down to the hand-crafted candles! Mark
> favors long walks and quiet evenings watching spectacular sun-
> sets from the porch (his own) nestled in a picture-perfect setting,
> horses grazing on the hill. Talk about stable providers! Your good
> nature and love of order Meg would complete the picture.*

The second: no photograph.

> *Dashing, optimistic Kevin is not a briefcase-toting nine-to-fiver.
> He views career as a series of ever-opening doors and he has*

the degrees to back up his entreprenure's approach: two BA's and an MFA from a special program that accepts only the most highly-gifted writers in the nation. The proverbial tall, dark and handsome Kevin will wow you with his easygoing ways and brainy style. You Meg will bring the common sense approach this one-of-a-kind guy needs.

"Look, she misspelled *entrepreneur*," said my husband Sam.

"It's a typo," Meg said.

"You can always run Spell Check," said Sam, who knows little or nothing about computers.

The third: no photograph.

Andrei (pronounced Andre) can take you to the stars! Andrei is a filmmaker who is going places. He has filmed all over the States, he's got the scoop on this nation and is ready for the big screen. About to pull up stakes here and take his visions south to Filmland, Andrei will miss the trails and mountain hide-aways of our state, and the shared solitude of exploring the rainforest. Ready to focus his lens on lovely You, Meg.

Of course we were uneasy. That recurring stuff about "this nation." Admittedly this was just after the planes hit the towers and stirred feelings of unity among unlikely allies. Patriotism was coming around again, Sam said. Looking back, he said, he remembered detecting a hint of it some time before, in the phrase *the power of place*. That was the title of a course at the community college that our daughter had taken over for her friend Stacey when Stacey had her baby.

But who was this Lali? We knew she was from India; what did she know of American dating customs?

"Her site isn't for dating," Meg said humbly. "It's for marriage."

And too we had to wonder what Meg had typed in about herself to produce this particular list of three. She *is* lovely. With her thick brown hair and big eyes she's a very pretty girl, but shy. In college she did well and had boyfriends, one of them serious, but in the next ten or twelve years the men dried up. Now she was at that stage between all the good ones being taken and the return of those same men, divorced, like salmon coming back up the river.

But what, Sam wanted to know, was the algorithm? Had Meg specified Stable Provider, Easygoing Ways, and the Outdoors? Or had she merely revealed her gentle, practical, perversely kind nature to Lali of DataMate?

Meg took them in order, one, two, three. The farmer was Lali's first choice for Meg.

From the dinner with him, Meg came back with muddy shoes and a sad mouth. She had not met him in a restaurant, she had driven out to his farm. When she found it, a big piece of land near the airport with an ACREAGE FOR SALE, ZONED COMMERCIAL sign on it, she parked on the shoulder, crossed a field on foot, and knocked on the door.

Here I tried to keep my breathing even. What was she thinking, driving out there alone to see a man she had never met? "Were you . . . apprehensive?" I said. At thirty-four she was too old to be screamed at.

No, it was in the daytime. Lali had visited beforehand. Lali e-mailed, telephoned, met in person, and visited the home of every person on her list. She was bonded. The agency was her own; she had founded it, and kept it a small enterprise. She was careful, dedicated, and, because she was a Bengali, attuned on a personal level to the subtleties of matchmaking. Meg had complete trust in her.

Lali had made an exception to the rule that the first meeting between her clients must be in a public place, because this man

Marcus (not Mark) could not be lured from his house. She herself, Lali, had gone there to meet him. Never, I said to Meg silently, Never, Never Go Unaccompanied to the House of a Man You Don't Know and Get Out of the Car and Go In.

He opened the door as if he had been standing with his hand on the knob. After a careful look at him and a handshake, Meg stepped into his house.

What did he look like? Oh, it wasn't his looks—he was better looking, she realized, than she had expected, tall and fair-haired. It was his loneliness. His standing there in the half-light cast not by candles but by a computer left on in the dining room. He was lonely. Lonely and dejected beyond her powers of description. Oh, she would, our daughter, have given anything to be able to help that man. Except that the only thing givable at that point was herself. At first he was unable to enter into conversation. Now and then he would dive deep and come up with a sentence in his teeth, while Meg talked easily and at length, as she would not ordinarily do, being shy despite her years of teaching.

True, they sat so long on the porch, she on a rusty glider and he on the step so she couldn't see his face, that they witnessed the sunset. They saw a horse plod along the fencerow throwing its head up and back as if to take a pill, and another one follow it with slow, fated steps. She asked if they were his horses. "Some are, for now," he said. "The two fellas at the fence, the bay over there with the herd." There were cattle in the field as well. "Some of the horses you see are boarders." She felt, as it got darker and he seemed to have dived for good, that she was in the presence of an almost-departed spirit making one last effort to stay in a human body.

His 4x4 was a pickup with a rifle rack in the back window. "At least," said Meg, who is a pacifist vegetarian, "the rack was empty."

"How did you know the rifle wasn't behind the door?" her father said, wringing his hands. "How do you know people weren't buried in the back yard? Who is this Lali that you would put this kind of trust in her?"

With the sunset over, Meg rose and took the man's cold hand in hers for the second time. Every mound had a callus, because he really was a farmer, had been growing alfalfa and pumpkins and keeping horses for ten years, and boarding horses and ponies owned by people in the city. Meg loved horses, though she knew them only from books. She loved cows as well, probably, she explained, because the brown-eyed white face of a stuffed animal from her childhood was stuck in her memory. A soft, floppy cow. Or possibly because the country had seen a mass production of china cows in her youth. They were everywhere; they were salt shakers, pitchers, key rings. People felt a love for the cow, Meg said, love for something a cow stood for or memorialized. This was the result—not the cause, which was commercial—of the herds of china cows. Meg could speak as an anthropologist while having a china cow on her desk.

Marcus had lost a wife, two years before. The wife had not died, she had left. She had turned her back on fields, horses, husband. One of her jobs had been to run one of those pumpkin patches with bales of hay, scarecrows, hot cider in an open kettle, and prizes for the kids who came out on school trips at Halloween. That's what the painted wagons were for, two of them beside the shed. Pulled by a garden tractor, the kids rode out into the rows of vines and came back with pumpkins on their laps. Marcus and his wife had had no children of their own.

Bit by bit Meg got all this out of him. The computer on the table had belonged to his wife, who had left so fast she didn't even take it, and one day he had been just fiddling with it and somehow run across Lali's service, DataMate. He didn't realize, as Meg did, that the site must have been something his wife had bookmarked. Later Meg had Lali look for his wife around the matchmaking sites, but Lali didn't find her.

"Goodbye, Marcus," Meg said. Goodbye. She felt she had known this man for many years, getting only as far in that time as she had in this one evening. It was all she could do not to offer him the friendship of e-mail, or a phone check-in. But something in his sealed lips kept her still.

The candles he had made were mud-colored things hardened in orange juice cans, from the melted stumps of other candles. There were so many on the windowsills and arrayed on the table-cloth and on the top of the refrigerator that she saw the candle-making was not a hobby but a tether to action, active life, life.

He had a lot of money available to him, and a college degree. How did she know? He told her. She had a sense of the complete truth of everything he claimed. He had been selling off prime land, but there was enough of it left, good grazing land, to lease to his neighbor while he was making up his mind what he was going to do. The sun had gone down but there was still light. Following her into the field of deep, wet grass to her car, he pointed out the driveway she could have taken, a few yards from where she had parked. She rolled her window down and said, "It was a lovely sunset."

"Dawn's where you see the real color." He punched a thumb at the mountains across the road, and then he faded back into the semidark as she backed and turned and waved. Finally he too waved and walked off in the direction of the fence where they had seen the horses.

THE SECOND ONE she met on the sidewalk in front of a café on The Ave, the main drag in the University District. This time

Lali was there to make the introduction, and when she was gone they went in and sat drinking coffee for half the day.

What did he look like?

Why did we keep asking this question? Because as her parents it was the first thing we could think of to ask. He too was tall. Tall and thin. Something in the way she said this made Sam ask how tall. Six feet, six inches.

"That's tall," Sam said. After a minute he said, "Does he have long arms?" He did. "Long legs?" He did. "Long fingers? Really long?" Sam said, holding his palm out an inch from his own fingertips. Long. "Well," Sam said, "I doubt you looked into his mouth to see if he has a high-arched palate."

"What are you getting at, honey?" I said. Sam is a doctor who likes to make deductions from physical description. When his sister and her husband visited, Sam made a bet that the lump they kept talking about in their German shepherd's neck was not cancer but a benign nerve-sheath tumor, and after the biopsy they called up delighted, as if he had been the one to spare the dog.

"Marfan's syndrome," Sam said.

Our daughter had no interest in Marfan's syndrome. To our dismay, however, she did seem interested in this young man, who, it turned out, had been living in a University District rooming house while job-hunting, but had been evicted, and had not yet found a place to live, even though he now had money in hand that his parents had wired. His name was Kevin and he was several years younger than Meg. For two nights he had slept in the open, getting to know the residents of Ravenna Park, who had befriended and sheltered him like the fairies who built the house around the girl, whose name was not Wendy, in *Peter Pan in Kensington Gardens*, a different book from *Peter Pan*. So he told Meg, showing her a copy in the university library where he liked to stash his backpack and stretch his legs out and read during the day. He showed her the thick novel he had written. "Did you read it?" Sam said, because both of us could picture Meg taking it home and reading every word as she would her students' papers. No. It was his only copy.

No address. No job. I wouldn't have put much thought into the words *tall* or *short* until Meg was looking for a husband. Kevin was too tall for comfort. Forced to travel along up above everybody else, too tall to be unnoticed, so tall his height might seem to account for everything he did or didn't do. None of this could be uttered, and I was ashamed of the forebodings her father and I were sharing behind our smiles.

It was all so old-fashioned, so tinged with the foreign; it had the flavor of the sluggish, mysterious comings and goings in an opium den, this search for a husband for Meg.

"I'd like to meet this Lali," Sam said. That would be a small step we might allow ourselves with Meg, some distance from announc-ing a wish to meet any of the three prospective husbands.

"Don't keep saying *this Lali*, please," Meg said reasonably. The awful prose of Lali's descriptions had made no impression on Meg, whose degree was in anthropology and comparative reli-gion but who was teaching composition at the community col-lege and should have noticed Lali's style. In less than a year Lali had become her close friend.

"If she's a friend how come she had to write up these . . . com-positions?" I said. "Why couldn't she just sit down with you and describe these guys honestly?"

"It was a formal arrangement," said Meg with dignity. "And the descriptions were in her database."

"I think she knows our Meg is a bit too kindhearted for her own good," Sam said.

"A pushover, you mean," Meg said.

"Not what I mean."

"These descriptions are honest," Meg said. "If you read them carefully, it's all there." She grinned. It was after she met the third one, the borderline, that we were having this discussion, speaking openly about Meg's decision to try to meet someone serious, someone to consider marrying.

BORDERLINE IS A PSYCHIATRIC diagnosis, not at all the ironic all-purpose label it is in lay talk. She's really borderline, we say, meaning somebody is capable of going, and might go, too far. But in the field of psychology it means something specific. It means a person damaged in childhood, usually, who has formed a personality consisting of impulsivity, paranoia, and avidity for affection.

"You mean in this entire city all this Lali could find for Meg was three creeps? For *Meg*?" Sam's blood pressure was up because the third one had proved to be a crazy man. Filmmaker! Andrei worked as a busboy in a steak-and-lobster restaurant. He was almost forty, a student at the community college.

That was when we asked if Lali was also a student there, and found out that she was.

With Andrei, Meg's good sense clicked in and she got away from him as fast as she could, though not before he wrote down her telephone number and started calling her apartment every hour. Then for some reason she agreed to go out with him, although she was already seeing Kevin.

It was Andrei's belief, as Meg assured us later it was the belief of many desperate citizens of Russia, bewildered and finally deluded by their own misfortunes since the collapse of communism, that the Jews were in charge and were intent on wiping

Christianity from the face of the earth. Christians must marry and produce children as fast as they could. Andrei had seen the card on the bulletin board advertising Lali's service and was ready on the spot.

"I am a Buddhist," Meg said, but in a friendly way. She let him film her. He did it with an expensive movie camera—a sixteen-millimeter, not a video camera. She didn't speculate as to how he might have come by such a camera, a man who wore a bum's old wing tip shoes, gaping at the seams. He had the camera with him at his first meeting with Meg; he lined up the attachments for her to see, taking them out of a case with sculpted compartments.

How tender on the part of the male, Meg might have told her students, if she had been allowed to teach a course in her own field: this open desire to win the female. This display, like a bowerbird's, this laying out of goods and assets. And the female approaching with some secret authority, to inspect what was spread before her.

MEG INVITED US to dinner. Lali was already there, demure on the couch. She rose to her feet as we came in, a beautiful child dressed in a pale gray suit, slim as an incense stick. Actually she was twenty-seven and had left her family and her fiancé in Darjeeling five years before to visit a married cousin in Seattle, and stayed. Sitting beside Lali, Meg looked large and vague and worn.

"Got many clients?" my husband said as soon as we sat down to dinner, before he had his napkin on his lap.

"Just now I have forty-six," Lali said, smiling at Meg, who must have predicted the question, and then soberly closing her dark lids big as awnings to think and holding up a finger. "Forty-seven."

"Uh-oh, that leaves somebody out in the cold," Meg said. We all laughed.

"So out of the forty-seven there were three who seemed to be young men who might have something in common with Meg," said Sam with a sinister politeness.

"Well, more than half are women. This is always the case, most regrettably. And while I am happy for women to meet, I am most strictly conventional in these introductions. Men to women. So the field is somewhat smaller for the women."

"How small?"

"I have, just now, fifteen men."

"Out of which three, a fifth, might suit Meg? I guess that changes my sense that three is rather few."

"Oh, Dr. Wagner, all fathers are suspicious! Of course they are! This is your daughter!" I liked the way she said *daughter*. *Doh-ta*, with soft consonants, expressing a degree of tenderness. "And my teacher!" She glanced shyly at Meg. "But I am most cautious. Very, very particular. It is not all done with computers, don't worry. It is done with the head"—she touched her smooth forehead—"the heart"—the neckline of her pink silk shell—"and luck." She rolled the startling whites of her eyes upward under their heavy, almost disabling net of lashes.

"What about karma?" said Sam, who had had many discussions with Meg when she was becoming a Buddhist—a lax Buddhist at best, with all of her hopes—and had been reading up on Hinduism for the occasion of Lali's visit. "Why would the person that Meg's karma has earned her have to be found or chosen by somebody else?"

"Ah, yes," said Lali, with seeming pleasure. "But karma will allow us also to meet those who will guide us properly."

"Lali is a computer whiz as well as an *A*-student," Meg said, as though she were making a match between us and Lali.

"And so how is it that this disturbed Russian crept in?"

"Andrei! He is someone I know! He was so surprised when the e-mail address from the bulletin was me, his friend from class!"

"Do you know him well?"

"Oh, I'm afraid I know him only well enough to like him. He is a silly boy, certainly, yes, in some ways, but he is quite trustworthy, of that I am sure."

"He climbed in the window of Meg's apartment."

"Well, I don't know, of course, but Russians are unlike Americans in many of their customs. That is impulsive, yes. But this boy has fallen in love. I can tell you I have heard nothing else from him for months and months but Meg, Meg, Meg."

"It doesn't matter, really," Meg said. "There's nothing between us." She turned to her father. "Seriously, think of how few people you meet who are instantly likable. Well? And these three, all of them—Lali is a magician."

We did not say that she, our daughter, found almost everybody likable.

"And what about this farmer?" said Sam. "Hard to see how he got on the list."

"Oh, just something silly. Something I was hearing when I went to see him," said Lali. "It was merely a laugh. His way of laughing. A most sober man, as Meg will tell you."

"And I liked him," said Meg.

"I'm not sure you were in a position to know that ahead of time," Sam said.

"But yet," Lali spoke up, smiling away Sam's remarks, "it is going to be Kevin, isn't it? Many of the signs were in his favor."

THE WEDDING WAS small, in a room of an old mansion popular for weddings in our city. Lali and Stacey, Meg's best friend, were the attendants, and on the big round oak table we set out champagne glasses and cake. Meg was almost a vegan by this time and had not really wanted a cake, but her training as an anthropologist made her reluctant to leave it out. "Cake is sacred," she said. "Pie is folkloric but cake is sacred."

"No one's advocating pie. But if you have cake at your wedding you want to be able to have a piece," said Stacey.

"And pie—why is that folkloric?" Sam wanted to know.

"Four and twenty blackbirds, Daddy."

Really we were all afraid that Meg would take on the job herself and bake one of those dark, wet soy cakes. Stacey was afraid it wouldn't taste good, but I was afraid it would sit there like an outward and visible sign of an inward and spiritual substitution. Kevin instead of the handsome prince. This was before we really knew Kevin and realized he was indeed the handsome prince and no substitute. By this time he did have a job, teaching English in a private school that didn't require a teaching certificate.

Two weeks before the wedding we found a bakery that could make a rich carrot cake that no one would guess had no eggs.

Andrei crashed the wedding but Meg was able to keep things friendly. She sat with Andrei on the piano bench for a long time in her white dress with her long neck bent towards him, talking quietly, explaining, I believe, her love for the man to whom she had just finished vowing herself for life, until the pianist came and reached in from behind them to strike a loud chord. It was time for toasting and dancing to begin. The talk stopped and the chord pulsed through the crowd while Andrei pulled himself together, unclenched his fists, and agreed to leave the bench.

How strange, it occurred to me as I watched Andrei during the toasts, that both of these men Lali had plucked out of nowhere for Meg had agreed, as if a spell had been laid on them, to be hers.

Two years later Kevin had published his novel. Meg was happier than we had ever seen her. She was trying to get pregnant; she even had an anthropology course to teach, in addition to composition and The Power of Place, which had become permanently hers when Stacey got a better job. One day Kevin was standing in front of his high school juniors happily scanning "The Wanderer" when his aorta burst.

In Marfan's syndrome the aorta can be as weak and decayed as a strand of old kelp, and no one will suspect it.

After he died Meg stopped going to work. She locked the door on the apartment where they had lived, without even cleaning it, let alone subletting it while there was no salary to pay for it, and came home. It may sound as though we were the kind of parents who secretly wanted their daughter back, but in this period we came close to telling Meg she might be happier staying with Lali, who had invited her. Because there was nothing we could do but get up and go through the day with her, while hopelessly trapped in the parental obligation of rescue, with Sam already wandering the house new to his retirement and susceptible to despair. She had not come home to be with us, though, so much as to be as she had been before, thereby repudiating, even obliterating, the happiness of two years. Finding this impossible, she mourned with a silent concentration.

In the spring, Andrei reappeared. He had finally gone to California and made a movie—we had read about it, disbelieving, in *People*: a documentary about megastores. First Stacey called Meg and said, "You know you're in that movie."

"What movie?"

"The movie Andrei made, the Walmart movie." There was a low buzz of talk about the film because it introduced scenes of nudity into a study of the giant complexes going up in small towns faster than the house the fairies built over Wendy in Kensington Gardens. Andrei had elected to film a long-haired woman wandering nude into these stores in various parts of the country. The furious or horrified response of supervisors or security guards, which he filmed with a handheld camera, represented defense of the status quo. The woman also strolled outdoors, past empty storefronts or among the backhoes on farmland being paved for parking lots.

That the film, as Sam pointed out, was the work of a man exiled from a ruined economy, who despised communism more than he hated the consolidation of wealth, was not mentioned in *People*, which addressed its readers on the subject of the Human Body. Why must a lovely woman be hidden from the great unblinking corporate eyeball? What did the corporations have to lose? What did they so fear from the Human Body?

The naked woman was not Meg, thank God. But Meg did indeed appear in one scene, her fingers leafing through a rack of CDs. The camera lingered so long on Meg, on the vintage high-necked blouse we knew Andrei had given her and we had advised her not to accept, her lowered eyes, the limpid, shy, music-imagining beauty of her face bent over the CDs, that Sam and I were almost in tears.

We had never met Andrei in the crawling-through-the-transom period, but now he was back and he had shoes and black shirts and a beard grayer than Sam's and a Saab. He was a success.

He came every few days with books and videos and flowers and plants for Meg. Orchids, impossible to keep alive, spilled over the dresser in the bedroom where she slept in the painted iron bed of her childhood. All she did through the summer, and the two more quarters she took off from school, was sit on the porch with the same book in her hands, none of those Andrei kept finding for her, but Kevin's novel.

Andrei was dressing in black cashmere sweaters, taking vitamins and St. John's wort, and drinking wheatgrass. He had put away any notion of the international Jewish conspiracy. He seemed to have rid himself of much of his original personality, certainly those things that had made Sam call him borderline—though not his obsessive notions about Meg.

By the time Meg folded up Kevin's shirts for Goodwill and found herself another apartment, a year had limped away. We swallowed our tears as she got into the Saab with Andrei and waved goodbye to us.

"Do you think she'll marry the guy?" Sam croaked. I said no. Of course she was only thirty-seven years old, and anything could happen. Not that she wasn't involved with Andrei; she was, by then. We had seen her cross from bare toleration of him—with his bitter asides, his sneers in Russian, his tender glances and sudden indrawn breaths of impatience, his palliating trinkets— to musing smiles as she listened to him.

Would neither one of these men have found her on his own? That was the question. What was marriage anyway, if it involved the yoking of two who would not have encountered each other naturally on the planet?

"Look, Kevin is a great husband, a great son-in-law," Sam had started in, in the early days. "But aren't there Kevins everywhere? Or not really, no, but I mean how did it happen to be Kevin?" In time we saw that Kevin came from somewhere and had a loving family and memories and a large place of his own in the world, as it is not so easy to see when you first meet anybody, especially your daughter's suitor. He had not been provisional at all; he had been permanent. In time we saw that he was in fact the man Meg saw clearly when she met him in the café: good, kind, and if less worldly than many, more upright than most. No, there were not Kevins everywhere. We mourned him. For months after he was buried, with Meg staring into his book on the porch, I would have to say to Sam, "Dear, go a little easy with the sighing. It's her loss." And he could have said the same to me.

"He was a son to us," Sam would say, wiping his eyes.

Lali comforted him. "It is so silly here that people say you are doing a good job when you do not weep." *Silly* was the strongest insult Lali would offer the United States. Yet in India her family was plotting every day to get her out of the clutches of this country. We had broken Lali of the word *nation*, though she had stood up to us, arguing gently that this was the only country, really, the word seemed to fit any more, not that that was an entirely good thing.

Now we knew Lali, she was almost part of the family; we knew she was not the child she had seemed, but a thinker, in her amiable, pragmatic way, getting her degree in political science in hopes of working in an embassy. A smiling thinker. Unlike our daughter, who was a sober feeler. At any rate the United States loomed forbiddingly in the thinking of Lali's family ("They are a bit less venturesome than I"), with its perilous cities and random mixing and licentious customs, as she reported, her accent deepening as she recited the warnings of her aunts. It was their immutable plan to lure her back to the chosen suitor, now past thirty and still waiting for his marriage to her.

THE BABY WAS a beauty. Our grandson. He had his father's well-shaped head and Meg's soft, thick brown hair. He had an easy nature, like Meg, and an absorbed, tinkering, solving disposition, like Marcus.

For she had found him again. Andrei, of all people, had suggested it, as a joke. When she had finally made it clear that she could not marry Andrei, he had packed up and gone back to L.A. He was working as a key grip while he made his own films; he had met a sound mixer who was comforting him. He still called Meg, and he called Sam and me to ask about her. He had become a man who took the time to call. He called to tell us to see obscure movies he had worked on, and then to tell us he was engaged.

Meg had gone back to the farm near the airport, back to the porch. Marcus was not only there, he had twenty horses boarding and had resumed planting the fields he had let to the neighboring farm.

It was spring. They walked in the fields and on into the woods where some of the horses liked to scratch themselves against trees. They climbed several fences. What were the steps over the fence, so perfectly fitted for climbing over? They were stiles. He had built them. Stiles. What were those big white flowers in the next field? Where? There, in the grass. He threw back his head and laughed.

The laugh, Lali had said, is an attribute of the man, and if you delight in it, go forward.

"Flowers! Those are calves." He was still laughing, bent over with it. "Herefords. That's their white faces." The calves were lying down, hidden in the thick grass.

"I'm a vegetarian," Meg said.

He remembered she had mentioned that. He had a good recall, it turned out, for everything she had said at that first meeting. He was ready to change many things, though the difficulty would be in changing himself. Never mind that, she said.

Lali, before she said her tearful goodbyes and went back to India for her own marriage, sighed with admiration as she held our grandson on her lap. "Oh, someday, Meg, I will come back for this, and you must say you will do it: you will let me find him his bride."

Choice in Dreams

• • •

M OLLY WAS HOPING to have a dream in which she didn't disgrace herself, in which she got to be an innocent tourist. There would have been solace in seeing her parents alive again, in one of those dreams that accept grief as a kind of heavy, immovable scenery but scour it of the peeling paints, leaving the sweet bare wood. Or she would have liked to ride a horse, as she had done effortlessly in childhood dreams. Or to see her beloved high school boyfriend and tell him she'd changed her mind, she didn't have to stay a virgin after all.

So many choices in dreams. But instead of seeing her parents or riding a horse she dreamed the usual dream, the one saturated in shock, relief, delight, and shame. In the dream, she did what she had only dreamed of. In abandon and selfish joy, thinking all the while "At last!"—she did disgrace herself. She dreamed of Mike O'Meara.

Awake, she turned over and pressed against her husband's back, as if he might have looked in through the window of his own sleep at her acts with Mike.

Why dream of someone else's husband? A man whose wife dragged him out of bed on workdays because he couldn't get up, he was hung over. A man who couldn't fix the washer in a faucet and left his towel on the good bedroom furniture in their run-down house, pieces that had belonged to his wife Alice's grandmother, because Alice came from a prominent family in their city, from one of the hilltop mansions of the philanthropic Catholic garrison, and Mike, a Catholic of a different sort, had carried her off. A man now bald, with legs atremble from chemo and radiation. A dead man. Is this a choice one would sensibly make, even in a dream?

On the positive side, a man who adored children, who could give you the hour of birth and the distinctive biography of each of his five kids. A man who made his living writing about crime and had been seen to shed tears in the morgue. A man who put his arm around his wife when she was telling the story of how they had to get married when she got pregnant, a man who said, "Thank God things used to be that way," and whose oldest, smiling son stood up at the table and took a bow. A man who went out on his own and bought his wife a garnet necklace he could not afford, because she loved red and all she had left, she said, was a good neck.

MOLLY AND JEFF got to know Mike O'Meara when he was dying. Jeff knew him for some time before Molly ever met him, because he showed up one day at the hospital to interview Jeff for an article about a corpse, and they liked each other. Jeff was a pathologist and Mike needed anatomical details. They got along so well that Mike took to stopping by the Path lab whenever he felt like it.

Eventually they took such a shine to each other that they made a plan to meet for dinner with their wives, and then the friendship of years began, beginning with the five Mike had left to live. He got his diagnosis soon after that first dinner, so almost all the time Molly was in love with him his death was on the way. She says "almost all the time" to herself because he seemed perfectly healthy the night they all crowded together into a booth and raised their glasses.

This was the period when food was first being served in a mound. Even in bars—they were in Mike's favorite bar—a plate arrived like a bed piled with coats. If you ordered fish you would have to go in with a fork tine and give a tug, disrupting the mashed potato in ruffs of chard, with slices of seared tuna forming praying hands on top. Jeff said it helped to be a pathologist. Alice was the first to plunge in and dismantle her pile, as Molly, laughing, picked up her fork without a thought and looked directly at Alice's husband for the first time since they had sat down. All she had noticed as he slid into the booth and shook her hand were stooped shoulders and dark mussed hair, like his wife's.

At what exact point did she put down her wineglass and feel a flowing engagement with all that was going on in the bar, downstairs in the street, and beyond that on the waters of the Sound where ferries were passing with their lit windows, because she was looking at Mike O'Meara?

A few weeks later, Mike served out the first of Alice's casseroles with a big silver spoon that had belonged to her grandmother, and they began on their friendship. At the O'Meara table everybody interrupted and spilled things and sopped them up with the grandmother's linen napkins and tilted back in the rickety chairs to laugh, distracted from whatever Alice was serving by the talk about crime and politics and religion, spun out of Mike's pronouncements and backed up by Alice's facts, and distracted too by each other—the three boys and two girls, the youngest already half grown, allowed from their earliest years to stay up late and shout their own opinions, or when they were older, to state them quietly with the irony of those newly back from college. And wine—Mike had to have a lot of wine, and Alice let him have it because she couldn't stop him and she wasn't one to fasten her hopes on somebody else's improvement.

Alice was a woman, Molly saw right away, in whose presence people including herself felt themselves amiable and worthy, at their best. Perhaps because of having been reared as she had been, in a kind of material and religious Oz, as Mike described it, and without seeming to will the condition on herself, Alice lived in a state of approval. She had known Mike since they were first graders at Saint Joseph's school. "She was the good girl," he said. He looked at Molly. "I bet you were the good girl too."

"I was," Molly said. "But not any more." They all laughed, Jeff threw his arm in front of her to restrain her, and for a moment she was safe inside the tent of marriage.

In the ninth grade, at a retreat in honor of the Blessed Virgin, Mike had handed Alice a joint and she had taken a deep drag.

"That did it," he said. "I was in love."

"In love," Alice said with a sigh. "I was the one. I was the pro- verbial slave. I had a lot of penance to do. They had me pray for him. Wasn't that smart?"

"And then the families got involved," Mike said. "I was too good for her."

Mike had not gone off to college when Alice did; he had skipped up a ladder of city jobs into the police department, where his way with witnesses and his regard for details worked their way into his file and landed him in Homicide. But he lost heart for the work. He knew something about crime, and because he could write, they took him on at the newspaper. You could do that then, hire on with promises instead of credentials.

Even though eventually he wrote a syndicated column on crime and appeared every so often on TV, few people in town would have recognized Mike or known where to find him if they had something to say about a crime. He wasn't at the paper, he was out and around, in courtrooms and jails and morgues. And bars, of course; he had a lot of drinking to do in the course of a day.

Molly had seen the danger in liking Alice too much, but it was too late for that; in no time she and Alice were in and out of each other's houses and Molly was reading through the youngest girl's poems because she, Molly, had once published poems in magazines—though sometimes the four of them did not get together for months. As couples, they had the kind of friendship in which regularity and obligation were kept at bay. Jeff was always saying what good friends that made them.

"That may be what men look for in friendship," Alice said. "Us girls want a commitment: call me every day or else." How could anyone harm Alice?

ONE NIGHT MIKE mentioned in passing that he was being treated for a disease. He had a lymphoma, a mild one. Hardly breathing, Molly looked at Alice. "They think it's the kind that can be relatively benign," Alice said after she took a drink of her beer. But if it was that kind, Jeff said when they got home, it didn't sound as if it was taking a benign course in Mike's case.

Five years went by. In some of them Molly was able to put Mike out of her mind for days at a time. In others it seemed she stood for half the year with her hand on its way to the phone. *It's Molly. I have something to tell you.* Of course he would answer sometimes, when she called Alice. At those times her own voice surprised her, greeting him with normal concern, asking questions about the chemo, the steroids, the possible dietary measures. Of course she saw him. He was getting sicker. She began to let her thoughts of him take her where they would. As for dreams, she no longer hoped for them. She would have kept him out of them if she could, because as often as not the man finally drawing her to him was breathless and thin, the chest like an egg carton when she finally lay against it.

In real life he was not yet that bad. This condition of his did not appear to worry him. Early in chemo his hair fell out. His daughters gave him a cashmere ski cap, which he wore a time or two until they went back to school. "Half the men we know are bald," Alice said. Nevertheless, Molly had a recurring dream of holding him, comforting him, enclosing his scalp in her hands.

His eyebrows and lashes did not fall out. Gradually his cheeks sank in an unpleasant way, though, high up under the cheekbone where it didn't look like the normal hollowing you might acquire in middle age if you went on a diet, but like an excavation, as if tissue might have been siphoned out. Molly knew his face so well by then that she knew where every cell belonged, and she was seeing them change, shift, vanish. She wanted to ask Alice how she could stand it. Of course Alice was watching. Then he was on steroids, and when his cheeks filled out the strange little hollows were still there, like thumbprints in dough.

ONE DAY THE doorbell rang. When she opened the door, with the chime still hanging in the air, there he was. "Come in," she said after a second. He walked in unsteadily—nobody knew any more which caused the gait, illness or liquor—and sat down at the kitchen table. He asked if Jeff was there, but of course Jeff was at work, it was daytime. Like many people who work on their own, like Molly, in fact, even without alcohol Mike often forgot whether it was the weekend or not and where people were who did go to the office. It wasn't that he didn't work hard. He was always on the track of somebody who could put him on the track of something before his deadline, and his big eyes, too big for a man really, almost in a class with Peter Lorre's eyes, were always searching down a street or around a room or over the planes of a face. If it was your face, those eyes were a snare. They were the famished, dreaming organs you see on posters of ragged children. They had down-sweeping lashes, black and thick, that acted on Molly the way the forest in a cartoon draws the scared kids in on tiptoe. Her body followed her eyes, her mind swayed, she stepped closer. Even a man—Jeff, for example, ordinarily a man of few words—would talk more freely, and in a more fervent way, with Mike as his listener.

"You've never had a friend like this," Molly said to him.

"He comes down there, he finds me," Jeff said humbly. Jeff was well liked, but nobody much hung out in the Path lab or saw a lot of him. But Mike would get him out of the basement and make him eat lunch. "Drinks his lunch," Jeff said. "I keep warning him. But you can't tell him. He drinks because of the things he deals with." Molly had never heard Jeff, who kept at a remove the worst of life that he himself dealt with, plated out on glass and magnified, make a psychological assessment of another man.

"Why deal with those things?" she said, clinging shamelessly to the subject.

Jeff said, "Fate. Fate put him there. Look at the guy. His whole life. What's he going to do? No money for school, smart." Another first for Jeff, generalizing about another's life. Usually he stuck with facts. In that way he resembled Alice, who read every page of the newspaper and knew what was happening in the world without any wish to remake it in her own words. "The guy should be teaching. When he's done with chemo I'm getting him in to talk to the students. Why not? They all watch TV, they all want to do forensics. Smartest guy I know." People said that all the time, because Mike had not gone to college.

Jeff could say that.

Molly could say, "Did you see his column today?" And so on. Nothing more. She couldn't say, What is it? What has happened to me?

Not for years could she ask anybody for confirmation of Mike's effect. Finally she brought it up with her friend Rita, who had known him. Even then Molly couldn't say anything about how she had felt. And what Rita said . . . but that came later.

On the day he came to her house Mike said, "Are you really busy?" Molly had been working at the computer but she said no. She said it several times. He said, "I've just seen something terrible. I don't even want to think about it."

She knew this must be the child everybody had been looking for. A six-year-old boy. They already had the man who had been seen with him. It had been in the paper for days, as helicopters circled above the woods of Seward Park.

Mike closed his eyes and made a tent over his forehead with his hands, as if he and Molly were sitting in the sun, and for a minute the eyelashes slept on the skin of his cheeks and drove all thought of what he might have seen from her mind. She supposed if he had been her husband she would have gotten used to the sight and maybe even been mildly irritated by it, as we sometimes are by a thing that once bewitched us.

Right away she thought he must have come from the morgue. Alice had told her his visits to the morgue figured in his drinking.

"I wish I could talk to Jeff," he said as Molly poured coffee. His eyes had opened. He shook himself like a dog.

She could have said, Why didn't you go to the lab if you want to talk to Jeff?

He and Jeff had a little contest as to which one had seen worse sights, though by then Jeff was out of the county hospital where gruesome events from the newspaper drew to a close in the cold rooms of Pathology; he was back at the university and spending most of his time looking at slides.

"Do you want to call him from here?"

"No . . . no." He swirled his coffee. "This was a kid. I can't mention this to Alice."

Oh? How come you can mention it to me? But she leaned forward sympathetically and cupped her mug in her hands. His attention swiveled down to her hands. She saw it. His mind would narrow like that.

In a low, despairing voice he said, "Your hands . . . they're nice, they're . . ." She set the mug down. He took hold of her hands. He folded the fingers in to make fists and raised the fists to his face and ground them into his eyes. A solemn shock ran through her, as if a comb had been dragged through her body.

All the blood had run out of her brain and into the skin and muscles of her hands, which were like invalids given up to a drug, and at the same time she had a marvelous clarity of thought, of almost disinterested pity for him. But that was quickly replaced by the familiar dazed longing. It seemed to her that he must know, having forced her hands to be the envoys of the secret, and yet something told her not to move, because assuredly he did not know, and would not want to know. When he stopped grinding her knuckles into his eyes and let go of her hands, it would shock him, she knew, if she spread them on either side of his head and pulled him across the table to her. No, he was like an animal that had come up to her in the wild, trustingly, and she had to be still.

"That's not really what I came about. There's something else I need to talk to you about," he said, still in the despairing voice. "Because of Alice." What was coming? She had to steady herself, try not to let her chest display the speed and shallowness of her breathing.

What is love? What is it? What is it? How can it be what it

seems to be, nothing? A vacancy, an invisibility, a configuration of the mind. But with a weight, perceptible to the body. And a married woman with a husband she loved and liked, caught under the weight, unable to breathe? And it wasn't even a *person* for whom she felt this nothing, this love, not a personality, a self, a man who drank too much and wrote for the newspaper and had five kids, but the face and eyes of a *being* of some kind who lived in the body and looked out of the eyes of Mike O'Meara. A being from an earlier life trapped in the layers of this one. Or a primitive version of a human being, say a Pleistocene man off the northern grassy plain, looking for the first time into the eyes of a rough creature on the same plain, herself.

It wasn't even that she wanted all that intensely to go to bed with him. Or it wasn't primarily that—though she knew a lot of people would have said so. "Lust," Alice herself would have said in a minute, hearing of these symptoms.

She wanted to see him. Just that. Year after year she had remembered and rehearsed and desired the sight of Mike O'Meara more than the sight of Jeff or her children or her dead mother or anyone else. She had wanted to know she would see him and for as long as possible each time and with some promise that he would come back so that she could see him again. It was a primitive feeling without very much of herself in it, like the wish to get warmer when you're cold.

She had other friends, who, if she had called them and wailed out what was happening to her, would have kindly said, "You pity him. He's dying."

"Tell me," Molly said to him. But again the doorbell rang.

It was Alice, at the door. "Hello, Molly," she said. Her voice was that of a school principal who stands up by degrees and comes out from behind a desk. "I'm surprised." She walked in. "I'm surprised."

Mike was coming out of the kitchen. "Hi," he said to Alice with a benign tiredness.

"Hi, I saw the car," Alice said, looking no different from the way she always looked, with her rosy cheeks and thick half-combed hair and her chin tucked into her neck in a motherly way. She had on her red necklace; her fingers were touching it. She didn't look angry. "I just didn't know *where* you'd be. *Who.*"

"Don't tell me you think I'm here with Molly." Mike sat down heavily on the bench in Molly's hall. Alice didn't answer, she just stood there. Molly can still hear what he said next. "Don't tell me you think that," he said. "It's not Molly."

"Sorry," Alice said, without looking at Molly. It was not like Alice to leave off the *I'm*.

It wasn't very long after that that Mike began to go downhill fast. He had to go for outpatient transfusions. Molly was one of those Alice invited to drive him and sit with him while the blood dripped in.

AFTER THE FUNERAL there was a long period when Molly contrived to have his name come up. Her friend Rita, who was a reporter at the paper, said, "O'Meara. Jeez, the poor guy. Something about him. He had that way. He never acted on it. Whoa, don't get me wrong. But he was always kinda playing. Those eyes. I know a couple of women who—"

"Oh, don't tell me that. Don't tell me that, Rita."

"Don't speak ill of the dead?"

"I don't mean that. I just don't want to know who. Who?"

"I think Marian. Yeah. She taught their kids. And Cathy Daley at the paper. They were always flirting around. She actually tried to get him to meet her someplace. He didn't, of course. He never would have."

Molly had never seen Mike flirt with anyone. Never. Was

there a world for each pair of eyes? Like a private screening for each person, and yours was tailored to you?

She tried to ask Alice about this, delicately. Maybe the woman was just a fling. Obviously his heart was still with his family. Was he a man who had flings? "No," Alice told her. "No. That, he would never do. This was serious. He was in love. He thought we could separate, for God's sake. He was trying to figure it all out. Whether I could take it. That's probably the worst thing he said. 'You can bear it, can't you, you're so strong.' He was in love. He could barely walk at that point, his counts were so low, and he was talking about *getting an apartment*."

"Oh, Alice."

"To be with her."

"Oh, God."

"I know. I know. But he didn't get to, did he?"

"No."

"He never got to. And I have to think it was because of her, because she wouldn't. And I never knew who it was. It was a freak thing. Oh, he had his deal, with women. That was just his way. But you know him, Molly. You know how he was, about his family. But one day . . . he said he just looked up one day and there she was."

"Oh, God."

"It was love. He couldn't think about anything else. She was younger than we are, of course. But she broke up with him at one point. When she told him she wouldn't see him any more he said that was like what he sometimes felt in the morgue. He would tell me these things. If he saw something unbearable in the morgue, his legs started to hurt. So I knew I had to let him. Oh, first I said, 'Maybe your legs hurt because of the lymphoma.'"

"Oh, Alice. His legs hurt. You thought it was me."

"Only that one day. Unbelievable. Sorry. I used to ask myself whether it was this person or that person, how young she was—I never could ask him her exact age—was she some friend of the girls'—but she was too sad-sounding to be all that young, she wasn't so ruthless, was she, or wouldn't she have gone off with him? Or whether she was somebody I saw in the grocery store, or at church . . . he liked Catholic women, you know, they were the kind he really liked because of filling the time at Mass when he was a kid, lusting over all those kneeling legs. But of course he didn't go to Mass now so how would he have met them? Molly—" She gave Molly a wolfish glare. "You would tell me if you knew, wouldn't you?"

Jeff said the same thing to her. "You must have known who it was. Women always know." He was angry at Mike; he wanted to have been told. He was Mike's best friend. "Think she came to the funeral?" But at the funeral, only Alice was watching. None of this was spoken of before he died.

Alice never apologized for saying "I'm surprised" to Molly, in her front hall. That one "Sorry" was for having even dreamed it could be her.

Molly got through the funeral. As a friend, she could be forgiven a choked sound when the priest said, "Receive our brother Michael." Alice held herself together, though she gave a little laughing moan a couple of times when they were all eating and drinking afterwards, and let tears run down her cheeks without wiping them. But she didn't stutter or gasp or double over; she hugged her friends; when she wasn't doing that she kept her arm around whichever of their children was near, or held onto Molly.

And who was she, the one Mike chose? Who leans on the car door when the thought of him stabs her, who loses her cart in the grocery store? Who lets out a groan in the shower? Who can't go into the part of the cemetery where he is buried, in case his family, his friends have come to visit the grave?

They would not despise her. Why will she not make herself known to them? Why won't she answer to them, Alice, and Jeff, and Molly?

Invisible River

· · ·

I.

A WOMAN STANDS at the mirror in a train station bathroom. Next to her a dark-haired girl is blending the shadow on one eyelid with a fingertip, while the woman marvels at the black pressed-down lashes, thick as a pocket flap. When both lids are done the girl pulls down her lower lip with two dark nails, perfect ovals, and examines her teeth and gums. Now she's making an O of her lips to cream on red lipstick, furiously round and round, not pausing at the corners. *All right, all right,* thinks the woman, *you're a beauty but that's too much lipstick.* The girl goes on a little longer and then without blotting her lips drops the lipstick in a little velvet bag and roughly cinches it tight.

She grabs the handle of a black leather suitcase on scuffed wheels, with a strap around it, and drawing her black eyebrows together yanks it on one wheel through the door a fat girl coming in holds open for her. *Whoever's out there waiting for you,* the woman at the mirror thinks, *he's in for it.* Or maybe there's nobody. Maybe that's the problem.

Of course nobody paces outside the door waiting for her, either. What train would she board, to what destination would someone accompany her, a woman of fifty-some who has laid a big brown purse in a puddle on the counter and seems content to daydream in a public bathroom? Finally she takes her hands out from under the water and pulls down the groaning belt of towel. She looks at herself. Despite her open stare she didn't get a fraction of a glance from the girl. She isn't old. If she were, a quick smile might easily have passed both ways between them, a small bow across time. She is unsure, herself, about applying lipstick, which may in this light have the effect of a label stuck on an orange, but eventually she does it anyway.

Unlike the girl, whose big eyes were red-rimmed under the makeup, she is happy. Or very close. She sees the possibility.

2.

GROUNDLESS NEAR HAPPINESS doesn't do anything for the Reader, if she comes across it on the page. She is looking for something with an edge.

The Reader is blond, healthily pretty in a laissez-faire way. At first glance her clothes look casual too, but they are carefully chosen. Two years in the city have taught her where to find clothes, which colors are hers, how to minimize her breasts. Intelligence and determination have won her the job she holds, not her first by any means, despite her youth. Having worked on publications for years, ever since high school, she has a long resume that belies her wide, crooked smile and her accent. Those in the ranks above her rely on her to hear a certain range of notes, in particular the notes struck by some of the newer writers, and convey it to them in the way of someone quickly transposing a tune. Some of her enthusiasms make them scratch their heads. "Take a look at this," they say. "What can I say, the Reader likes it."

When she has kicked off her shoes after work she stands on one foot with her knee on the painted tin cover of the radiator, leaning a shoulder on the glass. The sky narrows to a dark blue cone between buildings, with its tip in a river that can't be seen from here. But she relaxes. It is close by: a river. Full against its banks and then walled in, moving heavily alongside the streets with its own slow purpose.

The Reader grew up in a mining town with a river running the length of it. Until the age of twelve she lived in a house overlooking the river, which brought a shallow whitewater and a six-foot falls right into town. Two parents, three children, dogs, cats, trees, porch. Then her father died. After that she lived in several smaller houses, and finally, when her mother was getting into serious difficulties, an apartment above the café where her mother sometimes worked. No one called it a studio; it was one room, for just herself and her mother by then—her brothers were gone—and one cat. You couldn't see the river from the café but you could always hear it, hastening past the town where, with her mother, the Reader lived what she calls the sad part of her life. From time to time it rose out of its bed and flooded the town, drowning people's goats and pets and occasionally people themselves, sucking them through culverts, upending their trailers, and wallowing away with them before they could wade out to a rowboat—the peaceful golden brown river that gave them fish and black soil and green vegetable gardens.

Now she has made a second river her own, welcoming its tugs and barges, its measured progress into the heart of a city fit to be the destination of water.

Yet Nature has not been banished here, as people in her home town would claim; it haunts the city, especially in this season. Wet leaves plaster the sidewalks, some as big as the pockets of the yellow slicker she wears in defiance of all the city black. She springs down onto the yellow carpet every morning thinking, *My wedding*. Should she have included a flower girl, one of her nieces, to give more of an aisle-feeling to the space? *The space*—that's what the hotel's wedding consultant calls the long airy room where the wedding will take place. The same was true when she was looking for an apartment: everything, even the closet, was a space.

She doesn't miss houses with rooms, or anything else about the town she came from. Too much was known there. Even her mother is gone from the town, no longer on her stool in the café lounge late with the regulars and the two floozies and an occasional girl in overalls from the highway crew. Too much was seen in that town, too much gone over in stores and church circles and on the telephone. A widow didn't go on and on in the sloppy condition permitted in the first weeks; a widow remarried or took an interest in the church or the lives of the next generation, or all three, ideally. To do otherwise, to let a bad habit get the better of you, to drink cheap wine for months on end, certainly to be picked up out of wet grass before dawn and have the snails pulled off you by your own child . . . to do these things was to imply that your loss had exceeded the losses of others. That your husband had been somehow superior. That you, yourself, had been uniquely struck down.

The daughter, the Reader, was another story. In all likelihood people in town still speak of her, persist in expecting her. There, homecoming queens are remembered for a generation. But no one she would want to run into is there. Her brothers left early and never went back.

She can call the brothers . . . or not call them. Her boyfriend is on his way over. Her fiancé, now. *Husband*: sober word. But her boyfriend has nothing sober about him. He's like a dog, she tells her friends, a dog in a movie. Everyone on the set is making a movie, but the dog is at a picnic, sniffing, peeing on the grass, called back again and again to flop down, relax. Rewarded for it, for lying there panting. The dog thinks the picnic is real. And it is real. It's real when her boyfriend is around. That's partly because he's rich. *The story of Midas is wrong*, she thinks: *the rich touch things to life. They think what they're doing is real, and so it is. They don't get stuck in the wet mud of* was. Nothing had to be over, for people like her boyfriend, teased and admired for his appetites—too many green olives at the tapas bar, too much duck breast, too many girlfriends until she came along. True, new to the city, he had gotten himself involved with girls who were not as easygoing as he. But he meant no one harm, and his good nature always rescued him from these episodes, adventures on the way to her.

At the thought of him, and filled with the promise of blue, early evening, she does stretches at the window. All day she has read; taken notes; typed short, courteous letters that will go out under signatures other than her own. The stack she has left to read before the honeymoon is on the scarred steamer trunk where she props her bare feet when she sits on the couch. One panel of the old chest bears a Cunard White Star label.

It was a trunk she saw in an antique store, under a table. She knelt down, bumping her head, ran her hands over it, lifted the lid, and saw it was full of moldy magazines. She could hardly breathe. She bought it.

Just before that she had broken off with a man, a married man who had taken her with him to England on the *QE2*. He wasn't rich but he knew how to do things like that. He gave her books and jewelry, a big dinner ring and pearls that had been in his family and should have gone to his daughters. She knows that, now, though at the time she took the heavy pearl brooch from his hand carelessly, like a piece of fruit. And the fact that the big pearls were pears, spilling from a basket of gold, didn't charm her. The intricate basketwork, the braided handle—she didn't want these things out of a drawer in his house. She wanted him. "I bet this was your mother's," she said.

"It was. She had it from her grandmother."

In a way she had won after all, shaken him to the point that although he had sworn not to, he still called her from time to time, a year and some months later, just to hear her voice. She talked to him. She could do that now. A man older than her own father would have been had he lived, tall and half bald like her handsome father.

But certainly not, as her boyfriend claims, a father figure.

She doesn't hold it against her boyfriend that he can't *judge*. Why should he be able to? That, he always says of her long affair, was a bad deal. But—this can't be explained to him, ever—the disguise in which the older man moved, of someone unapproach- able, trapped in his own power, the surprise of him when he rose up and showed himself, streaming some element of his hiding place, as if other men were logs and he a crocodile . . . *that* had had a charm almost fatal to her. Finally she shook free of it, just in time. She met someone who could soothe her, free her from her concentration on the charming, intent, eroded personality of the man, and from his body—though athletic and graceful—so capturable by hers, so quickly made tense and still. A body marked off into distinct regions, unlike hers that has one surface like a heavy coat of paint. The dry skin of his face so unspringing- back, almost as if you could strip off patches of it by pulling, or leave fingerprints. The thin, dark, almost transparent skin around his eyes . . . maybe she would describe the skin as like the unwound cassette tape you saw for a while, shifting along the sidewalk or caught around the base of a fire hydrant. But she wouldn't go on and on. "Thin skin, bluish," she might write if she were the editor she intends to be, striking out lines of prose.

There was a time when creases, baldness, a graying mustache were things that acted on her heart like a drawstring. Probably he was one of many men his age she saw around her now, now that her eyes were opened, men getting out of taxis, crossing lobbies, who might laughingly admit to each other that they were learning in secret, from someone like her, how to be adored.

Thus also in the manuscripts she is reading: always the possibility that such a character, while feeling himself sad, his life-ardor waning, can be startled into explosive action. Especially with a guide—a Beatrice or a Tadzio. Maybe as he strides along the sidewalk with his hands in the pockets of his overcoat his heart is pounding from the cigarettes he can't give up. Or from longing, mortally pounding. Maybe he has children who are almost grown, almost not his anymore, with no interest in how wild he is inside. A crocodile, she called him. But not one of the "new" men, gratified by their ability to produce tears; no, his tears are real, his sad half-closed eye has fallen on *her*. But he won't stay long, mired in this sort of love. He'll saw the murky waters aside and swim away. Maybe the motor of his soul is idling with fast jerks, maybe he is sleepless with readiness for the new. In some scenarios he will burst out in another hemisphere, in Africa or Australia. Anything could happen to him. He may not know it. In plots of another kind, all that is needed is for someone who does know it to lay her hand on his and lead it to the new continent of herself.

These possibilities are not the same thing as a romance.

As for women: Often, the Reader says, it's simply that they're predictable. They're embarking on this or that, lowering themselves into unfamiliar waters, testing their freedom. Behind them there's always some ruin, some man has ruined everything, and then they surmount the ruin. You have to be wary of this material, now there is so much of it. It would be better if somebody gave us a devoted wife. That would be something.

So many ex-wives come streaming across her desk. So many half-crazy plotters, cast-offs, matriarchs without a household. Or the brainy, tough talkers, the intuitives, the solvers of murders. Rarely, a murderer. Revenge is of other kinds. So much revenge. Most of it imagined rather than carried out.

The bookstores are filled with these women. That's the strange thing, the Reader says regretfully: They're the readers.

3.

THE BRIDE'S MOTHER in blue silk. The groom's mother in a linen suit of a fawn color that doesn't agree with her skin—she knew it with certainty as she was having her hair done—and a necklace of small emeralds set in old coins, to redeem the unlucky color of the suit, because she is a doctor married to an executive, and has good jewelry, while the bride's mother is practically a street person. The bride bought her the silk dress and jacket and altered them; she got her on her feet and dried out and sober for a week, to arrive at this moment of standing with a fine tremble and a set jaw, in the grip of what is not yet dread, more an apprehension regarding the reception: whether she is going to put her lips to a glass of champagne. Whether, despite her promise to her daughter and her daughter's faith in it, she will tilt her head and swallow.

When the bride draws near on the arm of her brother, she turns opposite her mother and stops dead, swaying a little off her careful balance. This causes the brother to just miss stepping on her hem, and frown a warning that any delay could collapse the whole occasion on top of them like a tent. The bride smiles at her mother, a studied, down-turned smile of acknowledgment, like a child's stiff stage curtsy, for the guests to see. When she starts to move again the mother raises her hands to her cheeks.

In actuality she is pressing her fingers into her ears to stop their ringing, but the groom's mother beside her turns, sees the hands cupping the face in a classic maternal gesture, and smiles her agreement. She does this in spite of knowing her son said goodbye to another woman in his apartment last night.

In the pocket of his morning coat he has the squat figure of Yoda. Silly, but his mother was determined; she climbed on a chair to rummage in the Star Wars box in the top of his closet at home. Why should the bride be the only one to walk down the aisle knowing she had with her some invisible, unbroken tie to the past? As they got ready for bed she found the figure in her suitcase, and at her insistence they dressed and took a cab back over to his apartment quite late, without calling. When he came to the door there was a woman behind him sliding into the bedroom, tossing dark hair forward over streaky, made-up eyes and red lipstick. In the middle of his living room was a black suitcase with everything tumbled out around it, cosmetics strewn under the coffee table, a bra caught on the chair arm along with the cord of a hair dryer, clothes in a heap on the rug, as if somebody had hurled the suitcase at the table or gone at it with an ax.

But it's too late to make anything of that, to question her son or help him extricate himself from either thing. His mother has poured out the last of what she can pour into him. When she first saw him with his best man rather grim beside him this morning, he was pale and tired; she herself is tired and wondering if anyone marrying anywhere in the world during this particular hour could possibly see the thing through to a day like this, a child's wedding, thirty years down the road.

Her husband's glasses are foggy. She takes his hand. Few at the company he owns are among the guests today or have ever seen this side of him, with cold hands and sweating nose. It's too late for either one of them to finish all they were intending with this son, their only child. Although they have not put it into words between them they see him as hopelessly distractible, already swept away by the intrigues of his accidental job at a magazine—after so many applications to business school and medical school—and having no time for hard work, or for friends or sports or anything much other than the woman of the moment.

Was there something they did that made him turn out this way? Heaven help this girl he's marrying, pretty as she is. Is she pregnant? How nice she is, despite her one-upping of some of them at the table last night about this article or that book, despite those officious brothers—or one of them officious and the other withdrawn—at the rehearsal and the dinner, and the wives trying to pretend they're on good terms with the poor mother who didn't seem to know them apart. For the groom's mother knows, from her son—who is in the flush of an explorer's admiration for this brisk, unsuspicious girl with her brains and her ideals, an admiration his mother worries would be subtly altered by the absence of thick yellow hair twisted up on the head in a chaste braid, long waist, breasts verging on heavy—that the bride's brothers have repudiated their mother. Or one of them has and the other just follows along. They don't have anything to do with her. One of them has her power of attorney, she couldn't be trusted with a check if she had one to endorse; the other pays the rent on the room she has at the moment and is lucky to have—without it she would be little more than a street drunk—in a boarding house in Baltimore. A hole, the groom calls it, though he never saw it, or met the mother before this week, having stayed behind when his bride-to-be flew down to Baltimore to bring her back for the wedding.

Out of the hole into this hotel, old and fine, with its pleasing sconces and buttery sheets. The sons have seen to it that she move into a better hotel than the one their sister had been able to afford for her. Now she's staying in the one where the wedding and reception are to be held. Her sons are uptown in yet another, with their wives, having left all the children at home.

She ate her costly breakfast in the coffee shop. The groom's parents too are in the wedding hotel, but they didn't come into the coffee shop for breakfast. She didn't want to think they might have been instead having breakfast with their son and her daughter, who announced last night that they didn't believe in the prohibition on seeing each other before the wedding, and would meet in the morning. "Not tonight. Tonight we need our sleep," her daughter said.

They have dispensed with some of the wedding rituals. The reception is going to be free-form, but for the ceremony itself they've kept traditional music—a keyboard with an amp for the organ tones of the recessional—and language, phrases such as *Dearly beloved*, and *keep thee only unto her* which they would never, the bride said sternly, attempt to improve upon. For after all, as she argued to her boyfriend, whatever state her mother was in now, she had been the model for *till death us do part*. And they would not get into composing any special vows to close loopholes or leave them open, whichever, the bride said with a laugh.

The old, the new, the borrowed: these she has gathered. Her mother was to provide the blue. Instead of a blue garter she brought a blue glass bead from a broken necklace, a gift of her husband, a bead she had carried in the pocket of whatever coat she owned from the time her daughter was a baby, so that now it was rough and almost colorless, as if salt had etched it. "I can't believe you still have this! I used to go in your pocket after it and put it in my mouth! I loved to feel the little nick, see? But of course now little kids can't have anything this small, they could choke." Some of her friends already had children; the rules they lived by frightened the Reader a little even as she saw them as perfectly correct. They were what awaited her but did not yet have to be concentrated on. "Oh, but where will I put a bead?" Miraculously, the maid of honor knew that some wedding dresses had a tiny flat pocket, sewn into a seam somewhere or hanging on a silk cord for just that purpose, the storing of some talisman, and this one did, inside where the gores of the heavy skirt swung open.

Tomorrow before the airport taxi comes, the mother thinks, *I might just disappear.* Her younger son has slipped her an envelope and she has enough cash. She could take the train to Baltimore. It wouldn't have to be the fast one. She could make the trip last hours and hours, among the snores and smelly socks, sleeping or just looking out the window. Stay out of the club car. Get off in Philadelphia for air, and board another train later. Wander in that off-the-train daze in which for minutes, to the eye, even the marble walls of stations creep faintly, like the near land out the train window moving at a different rate from the far. What would she do in Philadelphia? Walk, look around her. Everything in cities was changing for the better, the maid of honor on her right had told her at the rehearsal. She was the best friend, who had a job in the mayor's office. Is everything changing? The mother has a TV to keep her informed but the changes are far away from her room, her path to the Minimart.

It would be good to be carried along tracks, instead of miles in the air with the destination rising up from below to stop her dead. She likes feeling herself pulled slowly away from where she has been, and all the steps of postponement.

The last time she took the train was six or seven years ago, to stay with her older sister in Baltimore. It was when she was first alone. Her daughter had left for school. A daughter, her sister warned her, had to get out. She had to go to college; she couldn't stay behind to manage for her mother. A daughter had to leave off being the steady little girl with an eye out for everything and everybody, steering her mother through the days into the blind evenings. This sister had stepped forward with an unexpected determination to get her straightened out, and she had agreed to it. It was something to try.

For a while, at her worst, after the quickly ruined time with her sister and before her sons stepped in, she shared a place not far from the station in Baltimore with two women whose names she doesn't like to remember, nor their red faces squashed in sleep, who tried to convince her to pack up and hop on a freight with them when spring came. They might know the switchman but what did they know about her? She was still major steps away from that.

4.

STATELY AS THE deep organ chords issuing from the keyboard, a little prow comes forward against her breastbone, or it may be the bone itself pressing there as she is borne to the heights of tenderness for her daughter. It doesn't matter that two men, her sons, are in the row behind, with wives beside them who had been carefully seated too far down the row of wineglasses at the rehearsal dinner to make themselves heard if they spoke to her. It doesn't matter that in their wallets are pictures of children who have not been told of her, and better so.

Next she is escorted under the arbor of woven ferns and rib-bon and led down the wide hall to the reception, the groom's mother following on her usher's arm with clear taps of her beautiful fawn pumps, not quite catching up. They are the first to arrive in the big echoing room; the bridal pair are behind a door in a private space where newlyweds can spend a few minutes getting their bearings before the reception. At the far end are waiters, with a forest of green bottles and the cake.

A tall man stands apart from them at the long table laden with candles and real autumn leaves, banked platters and swirled fabric, red and gold. Instead of greeting them when they came in he turned his back. He may be the wedding consultant, passing a hand over his bald scalp as he scans the table.

The guests will serve themselves and find tables of their own choosing. The real planner of the whole thing was the maid of honor, her daughter's best friend who works for the mayor. It was to be a little like a church supper in the bride's home town in West Virginia, she declared. But a sophisticated church supper, with wonderful food. This girl could imagine her way into a bride's intentions better than any hotel wedding consultant. Everyone agreed she should start her own business.

"Ohhh . . ." the mother had heard herself groan from the velvet couch in the bride's dressing room. "Oh, I didn't pay for anything." What a ridiculous thing to say, in anguish or surprise, to the daughter who came for her and flew her here and groomed her like a child and got her dressed and pinned jewelry onto her.

"Don't worry about that," her daughter said quickly. "You're here." Then her daughter pulled her close against the big white rustling dress and hugged her as if she were a little thing with stage fright.

She knows the bride and groom are to enter and greet everybody and then give the band a sign and just dance out onto the empty floor. There is not to be a receiving line; why should anyone "receive" anyone else? her daughter had said, over the groom's mild protest. It was exactly that, his assuming certain obligations could be laughed at but would be met, that got the best friend going with her changes.

A receiving line seems to be forming up anyway, with the bride and groom trying to present to his parents various young women in black dresses with thin straps. Then the lights go down and the bridal pair starts the inaugural waltz, in which they are to dance until some signal allows a tide of couples to rise around them. Alone on the floor they dance slowly and beautifully. She is proud of her daughter's dancing. On the porch of the house by the river, she had been the teacher, dancing with a thirteen-year-old stiff with grief, as she had danced with her husband in the evenings in summer before he was sick, with the record player lifted through the window and lightning bugs in the hedge, up and down the pine boards they had stripped and varnished themselves, around the corner and back, laughing and carrying on while the boys, joining in, jumped on and off the glider, bouncing the needle on the record, and the baby girl tried to climb up after them. Tipsy parents—waving to the neighbors. Tipsy, that unknowing pair, yes, but not drunk. There was no need to be drunk.

Over by the bandstand she can see her second son, the shyer, less successful one who pays her rent, but he's looking at the band and listening carefully to something his wife is saying. He's a big man, tall, but not handsome like his father; he has a disappointed, fallen face. She thinks, *I did favor your brother, just like you said. I did. I'm sorry. I'm sorry but he was so much ours. The first. I didn't know. I didn't know anything that could happen.*

Finally after a long time during which she can see only the bountiful rafts of stemmed glasses sliding among the shoulders— for they are not going to hoard the champagne for toasting, they are going to drink champagne all night—a few couples venture onto the floor and step carefully into each other's arms, and begin to rock slowly and move their feet in small squares, with concentrating smiles. As she watches them she feels a familiar sinking that means she needs a drink immediately. She will have to leave. Now. She's trying to retreat, but slowly, feeling behind her with one hand as if she's already had a few too many, or backed into one of the dreams she used to have, when each slow step led a few more inches back from some cliff or animal. She is suddenly so played out and heavy in the arms and legs that she thinks she might actually have to go to her room and fall down and sleep.

She plays with the idea. She thinks, *Then if I wake up it'll be morning and I'll hear the river. I'll wake the kids. I won't have this life on my hands.* But of course she's playing a game, a game of tempting herself. She knows she wouldn't wake up in her old house but she thinks in stubbornness and perplexity, *If I can't I'll die.*

But someone is asking her to dance. It's the tall, thin man, the wedding consultant. He crossed the room to her, shook hands, told her a name like Rodney or Sidney. He must have identified her as a member of the bridal party because of her gardenia and seen that no one has spoken for her. Perhaps that is his function.

She has not danced in years. When she gets out on the floor with him she is surprised at her memory of it, the alert that runs through her forgotten muscles. Some of that might be the man's doing. But here are her limbs stretching themselves, giving up some of their weight. In one of the smooth turns he executes, something catches, attaching her to his dark suit. At first it seems to be the corsage pin, but then she sees it's her other lapel, it's the brooch, her daughter's gift. Her daughter insisted that she take it, wear it, a big thick cluster of pearls in a setting the shape of a vase or basket with handles. "Lands," she says, "my daughter gave me this pin and it catches on everything."

He holds her away to look. The bruised eyes don't match his elegance. They seem to mock something, whether himself or her she can't tell. He says, "Looks like a loose prong. My mother wore one of those and it was always getting her into trouble." Then, so as not to place her in his mother's generation—for he is roughly her own age—he says, "And now they're all the rage again."

She decides he's not the wedding consultant after all. "Which side are you on?" she says.

"Which side . . . oh, the bride's. I had the pleasure of working with her at one time." The tray of champagne is tilting their way. He dances her away from it, bracing her firmly as his steps lengthen. The brooch catches again. "Uh-oh. Here." He pauses, and one hand secures her back as two long fingers of the other press her collarbone, lightly, while with the others he bends a tiny wire in the setting. She is flushed from the exertion and from having to arch backwards because of his height and stick with the conversation and keep her balance in a sequence that began simply but has grown more unpredictable as he feels her follow him. They start again, whirling a path through the crowd. "My daughter says it's junk, but I don't know, these don't look like any pearls I ever saw, they could be real."

"I wouldn't be surprised. Are you going to sell it?" he asks in a friendly way.

She almost trips. "Why do you ask me that?"

"Forgive me, I'm thoughtless, I was joking." But he isn't a smiler. He has her close, where without her glasses she can't really see him. He seems to steer her with something small, maybe the wrist bone. "I must be carried away, dancing with the mother of the bride."

"How do you know, you weren't at the wedding."

"I wasn't?"

"You were here in this room when we got here."

"Well, I'll confess. I said to myself, 'The prettiest dress. Eyes bluer than the bride's.' And I heard you speak to Mr. Weller there, the young groom, and I thought to myself—*Voila!* West Virginia!"

"Well, what about you? You're just as bad. You're not from here, you're from down south."

"So I am." With his mustache and sad eyes he could have been another of those soft-spoken Southerners you ran into in boarding houses, always polite, showing you some pocket watch or worn-out leather book they carried around. He could have been, if you didn't notice the halfway-mean pride that belonged to certain males looking to tease you into something—she was surprised to recognize it—and a kind of barely-held-onto patience.

He spins her into the center of the parquet floor, three times, so that she lies this way and that like a dress displayed on an arm. "What took you from West Virginia to Baltimore?"

"Things happened," she says, trying not to show that the burst of energy is deserting her and she is losing her breath. "I had enough of the place. My sister—how do you know where I live?"

With both arms he holds her in, against the strong outward pull of his wide steps in the turn. "I suppose I know everything about you," he says.

"I guess my daughter turned into a talker." Out of the corner of her eye she keeps seeing the white dress of her daughter, wide skirts sloshing up and back. Even in this first dance, the dance to complete the wedding and start the new, married life, her daughter is keeping an eye on her.

"No."

"She worked for you."

"Yes, she did."

She tries to lean back to look at him, but with his forearm along her back and fingers to her ribs he keeps her where she is. By now she needs her breath and doesn't try to speak.

Her ears are ringing so that she can't hear much more than the big double bass thumping. That she could feel even if she went deaf. The man seems calmly, even selfishly, attached to the idea of circling the dance floor with her for the length of this waltz, so long-drawn-out that other couples have finally started to fall back and gather at the round tables with their champagne.

"Well," she says, raising her voice to be heard as they whirl to the bandstand, where the mute on the saxophone is opening and closing, "you never know." She repeats it with each fluid triangle their twinned feet describe on the smooth wood. "You never know." The dulled feeling has moved off again and she's really dancing, breathing heavily but with ease. A wind has stirred up around them, holding the other dancers at bay. Even in stiff new shoes her feet move as if a current flowed under them, or from them, swaying her with little need for effort on her part. "You never—never—know."

"That's right. My, my. I thought so. You must have been born dancing."

She is getting used to his unsmiling gallantry. She is past making the effort to smile herself. There is a pleasure foreign to smiles, coming out of nowhere and going again, just as there is the opposite, for which tears are just decorations. With closed eyes she says, "As a matter of fact I was."

As soon as she could she left the ballroom purposefully, holding the slim black satin bag, her daughter's, with both hands like a dowsing stick. She looked over the brass rail of the mezzanine down into the lobby where a boy of nine or ten was waiting for the elevator, repeatedly jabbing the button. He kept his back to her; he had a thin neck tanned amber pink, with a small cloud of bone coming and going just above the neckline of his sweatshirt. She played a game that if he turned around she would see the fixed eyes of her first child, the one who had just taken his sister up the aisle. He thought he had escaped her but he hadn't. No, he had returned to her long since, un-grown, gazing over fat cheeks like a judge, or kicking with imperial joy, a baby again, on whom everybody stopped to congratulate them, tall husband, blond wife, and sturdy, golden baby, because of the seal on the three of them of his having been born at the earliest height of love.

She herself is steady for the moment. She has made it through the wedding, she has danced, at the edge of the floor a man has placed her hand in her daughter's, bowing. Her daughter has caught her in her arms and whispered, "My Meery." Nothing so tender as this old nickname made out of her name by her daughter as a toddler, whispered on a soft breath that warmed her ear, has been said to her since an AA meeting years ago, back at home. Three or four years after her husband died—or it might have been five—she was feeling the stirrings of a deep terror. Her daughter was applying to college. A seedy old guy was looking at her, on the bleachers in the high school gym where she and a dozen others made their confessions. Of course some of them might recognize each other, even though the meetings took place in a bigger town across the county line. He said, "I seen you and your hubby a few times dancing at the lounge." They weren't supposed to allude to any possible connections they might have. "I told my wife, I had my wife then, I said, 'That's a sweet gal.' She said, 'Yes she is and I know you wish we was all like that.'"

For that little space the tension had left her. She remembered that, leaning back until the knees of the person behind her on the bleachers cradled her for a second, and saying something like, "Oh, right, that's all we need. More like me. More drunks."

"Just hear what I say," the old fellow said. He was on his last legs. He had years and years on her, in the life she would have if she wasn't careful.

A cloud of gardenia encloses her face as she looks down at the boy until the elevator comes and he gets in. She stays with her hands on the rail, glancing neither left nor right as people come in and out of the reception hall. Her eyes, in which her daughter has put soothing drops, blaze the blue of her dress, her feet clench in the new shoes, she vows, as at her own wedding, eternal beginning.

Trespass

. . .

S TARK BONNEY WAS listening to a patient's heart when the woman took his hand in hers and placed it, stethoscope still in the palm, on her breast. He would have said he drew back, as a doctor accustomed to the occasional inappropriate comment or gesture from a patient, though in fact his hand stayed where it was. She took the other hand, placed it.

"Three times I have come here." The scope was still in his ears, the voice in it muffled and rather deep. The breasts seemed at the bursting point. "The orange aura that you have, I see it." She had some kind of foreign accent with a relaxed, insolent sound in it. "From one time to the next I wonder if you recognize me? Why do you think I am here?" She let go of his hands.

Of course he recognized her. "We're looking into your heart block," he said, holding her now by the waist. "By itself, it's nothing."

"No, no. Because of you. I am not Mrs. So-and-so like you call me. My name is Katya. You said that you were going to take care of me. That is what I want you to do."

A long stormy affair followed, interrupted by her death.

. . .

KATYA HAD BEEN a violinist. But she was not good enough, she said, to play with any of the ensembles for which she periodically auditioned, so she worked in a bank. She was good with numbers; numbers and music went together. "I play too much," she said. "Not the violin. That, I do not." And in truth he rarely heard her practice, though he had heard her cry in the locked bathroom after one of these auditions. "No, I play, you know, in life. I am not serious. Though I love most of all the serious musician. I am always dreaming about this one with the violin, this one with the cello." From the start, she could hurt him. "Oh, you must not worry. A serious doctor—that is the same thing. I adore him, with his blue eyes"—she kissed his eyelids—"his clean skin."

He went into the bank, not his own bank, to see her behind her window in her loud silk and tight leather, her streaked hair pulled back from the small, carved face. "What do you do all day when nobody comes in?" Because everybody used the ATMs now.

"I talk to the guard. This man is very sad. Not a good American. I gaze out to sea."

In Russia she had been a child of promise, taken from her village to school in Moscow, set apart for the study of the violin. But the collapse of the Soviet Union left her with no sponsor, no clear course to follow. She had no parents. Her mother had died in her thirties of an undetermined ailment, her father, "my beloved," in the war the Soviets waged in Afghanistan. At ten, she and a friend lived and worked with the cook at their school; after the cook caught them taking rubles from her tin they lived in a man's office, and in a downhill series of hideouts. The list shifted with each telling. "Don't ask me this! We fell through the cracks. As you say." She laughed. "Cracks! You know nothing." At sixteen, she came to the United States with a man three times her age, and quite soon she had left him, but of course, she said with comic despair, he was still on her doorstep. Still plying his Katka with gifts. "Katka": in Russian that meant someone more . . . more fun than "Katya." The gifts she threw into a drawer, where even Stark could recognize the touch of a pawnbroker—engraved spoons, medals from the Napoleonic campaigns, lacquered brooches, old pendants of amber.

After two years of a dizzying rhythm of jealousy and reconciliation, Stark had arrived at a new stage with her, in which the baring of reasons for their trespasses against each other went on in a kind of calm. His, now, were merely rote flirtation, undertaken more to retaliate than for any interest another woman could have for him; hers had more weight: confessed cravings, late-night phone calls, disappearances. He was outdone in what his ex-wife had called his "ways." Now he had no ways, only the relics of an old habit.

"I have good luck," Katya would say, on a day when she was soothing him. "Women look at him, this doctor." She had a rare smile, wide, with the mouth closed. He watched, with a dawning hopelessness, the slow elongation of the curved lips. It was a smile he thought of as Russian, the expression of a pleasure half savored, half scorned.

Gradually she came closer. The chases down the sidewalk—during which he gave thanks for his hours in the gym—the recriminations and avowals, the shouts and even slaps: all these, he told his partner Bernstein, had been leading somewhere.

"Right," Bernstein said. "Go for it."

Twice she had moved in with him and out again, but this third time her mood as she lugged in her houseplants was sober. She closed the door, leaned on it with her eyes closed, shutting out whatever had been going on with somebody he had not been able to identify, though he knew it was not the Russian or the ex-husband. She threw armloads of clothing onto the couch. "I will stay, now."

This final return came at the beginning of the second year, the brimming year when he told his friends, "Seriously, I know what they mean by 'a new life.'" They walked holding hands, or even with arms around each other. They produced, she said, an energy field of their own. "I won't even ask what you're talking about," he said. If his daughter Lynn had said such a thing in her New Age phase, he would have given an irritated chuckle. Katya said, "It is how we are, in my country. We are not closed to the great world, like you. We have souls. Look at you. *And*"— her homesickness, her simmering nationalism could surface at any time, out of the schoolbooks of the child she had been when she left—"if *we* fight a war in Afghanistan, everyone is thinking, talking about war. All the time. We do not let our little sons go to the war while we have a picnic. You don't know about this. You have only daughters." He did not remind her that she had no children at all.

He was not going to pretend to perceive an energy field, but his senses had indeed unsealed themselves. Backing out of the garage, in his own alley he caught the smell of paint, roses, individual Dumpsters, lilac. "Louder!" She turned up the radio. "This doc-*tor*! He must have quiet, that is what he likes, so he can hear little sounds with his—what-is-it. Loud, *forte*, he does not know. Music! What is that, to him?"

He found her a ring with a chunk of emerald set in ruby chips. She said she would marry him at Christmas. Early in the New Year, at the latest. "Right now is early in the new year," he said, for it was still April.

"Next year. But it will be a bad year. Another of your wars is coming."

He caught himself; he had almost said, "What does that have to do with us?"

Then, impossibly, absurdly, he was in a cemetery, walking alone to his car. He was at his door, fitting his key in the lock. He was on the stairs, he was in the bedroom opening the double closet she had taken over. He was stepping inside, he was standing draped in silk sleeves.

Impossibly, he was once more a man with a good car and a gym locker. Messages on his voicemail from women. The packed referral list of which he had once been so proud. Yet he was not that man. It was as if he had gone up the Amazon, or to Borneo, or some unvisited place, where he had landed without the labor of travel, and once there found every tie cut but the one to Katya. He felt as if he had been taken inside a cave, one where an unknown organism lived that had not yet entered civilization, whether poison or cure. Because Katya was gone—one minute she had been with him and the next gone, with her death somehow part of the cave—he found himself alone with what had happened. No one could see the organism in him, the way you could see a tan or a loss of weight when someone went away and came back. Death—of course everyone around him in the hospital and the medical school was familiar with death. Nothing exotic there. Yes, his girlfriend, his fiancée, had died, and they were sorry. No one knew he had not come back.

A shame came over him. In her harshness, her casual insults, Katya had been right: to be an American was to be a fool. To hear no warning. To have no idea what was wrong with you. To be overtaken by events you had never foreseen, and to smile. Others in the world did not smile.

She didn't mean anything political; she had no politics.

He saw that the word *adore* could be used for something

unrelated to love. Could it really have been he, Stark, who had tried in his heedless contentment to convert another person to decent, domestic, reliable love? At night he sat up in bed and grasped his head.

In the daytime he was filled with a dull apprehension, as if something were on its way that he must avoid. He had to hunch his shoulders and wait, the way he had seen so many do after an MI, not filling their lungs.

He didn't postpone any appointments; he went in to work every day. His clinic manager Shawna looked away from his eyes.

At home he would be standing in the light of the giant refrigerator Katya had chosen, in her love of appliances, and it would dawn on him that there was no food in it and the house was pounding with her music—audible no doubt to the neighbors—to which he had forgotten to listen.

"He does not know Dvorak from Debussy, the foolish man. The jerk. The musical jerk." She loved American slang. "It is all you have, in your language. I love this word you have, *jerk*! Of course we have such words! But we have so much more that you do not have because you have no souls. Oh, don't argue. You are nothing but—jerks! Listen, Doctor, what you call the bug, the ladybug, with your no imagination, we call *bozhya korovka*, little cow of god."

He had opened the case and taken out her violin, and now it lay on the bedroom chair. Something held him there scraping a string vertically with his thumbnail to produce a thin squawk.

At the funeral he had met her ex-husband, the man she had stayed with in that year, twice that he knew of. His hand was shaken by a man with baggy eyes and a paunch, who had come to the service in an open-necked shirt. He looked like a drinker. What did he do? Stark could not remember, though he could remember tearing at the phone book looking for the man's number, trembling with hatred. The man seemed to be sizing him up in turn, and finding satisfaction in what he saw.

After the funeral, Stark called his daughter Lynn. "You were talking to him. What did he say?"

"What do you care, Dad? He said she would have wanted to die while she was pretty."

"Pretty! Jesus Christ she was never *pretty*."

"He said *pretty*. Dad, I came to the funeral, OK? Katya was not my favorite person but I feel bad for you. But this is not what I want to be talking about. I do not appreciate—"

"Did he say she thought she was going to die?"

"No. God, Dad."

"What else?"

"He said she was about to come back to him. The guy's a mess."

"I guess she mowed him down," Stark said with a kind of pride.

STARK HAD AN ex-wife, Rosalie, but the years of getting through medical school and a residency and raising two children were far behind them both. Nevertheless, when their younger daughter Kelly was in town, Lynn got them all together. On a Friday three weeks after the funeral, early in the afternoon he called Rosalie and asked her to meet him for a drink. "No, not after work," he said. "I'm leaving now." He saw his stiff face glaring at him in the window glass.

He told his clinic manager, "Shawna, I'm going to have to call it a day."

"You should, you're getting that flu," Shawna said obligingly. Long ago, before her marriage, he had had a weekend or two with Shawna. She had suffered, liking Rosalie. But later he had seen her through her first son's atrial septal defect, and she was loyal. He tore off his white coat. He had never before left with patients in the waiting room.

Glimpsing the changes in Rosalie, he always felt a jab of protective dismay. Still, recently she had become involved with a fireman who, it turned out, was hardly any older than Katya. Rosalie had met him when, all alone in the old house, she had a chimney fire. Since taking up with the fireman she was using more makeup and her dark eyes had gone small and sparkling. When she leaned forward the skin at her low neckline formed crisscross lines. There was no way to warn her not to lean across a table when she was with the fireman. "She's talking about fires," Lynn said. "She quotes him. She's a nutcase."

Rosalie said, "What are you telling me? Is the family suing you?" From Lynn he had heard that when the fireman was around, Rosalie had a new, careless tone. She knew the pride he took in having had no lawsuits. Where was her soft heart? He felt tears come into his eyes.

"Good Lord, Stark. I know you didn't miss anything. I know you took care of her. I'm sorry, honey. Oh, dear." Rosalie had always cried when someone else did, even the children at times. She wiped her eyes; she had one of those manicures with white at the tips. "OK, look. Here's what you do. Go to the cabin. Go, and take it easy for a few days. Just lie around. There's a TV now. I got a satellite dish." The cabin was hers now; he hadn't been there since the divorce.

She said he didn't look good; he looked as if he had just crawled out of a cave. "Here." She dug in her purse. "Here's the key. Make sure you get it back to me because it's the only one I have now." In the old days they would have had three or four keys to the cabin, on hooks and stashed in drawers. But he couldn't inquire. Her tears had made him worse—and hadn't those eyes once seemed to fill her whole face when they shimmered with tears? He got up abruptly and went to the men's room. What was he doing leaning on a bathroom door with his eyes fixed on a hand dryer? With a diffuse spasm in his chest, a need to bear down after catching a breath, as if to keep something where it belonged. The dryer had a stiff logo of joined hands. From the wall the urinals gaped with their stains. How easily people ignored the real acts of the body, even people like himself, doctors who saw into the interior clenching, the explosions and expulsions. To how many people had he said the word *spasm* over the years, in reassurance?

When he opened his fist the key fell onto the floor. He picked it up and washed it. He dried his hands under the gasp of the blower.

"We haven't been over there in a month," Rosalie said when he came back and sank into his chair. "Somebody needs to check on the place. We were going to go this weekend but I can't, I'm off to lose weight."

We were going to go. She liked to hint at that part of her life. "You don't need to lose weight," he said. Her hips had squared a bit but she was small and still compact.

"Oh, now I do. Now I do. Lynn's taking me away to a spa. We're going to eat spinach leaves and do yoga and meditate. We'll have four days. So promise me you'll go. I mean it, Stark."

He thanked her in the parking lot. "Just go over there and take it easy," she said again, as if she were one of their daughters, looking out for him. He didn't go home; he drove straight out of town and into the mountains. He hadn't packed anything; he would have to wear what he had put on that morning. His feet hurt, in his good shoes. At Washington Pass he pulled in and changed into the running shoes he kept in the trunk. He left them untied. *Because he's a bum,* he said to himself, in Katya's voice. He walked on old snow that still, in May, covered the short path to the overlook, and gazed down at the dizzying switchbacks. If you climbed over the fence and dropped, you would go straight down hundreds of feet before there was a thing to stop you.

On the way back he made new footprints, in the grip of a childish, sentimental urge to point himself out to somebody.

At the cabin—which was not a cabin at all but a log and timber house built with the first real money he had made, with five bedrooms and a river-rock fireplace, quilts Rosalie had found in country stores, scattered floor cushions still in their buttoned denim—he realized he had brought no food. He found a potato to slice and fried it in olive oil in a familiar pan. He was not one who advised his patients not to fry. How would anyone who lived alone not fry? And Katya—who liked to present herself as a peasant and believed, or said she believed, that a fried potato was a meal if you had a glass of vodka to drink with it—Katya could have fried everything she ate. What use would any curbs have been? Should he have said more than he did, when he sent her to Bernstein? This was a young woman. A woman with nothing, seemingly, the matter with her. Before the day she seized his hands she had come to his office twice with the complaint of having lost or almost lost consciousness. Something about the lazy way she related this history made him doubt it. Nevertheless he proceeded, because persistence and care were what he was known for. He uncovered a common thing.

He must have suspected, by the time she made the third appointment, that she came only to see him. Over the years he had accumulated a few patients who did that. And had that affected his judgment, made him less careful? Exactly what had she said, that first time? And what about afterwards, with Bernstein?

"Nothing. Nothing but what we saw," Bernstein said. "The

thing might have showed up the next time, it might not. Could have forced it in the lab? You didn't do that; I didn't do that. A year she was my patient. Don't beat yourself up."

He should never have put his weight on her, with that heart inside her that was going to stop. He should never have raised his voice. What had he been thinking of? She had slapped him. He had thrown her down on the bed.

But he had not killed her by throwing her on the bed. She had stood up to slap him again and lived another year. Standing in the kitchen eating his potato from the pan, he groaned.

He made his way along the downhill path, overgrown now, to the river, which was running so high it had carved out a new branch. He couldn't see in the semidark whether the branch veered back to the river where the woods began, or tore on into the trees. In the middle of the two courses was an island, with a big cottonwood at either end. Loud, tumbling water had claimed so much ground that he could not be sure exactly where he was. It blocked his way to the sand between the two trees where he wanted to sit. Once he and the girls had dragged a picnic table all the way out to the river's edge. The table was long gone—stolen, Rosalie said. Bikers. They snooped around the empty vacation places now. A picnic table taken away on a motorcycle? "They scout stuff out and they come back for it," she said defensively. He had to consider the question of whether he had encouraged this kind of thinking in Rosalie, who had been so ready to take his word. How conventional he had been, despite his "ways."

"Thiefs should keep what they get." So Katya said, haughtily. "Or how can we have balance? Not like those guys in the movie." They had seen a movie about a heist. "Real thiefs, I mean."

"So should they get this ring? If they don't hurt this hand?"

Why had he said this? She had hidden the hand with the emerald on it behind her.

The branch was running fast, too deep to wade across. Deep enough to be black. You could see tall grass being rushed and flattened. There was no real bank. He put his foot in. Instead of dragging at it, the current lifted it like a leaf and pushed him onto the other leg, making him totter. Had the river ever come this far? He shook his wet foot, his body creeping with goose pimples.

His ears were full of the loudness of water, and for a moment on the path he had the sensation the river was moving up behind him. Lifting his head he saw, standing in the kitchen, a woman. Tall. *God, God . . .*

Of course it was not her. This woman was heavy. The woman was just standing in the kitchen without a sound, even though she must have seen him coming up the steps. She must have seen him at some distance, a figure approaching the house. She had his spatula in her hand, and she was holding the other hand out as if to soothe him. "Hi there," she said.

"Hello," he said. "Who are you?"

A man stepped into the kitchen. "I'm Ray Rollins."

"I said somebody was here." The woman held up the spatula with a surprising calm. "We were out there admiring your car."

"Whoa!" the man said. "I don't know, man, this is—here I thought we—thought we *had* the place. This weekend." So they weren't burglars. Or probably not. But then the man said uneasily, "What's the date, anyway?"

"Well now," said Stark, "it's the twenty-first, and I'm pretty sure I'm supposed to be here." He wasn't going to say "God damn it, I built this house," or anything like that. He wasn't going to say Rosalie had given him the key because that would give away her name, if they were burglars.

"Whoa," the man said again. Ray. Ray something. He had a crew cut. He looked like a football coach. "So now, did you . . . you must know the owner?"

Stark said, "I do."

The man came forward with his hand out. "Ray Rollins," he said for the second time. He gripped like a blood pressure cuff.

"Phil Bernstein," said Stark. He wasn't going to get into any explanations.

"This is Beverly," Rollins said after a second.

The woman said, "Beverly Lanier," and held out her hand. She smiled as if the situation struck her as nothing out of the ordinary. She turned to the man, and because she was big herself, Stark saw for the first time how large and muscular were the arms, now folded, of the man standing beside her, how thick his neck. Not somebody he could tackle, if the two were there after all to steal from an empty house. But wasn't the guy too clean-cut to be a thief? The girl, surely, too simple. "Well," she said cheerfully to Stark, "you were here first."

"Right," said Ray Rollins. "Right. So you're a friend of Rosalie's. Jeez I'm embarrassed."

All right. He knew her. Stark said, "Drive over from Seattle?"

"Yeah, we did."

"Quite a way," Stark said. It was a three-and-a-half-hour drive if you did it fast.

"Had to leave in rush hour, had to work." Stark could see the man placing him: older guy, white-collar, someone who left before rush hour.

"Well, hmm, what shall we do?" said the woman, Beverly. She had sat down on one of the stools Rosalie had had made to line the counter. The stools had arms, you could swivel in them and see the whole house spread out with its comforts. *Open Plan.* For months the words had echoed in their lives as they made trips to watch the place go up. "Not my room," Lynn had said, at twelve. "I want to be downstairs. I want the Closed Plan." Now Lynn was what, twenty-six? Twenty-seven? Older than this solid girl on the stool.

Stark waited for Rollins to answer her. He was going to back down, Stark could tell. He was the one who had made the mistake; Stark had received the key from Rosalie's hand that very afternoon. She couldn't have already lent it, if that was the only key she had.

It came to him slowly, as he was thinking of the key. He was bending, in his mind, to pick it up from the sticky floor of the men's room. It came to him who the man was. He raised his eyes from the counter where the girl had wrapped her square hands around the basket of river rocks Rosalie kept there. The man had stepped away from her, scowling. It was the fireman.

We were going to go this weekend.

So he had come anyway, the fireman. He had come without Rosalie. With a girl instead. He must have his own key. He had brought a girl to Rosalie's cabin.

Beverly said, "I'm sure we can find a motel in town." Hearing the word gave Stark a rude pleasure. Motel. Where this kind of thing belonged. Not in Rosalie's cabin, where Rosalie must have come more than once with the fireman, the bastard.

Ray slapped his hands together. "I need a phone book." His moment of shame and confusion was over. "And more important, where's the bathroom?" He grinned. Of course he knew where they were, phone book and bathroom.

"Oh gosh. But it doesn't matter." Beverly stretched and smiled. "I know the area, I worked up north of here one summer, with the Forest Service. I was a smoke jumper." So. It was out. Firemen, both of them. Firefighters. The bastard had brought a girl from work.

Hey, want to go over to a great place on the Methow River?
Hey, why not?

"No kidding," Stark said. He never said "no kidding." But he was Phil Bernstein. "That must be rough work."

"I liked it. I was young," she said, in the nostalgic way young people had of saying that. "They kinda made me prove myself a few extra times. But I like that." When she smiled the plumpness of her cheeks made the lower lids spring up and almost close her eyes. On one side she had a deep dimple. "You don't even want to know how much retardant is up there in some of those stands of Doug fir."

Without deciding he was going to do it, Stark said, "Why not just stay here. This is a big house. I have the room down the hall, there." It was Lynn's room. He hadn't wanted to go upstairs. "There's a big second floor. Four rooms."

She said, "Really? That would be great!" Ray was coming back. He walked with his hands on his legs, on the seams of the tight jeans, and a dreamy, private look on his face.

"Did you hear that?" the girl asked him. "Mr. Bernstein doesn't mind if we stay here tonight, if we want. It's late maybe, d'you think, to get a motel? We could do it tomorrow?"

"Jeez, I hate to do that. I don't know how I got this so turned around. What a dumb shit thing to do, excuse me." As if Stark were an old fogy.

Stark said nothing. He was doing it for the girl, with her dimple. It was the kind of thing Katya would do, and if he stopped there, if he didn't expose the guy, punish him, he would still be in the region of the kind of caprice that was Katya's. Katya did harm but she tended her victims. When she had her accident, for instance, a few days later she tracked down the driver of the other car. Not because the man was hurt; he was up and around and he was the aggrieved party, since Katya was a danger behind the wheel. She was trying to find out what the connection was between them.

"I don't know, Bev . . ." Stark could see the guy wanted to be let off the hook for bringing her here when somebody else had the place. He wanted persuasion, the bastard. "That would be . . . I don't think we . . ."

"I bet your neighbor just got confused about who was when," Beverly said.

"So Rosalie's your neighbor, is she?" Stark said heartily.

"No, no, I'm the one," said Ray, ignoring him. "I'm the one who screwed up. I bet it was next weekend. Jeez." He grimaced.

Stark was tempted to let him go on in this vein, getting himself into trouble. But Beverly said, "So, can I go get my stuff out of the car?"

"OK, I guess," said Ray, with a defeated look at Stark.

"HEY, LOOK WHO'S here." She had come down the path in the dark, by herself. "Look at this river."

Stark said, "This isn't the river. This is a spur. New."

"'*Well it's not deep nor wide*,'" she sang, "'*but it's a mean piece of water, my friend.*' You know that song?"

"I do not," he said.

"'Kern River.' Merle Haggard. '*I'll never swim Kern River again*,'" she sang. "'*It was there that I met her, there that I lost my best friend.*' I was awake. I looked out the window and I saw you out there. Then I didn't see you. I thought, *Gotta be a path goes down that hill because he's* gone. I don't know, I got a creepy feeling. You can hear this thing really loud in our room. The room we're in, at the front."

"The river's high," he said patiently. He was going to have to talk to her. If a woman got up in the middle of the night, you would have to talk to her. "It's made a whole new channel."

"Look at that moon. Ah." She held up her arms. "You've been here before. A new channel, you say."

Clouds had swept apart to show the lopsided moon, hanging at the top of a cottonwood, so bright it seemed it had arrived with a hiss, like a lantern. The woods were thin here, and the moon was so bright it had dropped black shadows into them.

"There are pictures of you, in our room." She had to raise her voice to be heard over the water.

"What's that?" he said, as if he couldn't hear.

"Pictures. Under the glass top of the dresser." So the guy hadn't taken her into the master bedroom, where he must have been before. They were in Kelly's old room. Kelly, the little one, the sentimentalist, with her photo collages and scrapbooks. "You know the ones I mean?"

"What ones?"

"All these family pictures. Two kids. Girls."

"Is that right?"

"They look like they live here. The man looks like you, a younger you."

He sighed.

"It is you."

"If you say so."

"Is this your place?"

"No."

"Whose place is it?"

"Rosalie's."

"Rosalie who? I don't know her, Ray knows her."

"He appears to."

"Why do you say it like that?"

"Rosalie is a good friend of mine," he said.

"Why did you come down here?" she said sternly. He could hear the voice of the firefighter. *Climb down. Do as I tell you.* "Were you going to jump in the river?"

"Was I—? Maybe I still am."

"I have my EMT," she said.

"That's good, if I do."

"I told Ray I got the feeling you were going to jump in the river."

"And what did he say?"

"He said you weren't. He said you probably came to finish some report."

"And that would be pretty lame, in his opinion," Stark said. "For a guy to do. Only you decide the guy is going to drown himself."

"You never know what somebody will or won't do. I used to guide on the Colorado. Some people—seems like they fell in on purpose. And fur-ther-more, ha ha, I figured it out. You're the husband, right?"

"I was. You're on the case. Are you a private investigator?"

"Yeah. I'm whatshername. Prime Suspect. Actually I'm a firefighter."

"I'm willing to bet he is too."

"Yeah. It'll be hard on our kids."

"Your kids."

"We're getting married."

"No kidding. Congratulations."

"Thank you," she said with a tuck of the dimple. "How about you? What do you do, Phil? It's Phil, isn't it?"

"I'm a lawyer."

"I knew it," she said.

"Is that a fact?"

"How do you know when a lawyer's lying? He's moving his lips. Sorry. Lawyers can't get a break. But hey, the ones I know are great guys." The dimple kept coming and going, but a girl like this, however she carried on in her own life, could be suddenly, mercilessly intolerant and proper. Yes, his daughters had taught him this, and a young woman or two who had turned on him.

"Lying would be something you frown on," he said.

"Not really," she said airily. She was getting into the spirit of things. She was not as simple as he had thought.

"Did Ray see the pictures?"

"No. I put my stuff on the dresser."

"Why didn't you show him?"

"I didn't feel like it. Why didn't you say you were married to Rosalie?"

"I'm not."

"She has a different name. I've heard it. I don't know what it is but it isn't Bernstein."

"I know that."

"So she took her own name back?"

"You're a very curious young lady."

"Nosy." She grinned. "I am. I'm whatshername." She put on a British accent. "Get me everything we have on the Bern-steins. And a shot of Scotch." Then she said, "You were down at the river when we got here. You used to come here a lot, I bet. I know you did. It's in the pictures. There was a beach."

"Out there, underwater. The river is supposed to be on the other side of that, where you see the cottonwoods. It's still coming up."

"Snow melt. We had that hot week. That's all it takes, up in the snowpack. River ever get all the way up to the house?"

"It never got anywhere near *this* high. Global warming."

She eyed him. "Ray doesn't believe in global warming."

"Why doesn't that surprise me?"

"What? You just now met Ray. Everybody likes Ray. Everybody."

"Especially you. You're going to marry him. You're going to marry a jerk." He was as surprised as if Katya had come up behind them and growled the word.

"Wait a minute. You don't know Ray and you don't know me. What is this? What's your problem?" Still she didn't walk away.

"The guy's a jerk."

"You better explain that."

"Just ask him. When you leave tomorrow. Ask him if he's a jerk. See what he says."

"No," she said.

"You're asking for it, if you marry him."

"Wait a minute, buddy. You know nothing about this man. You have no idea how brave he is, how he'll risk himself. Why am I talking to you? Hey, you're a lawyer. What do you know about anything good?"

"He's a jerk."

"Quit it."

"Jerk."

"I don't like that," she said. She stepped close, the way a man in a bar would, to start a fight. He knew that from movies; no one had ever squared off with him in a bar. "I don't like that one bit." She poked him in the collarbone with her fingers straight, as if she were playing a scene in a movie. She seemed to be kidding, or at least half kidding.

"Nevertheless," he said.

"*Nevertheless?*" she said, crowding him. "*Nevertheless?*" She was bigger than he was. She poked him again. He stepped back, off-balance, and the next thing he knew he had stepped into water knee-deep and slipped. He had gone sideways. How had that happened? But he was getting his footing. Then he couldn't get his balance at all and he was off his feet, going over.

His whole body gasped at the cold. First floundering and then rolling and then the thing swallowed him.

"Your feet!" He could hear her yelling. "Get your feet out front!" That was it. So the feet would hit and not the head. The time it would take to turn himself bore no relation to the speed of water. Ahead, this water was going to join the full force of the river. Something whacked him in the shoulder but it was too late to grab for it. He couldn't see and water had filled his throat. He was a thing to be filled. His legs crossed and recrossed, the feet were wrong, not in front of him. His shoes were off. Something with an edge tore past one leg. Tree stumps. The draw was where the stumps were. He knew where he was but now he was choking. It was too late. His shoulder ran against something loose and clashing, snagged on it.

A weight bore against him, rolling him up. She was in the water with him. "Gotcha!" she said. With arms like pliers, she was dragging him. From the splashing she seemed to be wading.

"Beaver dam!" At least she was out of breath. She had him splayed on the ground, with stones under his back. "Old beaver dam! So—yeah! So hey, the river has *so* been up this high. Beavers!" His eyes were glued shut. From the sound of it she was hanging over him, panting, stripping water down the legs of her jeans with her palms. She sat down. "I beat you to the dam! You had some close contact. Got some scratches. That's fast water."

He lay there with his limbs contracting and letting go. He wasn't cold. He got his wet eyelashes apart. He was in a half circle of flagpoles. No. Aspen: slim trunks pale as X-rays. Against the dark pines—the river had come up to the woods and some way in—the aspen showed tiny half-clenched leaves. The moon straight up was so bright he squinted.

"Hey, don't sue me," Beverly said, vigorously rubbing her arms. "Hey, Phil. Don't say I pushed you in a river and you lost your ability to earn your living as an attorney-at-law."

Why should a remark like that have a steadying effect? It seemed a way she might have hit on to comfort him.

"My shoes," he said.

"Forget the shoes," she said. For a moment it seemed there might be enough comfort in the world to get him through.

"Jesus!" It was Ray, running and shouting. "What's going on? Are you all right?"

"See? I was right," Beverly said calmly. "He jumped in."

"I mean *you*!" Ray yanked her up and against him. "Bev! You *lived* out here, goddamn it. *Flood stage*, baby. You heard the radio. There's range cattle going down that river. You could both—be in there—right now." He was rocking her from side to side. "Jesus," he said finally, holding her at arm's length. "Jesus, Bev. You had to do it. I know that."

He let her go and squatted beside Stark. "Hey, fella," he said. "You. Hear me?" Stark coughed and rolled his head. Water ran out of his ears. "Sure, cough. Puke. You're OK. Thanks to her. Do you know that? I want to say something to you. Do you see what you were up to here? You don't *do* that. No. You got it all wrong."

"Ray," said Beverly, not really chiding him. She smiled down at Stark with a bold cheerfulness. She had gone in, after all. She had done that, gone into fast water, pulled him out. With the little pit in her cheek she smiled at the matter of the beaver dam that would have caught him anyway, the matter of her having pushed him.

"I don't know," said Ray, shaking his head. "Jeez. You need help."

Now Beverly had squatted too, to rough his wet hair back and forth, the way a coach might after a game. Ray rocked back on his haunches. "Nothing's so bad you have to jump in a river, buddy." He squeezed Stark's shoulder.

Stark let out a moan. Now he was cold, but he wasn't going to get up. He was going to lie there awhile before he made any effort. He was the one on the ground, the one in trouble. He couldn't think how long it had been since he was the one lying down, with somebody bending over him, figuring out what the hell was wrong.

Phantom Father

• • •

S HE WAS A young married woman who fell in love.
   The man desperately wanted to take the place of her husband. He made scenes: he pled, commanded, threatened suicide. The trouble was that although she had fallen in love so suddenly, she also loved the man she had married, who was in the dark about what was happening and didn't even know the time had come for scenes.

Love, love. The same word for different things. Who can be sure what it is that is being felt? Love, like so much helium blown into a balloon. The further trouble was that, of three balloons, her husband had been blown fullest, stretched thinnest.

Having no way of knowing this, and weighed on by the truth, she confessed everything to him, even her suspicion that the miscarriage they were grieving, away in his family's place by the lake, had been the lover's baby and not his.

It was summer, the war was going on, and she was away for a last weekend with her husband before he was to go overseas. But in the morning, when he put on his uniform, instead of leaving for his train he drove the car down the boat ramp, where it lolled onto its back and sank to the bottom of the lake.

After the funeral, filled with horror, grief, and a remorse that overpowered her feelings for her lover at first, she asked for six months to go away alone. When she came back, her lover had married someone else.

Those were the elements. All of it happened in the space of those few years around the age of twenty, when one is barely out of childhood. All three, the wife Annette, the husband Alonzo, and the lover, still had parents helping them with checks and advice, parents who had come through a world war themselves and carefully planned that the children born after it would live unscathed and happy. The three, themselves wanting to be happy, went through these events while another world war was raging.

In time Annette married again, and the three children she had with this husband would find bits and pieces of these old events in themselves, like tea leaves.

The first child, Michele, inherited her mother's looks, olive skin with pale eyes and pronounced dark eyebrows, round placid cheeks in a narrow face, lips full and crinkled like sunned grapes, her father said, lying back with her, his first baby, on his chest.

He was forty years old, a surgeon. He had been a poor boy and now he had plenty of money—though never as much as Annette's first husband Alonzo would have come into—but he didn't care for money, he cared only for the wife and the child who dogged his steps, learning the fruits and plants, minerals and sea creatures and geographical formations that gave their names to parts of the body.

The child was impatient with books, though she liked to turn the pages of his surgical atlas with him and let him show her the cherries and mulberries and bulbs, islets and pillars and spindles. The body is old, older than the mind, he told her, and she got ready for a boring fairy tale. Because the body is volume, it is stubborn, he said. Its rules are those of water. Most of medicine is keeping water in or out. And for the most part the body, in its ancient way—here the child began rolling her eyes and banging her heels on the chair rungs—goes about its own business disguised from the mind and without consulting it. She gave a haughty laugh and ran away from him, out of the house.

But waiting for her in high school was a certain boy. He was a boy with a grudge: as a small child he had had polio. Although he recovered, and suffered very few of what her father called "the sequelae," he had a limp, and having been one of the last to get the disease, just at the time the vaccine appeared and saved so many others, he was bitter. When he got well he was wild, ahead of the boys his age instead of behind, known in the high school for his outbursts in the classroom, his stormy liaisons with older girls, even women, clerks or waitresses in their twenties, in places where the high school kids hung out.

MICHELE WAS SUNBATHING with her parents. Her little brothers played in the coppery foam of low tide while the three of them lay talking about her mother's marriage. Her first marriage.

Michele said, "It's funny, when you first told me about Alonzo, I remembered him!" Indeed she could remember the conversation, the slowly arriving, affronted surprise, at first, of the discovery that her mother had had another husband, and then a funny feeling coming over her, a recognition of the man they were talking about, as if he had come around a corner into view. "I remembered him!"

"You did?" her mother said musingly. She rarely contradicted her children or imposed an attitude on them that might be from another era, her own era.

"I know I couldn't have," Michele said, sitting up and leaning on her mother's legs. Her mother lay back, slightly overflowing the top of her bathing suit with the straps down, in her low beach chair. She had lost the narrow, bony shape that was her daughter's, except in the face. She was one of those women who keep a thin face. Men who passed glanced at her, the breasts, the plump tanned legs, tight-skinned and gleaming with oil. Michele looked down the legs to her mother's long, reaching toes; elegant and indefinably pitiful they seemed to her, the very keys of her mother's self. She leaned across and moved the pliant middle ones back and forth.

Michele was on the towel; her father had a hammock that separated him from the sand by just a few inches. He lay on his stomach on a yellow towel, idly running his fingers along the sand. They were all obliged to cover themselves and each other heavily in oil every hour because he feared skin cancer. He brought oranges to the beach to protect them from dehydration. He would cut them in half with his Swiss army knife and expertly squeeze the halves into his mouth and theirs, from above, the way people drink from a wineskin. Then he would eat the pulp, because it was good for you, and urge them to do the same. Once he had it on his hands, the bags and towels and sandwiches, even the skin of their own arms and shoulders, had the smell of oranges.

"So tell me what he looked like," Michele said. "Alonzo. Didn't he have thick brown hair?"

"She told you that." Her father's voice was muffled against the towel.

All of this was talked about in the family, not hidden.

"Did you tell me?"

"Oh, I probably did, Mish."

"Well, before you told me I knew. I knew what he looked like."

"Pictures," growled her father, consenting to appear jealous.

"I never saw one, did I, Mommy?" All her life she called her mother that.

"I don't know that you have," her mother said. "Eddie, has she seen pictures of Alonzo?"

"Bound to have."

"I have not!"

"Well, they're in the desk with everything else."

"Why was he named *Alonzo*? And did you know him, Daddy?"

"It was a name in his family," her mother said.

"The rich dream up names like that," her father said. They all knew he was proud to have been poor, himself, to have worked his way through college and sent money home to his mother. Yet he respected Alonzo, that was apparent to Michele. It was not Alonzo, it was the lover her father looked down on, the one who came on the scene and did all the harm. The man who had married somebody else after causing Alonzo's death. That man had no name.

"Anyway I knew he had brown hair, Alonzo," Michele said, "thick and standing up, and growing down in a point in the middle of his forehead, right? Right?" she cried, excited, as her mother dreamily, frowningly watched the boys drag a tree branch to a deep hole they had dug in the sand, their trap. Her father sat up. "Somebody's going to fall into that," he said to nobody in particular.

"Did he? Did he or not?" Michele arched her foot and flipped sand onto her mother's legs.

"He did."

"Like mine."

Her father said, "Annette, you don't suppose—she's his daughter by celestial insemination?"

"She may be," said her mother thoughtfully. "But actually I think she's got your nice lips." Though they all said her lips were her mother's.

"Really?" Her father lay down again on his back and pressed his moustache up with his fingers. "These?"

Her mother leaned over and kissed him. "Oh, you're burned. Your shoulders right at the neck," she said, kissing him there.

"Where's the oil?" he cried, sitting up. "And the boys—! Tommy! Eddie! Come up here! Michele, where—?"

"It's in your bag, Dad. It's right there. And he had one of those chins . . ."

"I couldn't say," said her mother, becoming aloof as she poured oil into her palms.

"My phantom father," Michele said.

Her father got to his feet, shook himself, and ran down to the water's edge to oil the boys' shoulders, fair like his own, not olive and immune to sunburn like Michele's.

Michele thought she did not just pity the stricken young husband with the rare, sad name Alonzo, but knew him as kin. Now she was only six years younger than he had been when he walked out of his family's summer cottage in the early morning, got in the car, opened the windows, and drove to the end of the boat ramp where the bank fell off sharply into a cave of water that sent up a slow obscuring cloud of mud. No one had ever said precisely this; she had imagined it for herself.

She felt she was like him, proud but easily defeated. She was more like him than she was like her own father, who had real power and could not be defeated. She would have to be very careful that she did not love too single-mindedly (and that doing so she did not, as her mother had, destroy anybody) and that the life she might have to lead because of the intensity, the near uncontrollability of her feelings did not overwhelm her. She would have to be careful, and already she had not been careful.

Just down the beach from the pit her brothers had been digging, a group of hippies lay on the beach. In a year or two Michele would be on a beach in Europe with just such a group, but at the time she was suspicious of them. They had stuck two poles in the sand and tied on a banner that kept coming loose, with a peace symbol on it.

The war in Vietnam had worked its way into everything, lifting many of the restrictions on what people wore and how they talked, even bringing a draft resister up onto the stage of her high school to disrupt the assembly. The girls had their bathing suit tops off and the boys were stretched out on the sand without towels, letting the girls rub lotion onto their backs. One of the girls waved broadly at Michele's father when he was loping down the beach, her dark-tipped breasts spreading apart and then flowing in the direction of her arm. He waved back with the same broad, lazy motion, and Michele could see that the girl had dropped her teasing face and was smiling as he got to the boys and scooped them up with their thin legs dangling. They clamored to show him their digging, so he put them down and fell to his knees in the sand.

Michele oiled her own legs. She shook her mother, whose eyes were shut and whose forehead would tan unevenly if she kept it soberly wrinkled the way it was. "I don't know why but I'm not interested in the other guy," Michele went on. "Your *lovah*. I'm interested in Alonzo. I mean you were married to him. He seems like part of the family."

"And the other one?"

"He seems like the other one."

"And so he was," said her mother. "If you think you might be pregnant we should go to the doctor rather than wait."

Michele lay back on her towel, slowly. "I don't think so."

"But you love him. You say you've been sleeping with him."

"I love him. I love him. I love him." She didn't want her mother to have to picture the car, the friends' cars, the logistics, so she said, "Just a few times."

"And so you'll want to have the baby," her mother said decisively.

"I don't think I'm pregnant. I'm thin."

"There's something about you that makes me think you might be. My first pregnancy . . ."

"With *me*! Or, no, I mean . . . no."

"No," her mother said. No, the first pregnancy had been the miscarriage that set in motion all they had been recalling.

"Here comes Daddy."

When her father had thrown his reddened body down again her mother began to speak thoughtfully with her eyes closed. "I was unfortunate. By that I mean I brought misfortune."

"Are we on that again?" Michele's father muttered.

"I learned my lesson very early, though I can't say what it was exactly. You'll find that. You can't say what you've learned, exactly, and whoever does—well, don't trust it absolutely. I learned too late for him, for Alonzo. It wasn't 'don't play around,' or anything like that," she said, with dignity. "I wish I could tell you what it was."

"I'll tell you what it was," her father said. "It was, 'Don't play around.' An ironbound rule. If you're married to a surgeon, especially. Because we are much more likely to do evil things to another than to ourselves."

Her mother said pensively, uninsistently, "It had something to do with life."

"Life is better than death, was that it?" her father said.

Michele said, "Aha, you're making Daddy jealous!"

"He's not jealous."

"I am too."

Her father had taken her mother's ripped-apart life and sewn it back into a piece. Her father was able to do that, Michele always said when she told the story, because in the 1940s and '50s men had the power to alter everything for women, or were thought to, and because life was better than death.

Michele had a baby and gave it up for adoption because that was what happened then, in her own era, even though her parents were more free-thinking than most; they had lived in Europe, and her mother, in particular, thought anything could be accommodated within the family, any number of people and memories of people.

Years later Michele would find herself telling her friends about the way her mother had suffered over the giving up of the baby, the son Michele had had at sixteen.

On the day Michele "relinquished," when she had gotten up out of the bed where they kept you for days at that time, and dressed herself in the clothes she had worn into the hospital, and they were signing her out, her mother had taken hold of the counter at the nurses' station and then, almost gracefully, let go and folded onto the floor. She had fainted.

When she came to, she got up clumsily, with all of them to help her, but she didn't say she was sorry; she withdrew herself from any talk about it. The nurse who took her blood pressure while she was lying on the polished floor gave her face a little stroke. Then the nurse hugged Michele, who had not been able to kneel all the way down because she was sore, and she gave Michele the baby's hospital bracelet.

The nurses told everyone standing around that it happened

now and again, a dead faint like that. Her father had seen it in a medical setting but Michele had never seen a faint. She had never known anyone who even said they had fainted. It was not an act of the time.

MICHELE GAVE UP the baby because of the time she was living in and because the boy she loved believed it was the right thing to do. He was powerful in argument. His disease had confined him for more than a year, and made him the boy he would be when he got up again: unbending, peremptory, greedy for every satisfaction of his will. To her on the other hand the polio explained everything, gave his bare leg in the back seat of the car, almost undetectably thinner than the other, a paleness that hurt her, his angry voice an echo of supplication.

She never forgot the absorbent force in this boy, shocking her with its drag, the *wick*—that was what it was—that had transferred her to him. If she were to see him again, it would still be there, she knew, if she saw him on some street ahead of her with his limp, or in a crowd, as she persistently imagined she would, out of which one of them would follow the other into a dark room—a room briefly illuminated and then lowered like a bucket into a well—and shut the door, and feel for a bed or lean back against a wall, and draw the weight of the other down.

Polio was a neurological disease but as far as she could see it had not affected his nervous system, which was tuned high, to gradations of pleasure not familiar to very many men she was to meet, men twice his age, and to pleasure given as well as taken, pleasure that seemed to have to do with the body her father had told her about, that was all dammed water.

How would this boy, for all his harsh charm, his casual domination of her and others, know what the right thing to do was?

How would he know what she should do? Why would she, so independent all her sixteen years, brought up to be, submit to his opinion?

You would have to be wiser than most of them were in high school, or for many years after that, to know what to do.

A year and a half after that, she was lying facedown on a beach in France. With her were a little group of hitchhikers who were translating for each other across her, one of them tracing letters on her steaming back. They were talking about their parents, the ways of parents in the various countries they came from. One of the French boys was already twenty, and the others teased him for calling his parents every week. Their packs were spread out on the hot sand all around them and one or two of them were rummaging for pictures.

Michele didn't have any. She had come away without finishing high school, carrying nothing that might hold her back. While they were talking on the beach she thought of her father's face, with the suntan oil on it defining all the wrinkles of the smile he had had, the day they were talking about her mother's past and he had said he was jealous.

She had not written to her parents in months. She had put them, too, out of her mind. She did not join the conversation; she had withdrawn herself. She was just beginning to see how she was going to have to labor to find the way back. This was the period she had been warned about, nearing the end of the first year after the birth, nearing the anniversary.

She was not even sure she was going to live. Sometimes at night in a hostel bathroom she would think she wanted to be annihilated, the way the birth had been. The baby existed; his birth did not. His birthdays would come; his birth would lie farther and farther behind him, unclaimed. And she who had never seen him, never been shown him: unclaimed.

It would have been impossible to open her mouth on this hot, anesthetic, foreign sand and tell what had happened, and no one pressed her. But she had begun to think about her parents. She thought, *My father is a man who cuts into people if they make a move to leave life. To capture them and bring them back into life.* Life was better than death.

He was no kin of the phantom father.

There must have been a picture of that man, the first husband, Alonzo, and she must have seen it, to give her the vivid idea she had of him. Turning over to get the sun on her face, and then letting the others pull her up by the arms so she could smear more cocoa butter on her thighs, she saw with a detached, sad approval how dark and taut the months of backpacking in shorts had made her skin. It had taken on a textured sheen like tent nylon.

She wondered, scratching white lines on it with her nails, why she had no idea of the other one, the lover, the one who had come into her mother's young life and then defected, like a driver swerving out of the way of a crash he had caused: the one who so suddenly, shockingly, *ordinarily*, after setting off the chain of events that was to color her mother's life, had *gotten married*. And yet that man was nothing but the precursor of her father, probably even like her father in some way. Probably in reality she was, herself, more like those two who went on living than like the phantom father. Ordinary. Likely, after all, simply to marry and have children as her mother had done, and as her son would do—she bore down on herself to imagine it—her son, a child just now setting his foot down on the ground somewhere and taking a step. If that was when babies walked. Didn't they walk when they were a year old? And then they fell down, they got up, they went to school, they went to high school; they fell in love and nothing mattered that had come before. That was what they thought, as they married and had children of their own. As he would do in his time, her son, having no conscious idea that somewhere in him were the boy's limp, the girl's ardor, the grandmother's body falling to the hospital floor.

Taken

. . .

A T THE TOP of the terrace steps Avery Mayhew rose into
view. No one in sight to stop him from wheeling his chair
off the edge. Perhaps the aides indoors, in their flowered smocks
with cigarettes in the pocket, wanted him to.

Or perhaps, more generously, because in the slowness of their
walk they seemed in some undeliberate way generous, they
wanted him to have the choice. All of the aides were immigrants,
from countries with little idea of places like this, Jane imagined,
and that was why they would pass her with the look, light as a
brushstroke, that said something was wrong—not here inside
the building but outside it, where she came from.

Mayhew never remembered her. He did retain a vestigial
politeness towards women; strapped in with a mesh harness, he
made an effort to sit up as she climbed the steps.

On her first visit, just after he had been moved to Calling
Creek, Fana, one of the Eritrean aides, had shown her how he
backed the wheelchair into his room when the meal trolleys had
to pass, instead of sticking out of the doorway where they all
liked to sit, claiming part of the hall as a kind of porch. Never
mind spit, harness, diaper, Mayhew was established as having

manners. Fana rewarded him with a spot in the shade between two boxes of geraniums, at the other end of the terrace from the water bowl set out for therapy dogs.

The aides had unfriendly words in their own soft languages for these animals. "It is not clean," Fana said. "But he like-es the dogs. Monday and Thursday they will bring them, they will take them in-to the bet-rooms." Jane liked to hear her *T*'s, they were so delicate, so refraining; they held a suggestion that everything would lie lightly upon one, never pierce.

While her husband Avery was in the hospital near death, one article said, Mrs. Mayhew had taken his dog to the vet and had her put to sleep. She told the reporter who knocked, "The dog was old and she was sick. And don't let me see you on this porch again."

"Hello, Avery," Jane said. "I'm back. Yes, it's me. I'm back. I'm glad to see you."

Without gladness, his blue eyes saw her. The rims and whites were angrily inflamed. "He rubs his ey-yes," said Fana, crossing the terrace with a Dixie cup and a pill. "You do that don't you, Mr. Mayhew?" She put a lament into the name.

He was dressed in a blue plaid shirt with a terrycloth bib; his feet were in what looked like women's slippers lined with bunny fur. "Comfees, we have put," said Fana, indicating the slippers. She turned her face to speak out of the side of her mouth like a comic. "On the heel. Bet-so." Bedsore.

"Oh, no," Jane said. She quickly clamped her teeth, which often chattered when she first saw Mayhew or heard physical details offered about him. Who did Fana think she might be? Not the wife. The wife, Doris Mayhew, had never come, after the state removed him from her care. The removal was Jane's doing. Why had she involved herself? For her niece. Because her niece Tara begged her to. Now she had her brother's sad warning that this particular caprice was one he found it hard to excuse, when everyone else was rebuilding, after seven years, had rebuilt. Rebuilt what? She bent towards Mayhew. "Today, I came without my paints. But next time."

He heard her with the dull look of an old horse. She was several years his senior, but she wore high-heeled sandals and a toe ring, the gift of a man, her lover Karel—or Karel who had once been her lover—while Mayhew wore slippers, a bib, and on his wrist a Wanderer's Alarm. Mr. Mayhew, the history teacher. Seven years ago her niece Tara had been one of his students.

Then for more than five years he had lived in a chicken coop. There was legal proof of that. Days after the accident—still called that, in town—the Mayhew family had disappeared. It was as if they had never lived on a named street in town; never attended the Methodist church; never passed, the sons, through the gauntlet on the steps of the school where their father had taught. Doris Mayhew must have made a trip back to get him, because the hospital, which was in the next county, had a record of his release to her. It was not as if anyone had been visiting him to notice. Of course a wife can sign out a husband.

Then it took a long time for word of them to reach town, and longer for any sense to be made of it. She had bought herself a piece of scrubland, it was said, down near the Tennessee border where her people were originally from. Gone on teaching the fifth grade. How could she retire? Mothers recalled how you could hear a pin drop in Doris Mayhew's classroom. Not to excuse him.

"I redid the whole place," she was reported to have said, holding the door of the chicken coop for the girl from the Health Department. A toilet, a tin shower with a chair. Doris Mayhew lifting, soaping: Jane tried not to imagine it. If anyone washed the man. Maybe the sons, while they were still at home. Maybe the sons rebuilt the chicken coop. And had they had any say, when the dog was put down? Boys who had gone to school with Tara, one of them in her class, enduring World History with his father at the blackboard and the girls listening with their heads back, their eyes half closed or sliding sideways at each other, as girls' eyes always had, in his father's class. The girls raising their hands, teasing for his father's notice. The son must have figured he could get through that, his father's following. His brother had. He must have thought that was the thing that would be asked of him that year.

"When you will paint," said Fana, "I will watch." She lowered her voice but kept it loud enough for him to hear. "It is good you will paint Mr. Mayhew because he is hand-some." The metal chair she was dragging gave a screech on the flagstones. "For you." At the other end several women came out in floppy gardening hats and walked on their own to chairs in the sun.

The Residence at Calling Creek stood over its built-on wing of red brick like a cow with a calf not her own. It had been a farmhouse, one of the big old fieldstone places parting with their fenced hills one by one. The old porch had given way to an open terrace, and the double-hung windows had been replaced and stripped of their black shutters; with a gaze like someone missing her glasses the stone face of the building looked out over the circle drive and the parking lot. In the yard was a buggy, shafts in the grass, left over from the period when the place had been an antique store. Beyond the parking lot was a small field, leased to somebody now to finish his Herefords. Thick with clover, it sloped in its square of board fence down to bulldozers and the close-ranked new roofs of Calling Creek Acres. The creek itself was nowhere to be seen; it ran under the tangles of Virginia creeper somewhere at the back of the original farm.

Her brother Dewey said, "I'm not sure why you're going down there at all. And you're taking your paints? I can't altogether see why you feel you need to do that."

"Not need, want. I just want to paint a couple of things."

"Like the buggy?" he said, aggrieved but optimistic.

"No, not that." Could he ever have looked at her paintings, and think she would paint a buggy?

The next minute he said, "Anymore, you don't ride hardly at all." He lapsed into his country lawyer talk when he had a point to make.

"It was disagreeing with my hip bones," she said. Dewey could accept that, rather than "I got tired of it," or worse, "I stopped loving my horse. All that time I could only love one thing." Of Karel, Dewey knew the name, nothing more. "Carroll," he spelled it, e-mailing her in New York to say that she should of course bring him or someone else of her choice to the wedding. Dewey's theory, endorsed or more likely proposed by his wife Maggie, was that New York was full of men standing ready to occupy Jane's time and attention. Many men, not one. Maggie would never credit, in Jane, a paralyzed longing for *one*. Dewey shook his head; even though he and Maggie were in the midst of an addition to their stable, he pitied his sister for letting him have her horses.

"You know, Jane . . ."

"It always begins with 'You know.' Something you don't know, that's going to make you feel bad."

"I think you blame yourself for what happened."

"No, Dewey."

"It may be you do."

"You mean Maggie does. Just because Tara was over here so much, just because I—" She almost said "love the girl," but that would be reported to Maggie and Maggie would see it as envy.

"But honestly I never passed on any of my black arts to your daughter."

"Now Jane." He wiped his face as she had seen him do in court; with him it was sincere, it had something to do with thought, the draining quality of thought. "Tara was a . . . she was fifteen, she was just a silly girl."

"No she was not. She was a wild girl, maybe she was an awful girl. Silly she was not." *I was never so careless, so fearless as Tara, no. So merciless. If I could have been, I would have been.*

But she must stop, she must not keep on until she brought to the kindly face of her brother, who was, after all, the father, the old look of baffled shame.

VERY EARLY THAT morning, Monday, someone had called from the front desk and put Fana on, because Jane had said a month ago that she would be back. "All day he was wai-ting," Fana said. "Mr. Mayhew."

Jane knew Mayhew had not been waiting; to wait you had to have memory. Fana said he talked, and Jane defended herself. She knew the man did not talk. "My dear, I don't have my calendar with me"—she was still in bed—"but I feel sure it was today. Yesterday we had a wedding here." She didn't say, *My niece Tara got married. Ask around. Somebody there can tell you about Tara.*

She had given up her habit of agreeing with people when it made her the culprit. For some time she had been saying, in fact, whatever came into her mind. There was no reason not to, now, no reason to be charming or even particularly civil. There was no reason to have her hair cut and colored and know the plots of operas and be ready to book a flight.

It seemed all she had done for years, even putting paint on

canvas, had been done for the sake of a man. A man whose name she must not mention, because it was foreign and unusual, and in some places a known name. A man she must not write or call or imagine leaning on her in a cab in desire so long-established it was almost lawful. And now there was no reason to do anything but paint and sleep.

But the phone had cut off both sleep and the images that formed on waking, and she got up quickly and wandered in her nightgown into the early sun, among the white almost weightless chairs you could rent now, arranged in curved rows in the garden.

Petals coated everything; Maggie had made sure the little girls had their baskets full. Jane picked up napkins, cigarette butts. She brought one of them to her nose. Karel. Karel had given up smoking with the greatest difficulty. Gum and patches and hypnotism, and finally a therapist. Some of the same aids he had required to give up Jane. He admitted such things. "I'm weak." To love her was weak.

"You're strong," he told her. "Don't worry. You'll wonder how you ever wasted your time on me."

"I'm strong," she repeated.

"It's in the paintings." Karel was a connoisseur; he gazed, he selected; years ago he had followed her into the coatroom of a gallery, taken her by the shoulders, pressed her into the coats. "Who are you?" she had said, out of breath.

"Don't worry, we have been introduced."

"I'm glad of that," she said, testing the thick white hair with one finger.

"It was in another gallery," he said, smiling.

"I wouldn't have to know you to know these things about you," he said later, caressing her. "The rashness, the sympathies . . ."

"Ha. That's anybody. Sympathies? I could be Hitler. He was a painter. I could be a murderer like Caravaggio. You would never know."

". . . the appetites," he went on. "I would know," he said, with the combination of pride in himself and submissive tenderness that she had come to know.

In the rock garden the two lizards, whose cream stripes somehow turned over like ribbon and flashed into turquoise on their tails, sat in the sun. She had narrowed down; she was not the person he described, she was a woman who stood at a bedroom window, forehead on the glass, and watched for flickers in the rock garden while the big clock in the hall struck the quarter hour, the hour. She could have put those lizard colors on canvas in two, three strokes of the palette knife. Yet why would you? Hadn't Dewey been asking, in his muddled way, why you would paint at all? Why paint anything? What if you had lost the sense of how to paint what a thing meant to you?

Now her mind was going to crawl in a low determined way through French doors into a room where it could lift its eyes to the painting hung alone, emblazoned with gouts of cadmium yellow, a sunroom where the man who had sworn himself to her sat on Sunday morning reading the paper with his wife. Where now a mind could crouch—a small replica of herself that was also a lizard, tail lashing—in the dark behind the glass panels of a bookcase, and watch the small, the trembling wife, the wife who spoke with the same accent he did and who was kind and good, holding a treasure, her own life, always in her hands before him like a cracker she could break.

Maybe his children were there. No, they were away at school, in lives of their own. Old enough that they could have managed without him. Of course they could.

Yellow had filled her paintings at the time. Yellow of celebration, of summer, of ease and satiety. None of them the yellow of today, flat and wintry, hers before she noticed it. Northern, like the yellow sky over Friedrich's abandoned landscapes and cold seas. A color for never. *I attest to it,* said the color. *Never.*

Yet from her painting above the mantel one of the old jubilant yellows was shedding its light on him, and on his wife. A wife so fragile, trembling and silent, so huge and powerful, that she could never be left. *She would kill herself.*

"I know how many men have said that," he said humbly. "About their wives."

"Over the *centuries*," Jane said.

"Jane, for God's sake, Jane. You know." He too could plead. "You know her. She would kill herself." The unsaid thing was that she had tried before. So he had given her reason to try, before.

Jane did know, of course, that there were people who would kill themselves. How had he found the one person who would know this as she did?

There were people who would not give a thought to being dragged out of a car like sandbags while other people did the screaming. They would think only of dying. They would have set their sights on it. Dying, rather than going on, the way everybody else had to. Obsessed people, with no mercy for whoever had to yank hose from pipe and attempt CPR, rightfully howling at the sight of the human face turned demon red by gas, slapping that face, again and again—a bottom-heavy schoolteacher in a pantsuit, home from Parent Night and down on the cement floor of the garage beside the corpse that firemen were going to bring back from being a corpse. Those dreary others, neighbors, parents, sons, gathered in the hospital cafeteria. No mercy for them.

• • •

THE BRIDESMAIDS WERE pretty, all of them. Slim in their gauzy togas of green and lavender, pliant. Yet certain ones, she knew, were made of something invisibly resistant, like the polymers that hardened paint. Not pliant. One or two were liars.

A tanned girl bumped her, spilling champagne. "Oh, sorry, sorry," the girl said in that high voice they all seemed to have, though it was Jane who was dizzy, not the girl with skin so smooth the ball of the shoulder gave off light. If she were forced to paint them Jane would paint their bones: curved little skull barely fused, clean jawline. The glowing collarbones of Tara. Of course if you loved beauty, if you had married badly, if you yourself were known for your black hair and your creased smile, if you had taught World History to tenth graders for fifteen years and still you loved beauty, beauty and daring—if this girl, of all of them, came to your desk after school with those collarbones lifting as she breathed, would you not think of putting your lips there?

Half the dresses in the garden were strapless; the ones that did have straps or sleeves showed bra straps as well. How many years of safety pins, of shamed pulling and tucking had gone into the concealment of bra straps, only for them to emerge finally as part of the ensemble? Although there was no finally. Or not in fashion: had not the tippet reappeared? Given a small twist, brought out as luxurious or perverse, and in the right colors, the parasol could return, even the bustle.

What was the matter with her, scolding like this in her mind? She had reached the side of the rabbi. He was standing by himself at the end of the walk where the paving stones led up and out of the garden. He was a heavy man; things moved around him. Before Tara and her bridegroom Josh he had stood as if to block a door, though his hands had been peaceably folded. She had an urge to sit down heavily in front of him on the scattered rice, at the level of the milling legs. She knew all these people, though not so well as she once had. They were mostly people her brother's age, from the time when a gap of four years at school was the same as decades.

She looked for Josh's mother, Elaine. She had sat with Elaine at the rehearsal dinner. She felt some responsibility for her, a widow, a short, friendly woman who had inadvertently crossed into the region of Maggie's fiercest smiles during the planning by saying that she hoped to wear peach. Peach was Maggie's color. "I've never visited the South," Elaine said when Maggie steered her to Jane's side in the garden and left her there. "Look at this. You've done it all so perfectly."

"Maggie did it," Jane said. "I'm in disgrace. I lettered the place cards in a hurry. They're messy. I'm the next thing to a visitor."

Elaine waved that away and said, "Look, just look." Two faces, close together, white as plates under the paper lanterns: Josh whispering to Tara. He had her hands in both of his. Elaine laid her own hand on her heart. "Excuse me, I might have to cry tonight so tomorrow I'll keep my makeup on." *Cry now*, Jane thought.

When it was all over the young people drifted out from under the lanterns and down the hill to the empty stables. "I bet they're going to smoke a joint," Elaine said, patting her hand. "I wouldn't say it except to you."

"Not to Maggie anyway," Jane said.

Elaine had asked for a tour of her paintings but there had not been time. "I was studying design before I married," she had whispered, before Maggie found her shawl for her and took her away.

THE RABBI DIDN'T have the generalizing social gaze. His eyes settled on a person, then another. Now they were on her. Under the thick eyebrows the half-hidden eyes seemed to be green. On the way through the house to the rehearsal, he had stopped to say, "Is this your work?" Eternal question, followed by "Interesting." Or "Lovely," when none of it was lovely. "Jane's colors," you would hear them saying, with the musing calm of people under no obligation to like what might be liked in New York. A sympathy almost, for Jane in her dependence on such colors. He didn't say anything, though he put off going outside, and ventured into the dining room with his fingers together and tipped up in what she would have said was a priestly gesture. But a rabbi was a different thing entirely. He must have a wife.

"How is this done?" he said.

"With a knife."

"Aha." Next he would say his wife painted a little. But he didn't; he said, "You're a bit of a Fauve."

His name was Israel. Israel.

Somewhere in the bookcases was a Bible, her prize fifty years ago for a drawing done before she could read. Where was it, with its zipper pulled by a cross, its words of Jesus in red letters? Inside, pale reproductions of unknown paintings, one of them her favorite for copying in crayon, with her thumbprints on it and her memory of smelling the page: *The Children of Israel.* Men, women, and children were pressing forward across a pastel desert, colored shawls blowing. The sheep, the tents, the wells: as much her own as her horse. And Moses spake, and his rod had a serpent on it. Men broke the earrings out of women's ears to melt for a golden calf. King David sang the Psalms. *Selah*: a word that stirred her, a word with no translation.

The Psalms, said their father, who alone among his law partners did not sit down in a pew on Sunday, were songs to pacify God, make him stop.

And God did stop, stopped existing. For a while, to ally herself with her father, she had thrown herself into argument. At the dinner table her mother could not clear up the matter of Jonah, and cried with the effort to draw them into the story of Ruth. Shaking out his napkin her father said Ruth was no different from Cinderella.

After his stroke he didn't remember, and why would she tell him he had left a daughter empty-handed at ten? King David flown, and the angels of the Lord in fours and sevens, leaving a vague sense of maneuvers repeating themselves on a map, in map colors of pink and yellow and tan. And words—*cubits* and *beryl*, *Nineveh* and *hyssop* and *concubine*. As if a god would ever have cast an eye on one rock in space, and chosen some there for himself and left the rest sliding to their doom. As if a god would fashion a smaller god and send him down to test all the scrambling creatures with their slaves and wars. And they would fail the test and the god would fail at the job of testing them.

As if, Tara would say. Tara had never gone through a painful believing phase.

All this Jane would have liked to bring up with the rabbi, because of his green eyes. Because it was never too late to complain childishly of things taken away from you. But not only that. An awful temptation could come over you to confide in a stranger, some doctor or priest on an airplane who gave off the benevolence of authority. The temptation to start right in, ask for a judgment. To say, Help me. A man told me to go. And I wouldn't go. I went into his closet. I picked up his black shoe with a scent in it like alcohol. I put it over my face, breathed, it was my last breath of him, his wife was coming in twenty minutes, he made me leave, he was protecting her from me. From me. And he— who was he? I'll tell you. I'll tell you—

But no, this rabbi's smiling eyes could not be taken for his conscience. He would have his duty; he would be no latitudinarian. Shame on you, eyes like that might say. He was there, after all, to officiate.

"No, we can't have the wedding on a Saturday. Josh is observant." It had taken Jane a minute to know what Tara meant. First she thought, *He'll have to be.* So the wedding was on a Sunday, with that stupefied feeling the day would always have for her. The stopped gears of the week, the gloves, the stairs down to the paste-smelling rooms of Sunday School, where her own drawings, copied from the Bible and framed by her mother, hung on the walls. "We don't want to be proud," Miss DeJong said to Jane's class, "just because our pictures were put up last year."

"New shoes," said Miss DeJong.

"No," Jane said, hiding her feet.

Her mother always knelt and brushed the tops of her Mary Janes. Her toes recalled the soft scuffing of the black brush. Was this Christianity? And the buckle being loosened by her mother's fingers when she had the strap too tight. Why, her bending mother, already sick, would have been young, decades younger than Jane was now, and not that much later would close her copy of *The Upper Room* and die in her hospital bed, spared any knowledge that this child was going to run away at eighteen and be married for a winter to a boy known to have peddled drugs in the schools of three counties. And then come back, abandoned.

"*Taken*," people said in town. "She got taken. Thought he'd get the money."

"Didn't though."

"I bet he got some of it. She's that way. Where did that boy take himself anyway?"

"She'll never say."

Dewey was married by then, and his new wife Maggie repeated these things to Jane.

Some things could not be spoken of to Maggie. Certainly not a childish sorrow unable to complete itself after years. No, for Maggie everything had a beginning and an end. A wedding, for instance, tied a ribbon around the past and put it in a drawer. Even such a past as Tara's.

What could Maggie be expected to know about drugs and hiding and debt? What could she know about the soiled childhood, the shame and sweet apology that boy Jane had married had had in him? The beauty of face and body. Ha! Maggie would say, for that was surely gone. But still the letters and phone calls came every year or so, from hostels and bars, from jails, from towns in Mexico, and were answered.

All Maggie knew was that Jane had come back, that year she was eighteen, to tend the big house, tend the garden, tend her father. And paint. Oddly, to come accidentally into a reputation elsewhere as a painter, or so it was said. Certainly the trips to New York began to stretch out, the trips back, in the company of one man or another, to shorten. After their father died Jane would shut the house up for months at a time. She was not around enough to keep the horses worked, and eventually Dewey trucked them, with their dusty tack, to his own stables.

Dewey made up for whatever it was she was up to. A brother well married who practiced law in his home town could all but undo a sister's effect. In time he could undo even the effect of his own daughter, who had persuaded the high school history teacher to die with her.

"I LIKED THE service," Jane said to the rabbi. Was *service* the word? "When she circled him. And 'I shall betroth thee unto me forever.'"

"'Yea, I shall betroth thee unto me in righteousness.'"

"What was the other passage?"

"That was from Tobit. The story of Tobias and the angel. The angel takes him to his wedding, helps him through it."

"We all need that."

"He marries his cousin Sarah. Seven men have previously married her and died on the wedding night, when they went in to her. Into the bedchamber."

"I see. A risk."

"The angel drives away the demon who's at the bottom of it. He does it with a fish liver. The smell. You know how fish smells. Imagine how fish *liver* smells."

She laughed. "You should have read us the whole story. I don't know that one."

"It's in the Apocrypha. What you call the Apocrypha. Those books in question."

"And the rest is fact," she said casually, but she couldn't provoke him.

"It contains some famous prayers. A lot of screwy stuff has gone on. You've got a fish grabbing the guy's foot, you've got an angel, you've got marrying your cousin you never saw before, and this and that. But you've got these great songs of prayer. Two of them prayers for death. Prayed by characters who are going to live long and prosper."

"Prayers for death," she repeated.

"Some aging, some death. But you've got a wedding, and much rejoicing. Property changing hands. 'You have dealt with us,' they pray, 'according to your great mercy.'"

"Which part was the great mercy?"

"For them"—he held up both palms to excuse them—"a wedding. For us? Who can say?"

"So . . . a demon. Of weddings."

"Demons. A wedding could call them out. Not just out in the desert where you have mirages, crazy hermits, guys you might *mistake* for a demon. In Rome they wrapped the bride up in a veil to ward off evil spirits." He waved at the chuppah now folded and leaning against a hydrangea. "So tomorrow, somebody comes and takes all this off your hands, and it's all over and you can sit out here and drink the rest of the champagne."

"I'd love to," she said, raising her glass as the waiter came to pour, "but see all those bottles? People are abstaining. A statement, I bet, a little reminder to our family. Kindly meant, of course. 'We'll celebrate, dears, but we'll reign ourselves in just the tiniest bit.' No, tomorrow I won't be here. I'm going to see Mr. Mayhew at the home. Mr. Mayhew who taught history. He's at Calling Creek now."

"The Residence," said the rabbi with a flourish of his big drooping hand.

"Do you visit?"

"So far," he said, drawing down an eyebrow, "they have not sent for me. No, I do a little Hebrew class in the development down there. I've seen the place."

"Well, it's not a chain, and it's better than where he was."

"I believe you're right. I believe that is safe to say."

As soon as Tara had thrown her bouquet and run with Josh under the shower of rice and away, the garden had gone slack. The musicians sat slack in their chairs until Maggie went over to prompt them, people were eddying onto the screened porch or down the path to the steps where Jane and the rabbi stood looking at each other tiredly but with attention.

People came to thank her, and press their cheeks to hers. "Jane, dear, your pretty dress, now what do you call that shade?"

"Green," she said.

Now Maggie was supervising a grouping of the attendants for

a photograph against the rock garden. Elaine waited where she had been placed nearby for a last pose. Dewey was weeping behind one of the tall flower stands. Because this daughter, his favorite despite being the most difficult, in her hair-trigger readiness to give and take back, the one who had very nearly ruined herself and the family before her belated decision to go away after all, go to school as they had begged her to do, a northern college where despite having little intelligence to speak of, she had had great success—this daughter who had gone halfway to death and come back, who had filled a hospital waiting room to overflowing, had a formidable beauty.

Could that be all? Some configuration of eyes, nose, and mouth, some arrangement of colors? No, there was a violent health that let Tara go on swimming lap after lap when her teammates had dragged themselves out of the pool, let her hemoglobin purge itself of carbon monoxide as Mayhew's would not. There was an almost mindless strength of will. But beauty was the thing on which everyone, even Jane, could pin some generalized longing. Tara in white coming on thin heels belying the slow power of her walk, her arm laced through her father's without holding on, had caused a deep indrawn communal breath. So much seemed gathered in her, and ready to be strewn on all of them like the petals out of the little girls' baskets. And yet what was strewn? Nothing remained of whatever it was, to be theirs, or help them.

"HELP HIM," TARA had said, her voice a croak.

"How can I help him? You help him."

"How can I?"

"What will you do if I help him?"

"What do mean, do? Pay you back? Dad won't let me have my money. I'm teaching swimming. Josh has another year of medical school." Tara drew herself up proudly. "We're going to have kids right away. God, Jane. We'll pay you back. Don't think Josh doesn't know about Avery. He knows everything. He understands. He's the first one to really understand."

"Ah, the first," Jane had said, thinking, *Must I help her? Just because a black-haired amorous little girl ran into my house whenever I came back, ran into my arms, followed me, gazed as I painted, and sent me valentines?* "It's not the money. I'll get the man moved. There's Calling Creek. I don't want to be paid back."

"What then. What do you want."

"Redress. For him."

"But what, what, *what*? I wish I had died."

"I don't think so."

"Why didn't I, why didn't I die?"

"You must not have wanted to."

"Jane, you are the cruelest person in the family."

"No, I don't think so."

But Tara had known what to say. She had said, "I love him. I do, I still do."

THE RABBI RAN finger and thumb down the lines on either side of his mouth. "I knew Mayhew to say hello to. I had a son at the school. The boys were not as hard on him."

The girls had formed a pack, and turned Avery Mayhew in. It was Tara's fault, though the town had stood behind her. And then the first girl admitted that she had exaggerated, and then they all said Mayhew had not flirted with all of them, or with any of them: they all said they had lied outright. To protect Tara. And then, after her screamed admissions—motels, cars, her own father's tack room—Tara would not give him up. She went on, after ruining him, to further ruin.

"We'll have to kill ourselves." That was the testimony. The

paper ran it under two pictures from the yearbook. The words of a fifteen-year-old sobbing into a phone, the plan of an uncontrollable girl to which a grown man, a married man, had acquiesced. A teacher.

"Well, I'm getting ready to paint him. He has agreed to sit. More or less agreed," Jane rambled on. That was not true. "He was so handsome, if you remember."

"Hmm. I looked at your portraits in there. You don't have a whole lot of interest in the face."

"Well, of course, portraits are about more than the face."

"There's this," he said ruefully, clasping his girth in both hands. "But it used to be we thought the face gave you away. You couldn't hide, say, the fact that you chased little girls."

"But of course he didn't chase them; they chased him, and they weren't little girls."

"No? When does *little* end?"

A girl slid past them and out of the garden, wearing two scarves tied together. "Well, I'd say by the time you wear that," Jane said. Of course it was not two scarves but a sundress. The girl was carrying her shoes and somebody had wound the ribbon from one of the stands of dahlias several times around her upper arm. "And your son who was in school here, where is he?"

"Philadelphia. Married. Studying to be a rabbi."

"That must make you proud. That he wants to follow in your footsteps."

"Far from it. He doesn't see much of us. They're Orthodox. It's not to punish us for how we did it, it's just . . ."

"Does God see these things?" she said conversationally. "See who gets punished and who doesn't?"

"I don't know. God is far from us. I don't have my own congregation, you know."

"No, I didn't know."

"Why should you? I just didn't want you to assign my views to the community."

"If my community heard my views they'd run me out of town."

"You mean the rich?"

"If they'd claim me." *Why strike the pitiful note?* she asked herself. *There's nothing pitiful about me.* But there was, the pitiful wish to be looked at, appreciated for burning-out pigments of skin and eyes and hair that had at one time caused a stir.

"Artists. There's your community. Art, as we know, is taken very seriously here." He grinned. For some weeks that summer there had been a furor in the papers about a statue in front of a bank.

"Art by people from somewhere else."

"Naturally. That's where art comes from, somewhere else."

"Far away."

"Overseas." After a while he said, "I would have said she was your daughter."

"Well, thank you." Then she thought he must have meant because the wedding was at her house. "She is my favorite. I can't help it, she always was. Her sisters were married here too," she said hastily. "It's a tradition. I'm sure you met them last night. There they are, over there with Maggie."

"No resemblance."

"I have no daughters of my own. I don't really live here. When I was growing up I loved it so. I would *race* out in the morning to see my horse. I would ride with my mother. She named the horses after people in the Bible. Mine was Dinah. Dinah!" she cried, as if the mare could be summoned. "One day I turned my back on her. My mother. Everything is ruined. I hate my life."

"I myself am in the midst of a divorce," he said, as if to fortify her.

"Oh, no. I'm sorry."

"It's best," he said, bending his head and examining his hands. His broad ribcage expanded in the black coat. When he looked up it seemed that one of his eyes had filled with tears but the other had not.

"I'm really sorry. God. My horse, my life . . . stop me, somebody."

"Stop with the horse, the life," he said.

She laughed. She looked at the sky. She saw a vision of the parting of Tara and her shy, stern medical student, with shouts and tears. You could never say that, even if, like Jane, you were getting reckless in what you did say. Never say a sliver of ice from the future blew into you in the middle of these ceremonies so that you knew beyond a doubt that the end was coming and sometimes not even from afar, not even decently loitering while the marriage got on its feet.

He was thinking. Now both eyes had filled, and reflected the low sunlight. She had better leave him alone. She had better leave everybody alone. Over there her poor brother was fingering his boutonniere and wiping his eyes with a napkin.

"Could I ask you something?"

"Ask me."

"Didn't you have to instruct them? Prepare them? I know you know her story but do you know her at all? She's reckless. She's driven. She doesn't think. Did you caution that boy? Do you know him?"

"He's from Connecticut. We don't all know each other."

"That's not—"

"He'll do his best. So will she. It's a genuine enough conversion. She's way out in front of him with the Judaism, by the way. She went into the mikvah, she purified herself. And the parents, you notice they're not that worried? That's half the battle."

She didn't say, Elaine is a romantic and with Dewey and Maggie it's relief. She said, "You got to know them, the parents."

"What is it you're asking?"

"I don't know."

"This could help her. The girl has a burden."

"Tell me what you really think."

"Betrothed in righteousness," he said, and winked at her.

She talked to Mayhew, where he sat between the flower boxes. She talked about the heat, the steers grazing in the fence-row. She counted them and told him the number. She said she hoped he wouldn't mind sitting right where he was, on the terrace with the red geraniums, for one or two short sessions while it was still summer. But with field and sky behind him. In that blue shirt.

There was a certain peace in not having your smile returned. You could go ahead and drop the subject and the smile. When had he begun the unpleasant skewing of his head to stare at her? He was going through an awful simulation of a tourist trying to follow in a phrase book. The head went still, a stare took the sag out of the features. Something like horror passed over them. Horror at *her*? Something he saw.

Then he couldn't take his eyes off her.

Someone came and propped the doors open. The women in hats helped each other up out of the chairs. Fana came out to say it was his nap time. "But first I will smoke one cigarette on my break, and then I will come back," she said. Before Jane could stand up and say, "Don't go, I'm just leaving, let me leave," Fana had drifted down the steps past the OXYGEN IN USE, NO SMOKING sign, crossed the lawn to the buggy, and lightly mounted the iron step, where she waved out her match and faced the little field, or perhaps her own country, where women did not smoke and those too old to be useful might be left sitting in their own yards, with children around them instead of dogs.

Mayhew had begun to struggle against the mesh belt. He kept swiping at his neck and chest with his claw hand. Was something running down his throat? He seemed to be after the bib, but the Velcro at the back of the neck wouldn't give. Finally he got the hand to his eye, rubbed viciously. Then the other hand wavered out and she felt it dab at her slacks.

She moved her leg, the hand came on. She had to touch it and finally lift it in her fingers. The palm was slick with sweat. The blue shirt stuck to him under the arms. His eyes had undergone a change. "Tara," he whispered.

She kept the hand in hers, holding it loosely to let it dry, but she didn't answer him.

"Tara."

"No!" Jane shook her head. "No. No."

"Tara."

She leaned away from him.

"Tara . . . are we old?"

She dropped the hand. She stood up, steadying the backs of her legs on the planter. The red eyes kept up their demand. "Yes," she said, finally. "Yes, Avery, we are, now. We're old."

Tearing now from being rubbed, the eyes undertook an examination of her face and body. With care, she sat down again, folding herself away from view. "But . . . but listen to me. We've had a good life." The stare dropped to her breasts, rose to her face. She clenched her teeth. "I know you don't remember." *Stop that. God help you if there's a mirror in there, if you think I'm old. Do you think I want to come here? I don't know why I come. I come because I can't see the end of this. Is that it?*

She made herself look at him. She let her stare grow as bold and sickened as his. Nevertheless she kept looking. Somewhere behind what she was seeing was the face from the yearbook, the face Tara trusted her to comfort. The beloved.

"Avery," she said finally, as if in the long habit of coaxing explanation, wifely forbearance, "everyone gets older."

From the buggy, Fana called to the women at the far end of the porch, "Time now, time to get ready for your meal." They had their dinner at 4:30. Fana didn't come right away; she let them pretend not to hear. "Are you ready, Mr. Mayhew?" she called.

"The important thing is"—Jane came out of the chair, sank to her knees on the flagstones and crushed his hands in hers—"I'm here. You see? I'm here."

"Tara." He leaned down as far as the harness would let him, and sighed with a groan that stirred her hair.

There was a bloodstain on the fur of his slipper. Through her hair she saw the bones of his foot move in the thin white sock. The beloved. She raised her head. "It's all right, stop it," she whispered harshly, intimately, to the shut eyes. "Oh, it's all right, Avery. I'm here."

Behind her Fana said, "We will go in now."

He kept his eyes shut. Jane got to her feet. Fana took hold of the handlebars, bent to the back of his head. "Today, Mr. Mayhew, is the day you will see your friend."

"His friend?"

"His friend the dog." Fana made a face. "For this friend, he is waiting."

THE RABBI WAS in the parking lot, standing beside his car. Neither of them showed any surprise. "Hello there," she said.

"So, how did it go?" he said.

"Well, I have a question for you. What was that about 'great mercy'?"

"'You have dealt with us according to your great mercy.'"

"'You have dealt with us.' That's it. That's the part that applies."

Across the hot concrete from them the sun had turned the sweet-bay trees along the fence a tropical green. Phthalo green yellow, it might be. You could put in a red sky, filling up most of the space, keeping the strip of field a blue green inch at the bottom of the canvas. If you did it small, and got the red right—red could combine torment and calm—and put in no human figure, you would have a tiny painting of still, intense memory. *Farm.*

"Mercy," she said, combing her fingers through her hair and shaking it as if the groan might have lodged there. "I don't think so."

"Who are you to say?"

"Who are *you* to say?"

"I'm the rabbi."

"I see."

"I came because I thought we might want to walk down to the creek."

"There's no creek there any more," she said bitterly. "Oh, a trickle."

"Clean, though. They cleaned it up. The fish have come back, I'm told."

"Fish," she said in despair. "I couldn't read that fish story of yours. I looked in an old Bible I have and it's not in there."

"I will read it to you," he said.

Behind the house, Queen Anne's lace and milkweed nodded through the rails of the fence at the mown grass with its sprinklers. If he knew about the creek he must have walked here before. By himself. Thinking of his wife, who was divorcing him. Jane felt sure it was that way around. He was not a man who would cast somebody off. He already had his foot on the fence rail and she had to show him there was a gate farther down, at the corner of the yard where the fence met another coming up from the barn. She showed him the thin path made by cows, leading downhill to the barn.

"When?" she said, opening the gate for him as he tried to figure out the looped wire on a stick of wood.

"When what?"

"When will you read it to me?"

"Today," he said. "You'll come to the house. The apartment. My wife has the house."

"I'm sure she does," Jane said.

"So. You like him maybe a little. Mayhew. This guy who gives up everything. And for what does he do this? For a woman."

"A woman!" she said. But she didn't argue. There was more to it than an explanation, however long, could cover. Often it seemed to her the explanation of anything that came to pass would have no beginning and no end. If you painted a thing, that was the shortened explanation of it.

When they sat down beside the creek, almost invisible but gurgling under the vines, she held up her foot. "I wore the wrong shoes." He studied her sandals, her toe ring. He had been panting as he walked and he was still breathing hard. About that, she would talk to him on another day.

Luck

• • •

H IS DOCTOR PUT him on the plane and he flew home to Seattle alone. It was September, and he was well.

Your mind can rush you like a tackle. His mind had been warning him, and his mother, for long enough that on the day she came in from work and called his name twice from the door, she knew.

He had been shooting baskets with Chris. Then he was walking home from Chris's house, but walking on and on and not getting there, not getting home. By the time he got to the porch he had a shrunken, sickish feeling, light-headed and hot. His memory of it was from describing it. At the door of his room he had braced himself against the onrush of something, a kind of furious speech, close to his ears yet too faint and tinny to make out, that he had been staving off all day. He got down on the floor and covered his ears. The next thing he knew his mother's hands were loosening his fingers and he could find no answer to the normal words she appeared to be saying.

Quickly, somebody had been found who knew the best place to take him. Even though the place was in Chicago, his mother had taken him. She was so pregnant she had had to lie to get on the flight.

All he remembered of the trip was her getting up to go to the bathroom five or six times, and taking his hands back into her own cold, washed, half-dried ones every time she sat down, and saying, because he was whispering on and on, he couldn't shut up, "Shh, shh. You don't have to worry, it's all right."

She thought flipping out had made him afraid, but that wasn't it. He liked planes. It was said that as a baby in a stroller he had shouted and pointed them out in the sky, and he could remember himself in a certain grassless spot in the playground near the slide, in what must have been kindergarten because his father was already dead, staggering backward to look at a plane going over.

It wouldn't have been all that crazy for a little kid to get the idea that catching sight of a plane in the sky brought him luck. And then he had had the ability to dispense the luck. That was his game, to bring them luck, to offer safety to passengers who could not be seen, who were so far off and miniaturized they were turning into nothing. But if he saw their plane in time, they returned to existence.

Was anyone looking up at the plane he was in now, coming home by himself? He shook out his shoulders, rocked his head. Relax yourself. Relax your body. Relax your mind. If you could relax "your" body and "your" mind, where and what was "you?" You, you were not there. You were not on the plane. But of course he was there, in the seatbelt. What had etched the glass of the window in just that way, thousands of silver hairs trapped on it? Every once in a while his gaze went through the glass, like a finger breaking the surface of water, to the banks of cloud just below the wing. As the plane veered downward into them they streamed sideways, bathed the windows, and pulled apart suddenly into dark, wooded land, where you could see roads, huge lots full of tiny cars, even horses in fields.

The noise snapped into a higher register, the wing fiercely dropped its angle, and quite suddenly they were down. Until he had the floor of the gangway under his feet, he didn't think of being home. He didn't think of his mother or the baby until he saw them.

His mother did not hold the baby up to display him. She had him in a corduroy contraption on her chest. She put her arms around Gabe with the baby between them and said just his name; she didn't say how he looked—his skin had broken out—and he didn't say how she looked, which wasn't very good, with gray hair in her bangs and her eyes set among creases.

She kept her arms around him, resting him. He was tired, but in a normal way, without the tinny commentary. His drug had gotten rid of it, the quiet racket too fast and just too far away to be unscrambled. "So, is this Lars we have here?" he said.

"That's him," she said. "Sixteen pounds of lead, when he's asleep."

A baby. And she its mother. But in fact she had left it once to come and see him, and barely spoken of it, the result being that Gabe could not say he had firmly understood its existence. He studied the wad of cheek against the sling, the large ear, bigger than his own. He said, "He's pretty cute."

"You can't really get the full picture. You'll see him at home. And we'll see you. Oh, Gabe. I'm so happy, I'm so happy you're home."

"This is all my stuff," he said. "I didn't bring anybody a present."

"A present!" She stopped walking and he thought she might hug him again but she didn't. Roughly she pulled down her jacket under the sling and set off again, walking fast, as she always did. Nothing woke the big, jouncing baby. Gabe said, "How's everything at school?"

"All right."

"All settled down?"

"Oh, they'll get used to anything. They haven't but they will. I can't go into my office because it's locked. The district is worried I'll sue. They've got me in the back transferring test scores, won't let me see my kids." She glanced at him. "I mean particular ones, who need me. They have to come in and lurk at the counter and get sent away and leave notes on my car to ask me if they should report their uncle for raping them."

A lot of people knew it was Mr. Lofgren's baby. The principal knew. Still, his mother had been written up in the newspaper for her work as a counselor in the school—it was his own school—and she had gone to Washington, D.C., to get an award, and in that way she was more important than the principal. And Mr. Lofgren was important, of course, because of basketball.

In the parking garage the wet tire tracks were like attempts to draw something very large on the floor. "Well, so. Did he move in?"

"No, no. No, he's still at his place."

"I bet he still has *his* job."

She chewed her lip sadly, unlocking the car. "He . . . yeah."

He helped her disentangle the baby's legs from the carrier. He was surprised at the baby's weight. Once she had it in the car seat in the back he got a look at the lolling face. Evidently it had a cold; the big cheeks were chapped and smeared and the pouting lips had a crayon red outline. Huge ears, flimsy looking.

Soft ears. Familiar. He had just read in a magazine, while he waited for his haircut before coming home, about a study showing that criminals were likely to have large, extra-soft ears. Certain kinds of criminals. Serial killers.

"Lars," he said. "Isn't that sort of a weird name?"

"It was Carl's brother's name. He died in Vietnam."

"Uh-oh. But old Carl was a hippie, like you."

"He was in Vietnam too."

"So how old were they?"

"Eighteen and twenty. Carl was eighteen."

"Ha. I could join the army."

"You're fifteen. And don't pretend you want to join the army at any age."

"I couldn't get in the army. I'm crazy."

"That's good, if it will keep you out of the army." She wrenched the car into the freeway traffic. This was the way she drove; he'd be better at it. He'd be a little behind when he got his license but he would have it by '93. She said, "I got mad while they had you. Mad at the clinic. They had you and I didn't. I missed you so much."

"Anyway the whole thing now is what drug you're on," he offered. "That's all they do. I could get admitted any place for that. Did they tell you that?"

"Yes, they were pleasantly modest about themselves, they told me that."

"When?"

"Towards the beginning. But that was the best place."

On their block, a hand went down the middle of the street. Though it was only a leaf, it moved so formally, as if along a keyboard, that he stared after it. He felt a sudden energy of longing. "You know what I always liked? When I was like three? See that?"

"What, the Toyota?"

"The window. See how the tree branches like slide off? In the back window? Every once in a while a plane goes across. I used to think the plane was there in the window, *in* the glass. I had to make sure it got across. Man I used to watch for those little guys."

In a voice almost of tears she said, "You always looked at things."

That made him seem to have been gone longer than he had been. She went on dreamily, "You must have been five. That's when I let you in the front seat with me. Now they say not to. They probably did then. I was so out of it that year, who knows what else I did."

"It was lucky. Luckier than seeing a real plane. I used to wait . . . I used to almost pray to see one, for a while there."

In the driveway she said, "Can you pray at that age?"

HE GOT UP early and went down the block in the near dark to shoot baskets at Chris's old house. While he was gone Chris had moved. His mother blamed it on Chris's dad. "He got a raise. So right away you *know* Katie had to have a *horse*." Katie was Chris's little sister and nobody could stand her attitude. "So now they have one and they board it next door. Couldn't be more convenient for Katie."

In front of Chris's old house the hollow bashing of the ball was a shock, in the quiet. He saw lights come on next door, and he tucked the ball and left. He saw his mother through the fogged front window—she was keeping the house hot—sitting very still on the couch in the T-shirt she slept in, with the baby on her lap. She was looking through the window at him, her face puffy and blank. Suddenly she snapped to and waved.

He took off his coat. "Look what I found in my pocket."

It was a pacifier. She smiled her old smile. "I snuck that jacket while you were gone. Do you mind? I won't wear it anymore. It's too big for me anyway."

Holding the ball, he flopped down at the other end of the couch in the steamy room. Across from them was the broad, high-riding armchair he had noticed last night, brown leather or something that looked like leather, with a bulging headrest and sleeves on the arms, and a handle like a gearshift on the side of it. "Where'd you get *that*?"

"I bought it. It's a recliner. Do you think it's ugly? It *is* ugly. I just wanted something . . . substantial in here. Bad, huh?"

"It's OK."

The baby was awake on her lap, staring at him with its blue protruding eyes, like Mr. Lofgren's. And the ears. It screwed up its face to cry, but instead of crying jerked the big head several times in a kind of pitcher's windup.

"He's too sleepy to nurse. Did you hear him in the night? He doesn't get up much compared to most, do you, buddy, do you?" She picked something off the faded yellow sleeper, which looked as if the baby had already worn it out in his crib life. Now the crib was at the foot of her bed, but Gabe had the feeling she had had it in his room. Everything was where it was supposed to be in his room but there was a sticky smell when you stepped inside the door.

"He's cute."

"Honey, you don't have to keep saying that. He's funny-looking at the moment, if the truth be told. Well, I'm going to get him ready."

"Ready for what?"

"He's going when I go."

"But I'll be here. I could keep him."

"Honey, I'll just take him to Mattie. His sitter." For a second Gabe thought, his *sister*?

"He has a sitter who takes just two others, two babies. He's used to her; he does this every day." She dropped the blanket on the rug and swung the baby above it, causing him to kick and stub his feet on each other, rasping the cracked vinyl heels. Why didn't she dress him in something newer than that?

The baby didn't want to be on his back; he thrashed, grunted, and rolled his eyeballs at her in a ridiculous, threatening way, like a fish scowling in a bowl.

Even serial killers had their diapers changed at one time. No one changing them knew what was to come. No one had any idea what was cramped up in a little shrimp body waiting to unfold. A baby did not know it was not innocent.

"They were going to give me a leave but it never materialized. Then they were going to let me take him to school with me because I don't have anything to do, but no, dammit. Bad example." She unzipped the suit and peeled it down, releasing a rich, sour smell that seemed to excite the baby, who flailed his arms and made a trilling noise. His tongue was another limb, so active it made his chin slick, as well as the creased area that would have been a neck if he had had a neck.

"Hand me those." She wiped the yellow paste off the baby's tapered buttocks, which were remarkably smooth and clean-looking under it. "I know you could watch him. But it's hard to take care of a baby this age. They're irritating. They tire you."

"Hey, whatever." He bounced the ball off the new chair.

"Gabe, I haven't explained anything to you. About Lars."

"You don't have to explain to me."

"I feel as if I do need to. Give me a chance to do it. Look at me. Listen. One child was all I ever needed. One. You. I was . . . it was . . . I said to myself, that was stupid, you got pregnant, but you're thirty-nine, you can either do this or forget that whole side of life. Babies. The part of life that ends. I mean it *ends*. I know it's hard to see that, at your age."

"Hey, I think you should do what you want. So when do I go back to school? I might as well get started."

She had her chin on the baby's head. "Let's wait awhile. A few days. I called to see if Chris could come over this weekend and his mom wants you to come down there instead. Tomorrow. See the new place. He's out of school for parent conferences. She's taking off work to see his teacher."

"How come?"

"Conferences. Just the routine thing where they tell you your kid is distracting everybody, or everybody is distracting him, that stuff. But she's worried about him. You know how she is. The music worries her, the swearing, the drugs, she thought the suburbs would be safe, blah, blah."

"His crazy friends."

"If you say that all the time, you'll convince yourself, honey."

He moved closer. She saw he was going to touch the baby and she smiled at him. He said, "I just want to feel his ears."

HE WAS COLD, waiting in the shadow of the garage across the street, behind a recycling bin. The ground was yellow with wet leaves. Mr. Lofgren lived in an old neighborhood; all up and down the block the old trees with fat, knotted trunks had burst the sidewalk and pried up the street with their roots. Right at that moment he was up on one of the roots, balancing himself.

The windows of the Lofgrens' house were steamed up just like the windows at his own house. Two or three of them had sheets of plastic nailed up around them in preparation for winter, and there was a ladder propped against the house. There was no garage, or he could have turned on the ignition in Mr. Lofgren's car—though he would have needed the car key—and locked the car and, when Lofgren came to investigate, shut him in with the exhaust. He had seen this done on TV. Though what had prevented the victim from leaving the garage the way he had come, through the house? Or just opening the garage door from inside?

Would he want to do that? Not that. But something. He knew Mr. Lofgren got off early on Thursdays because of the extra time he put in coaching. His car was on the street so he was home, though no lights were on in the front room. Gabe imagined him in a den in the back, sitting in front of the TV. If they were home from day care his younger daughters would be in there, little droopy girls hanging around not knowing enough to memorize what he looked like: his big forearms thickly covered with blond hair, his quarterback jersey with the white latex 11, his size 13 feet. Gabe probably knew more about the man than they did.

At the beginning of his ninth-grade year Lofgren had said Gabe was turning into a good ball handler. But he had not built up the speed that was expected of him, and almost as quickly as his ability to grab rebounds had come on, it was gone; his mind had robbed his body of it. When he got out on the court in PE his brain locked on to some string of words—even some rule stamped on the equipment bins—and ran them, until at a certain point the rhythm would get in the way of what his body was doing and he would be shut in with the sound, and a nearly irresistible feeling that the others were not on the court with him, were in fact far enough away that he could not tell for sure what they were shouting. With each occurrence the sensation had an added power and reasonableness. And there was a certain way Mr. Lofgren came to eye him, and slap him on the back, and pick him for errands, that made him think Lofgren—always ready to kid around but not, Gabe thought looking back, really as funny, or smart, or tuned in to his athletes as most of the kids considered him to be—thought something was the matter with him, something that had to be talked over with his mother. So, the telephone call. "Gabe? Carl Lofgren. Is your mom at home?" So that was the beginning of that.

Two hours had gone by soundlessly, except for the tap of pigeons' beaks. Something had attracted a flock of pigeons and all afternoon they had been stabbing at the pavement, near enough to his feet that he could feel it through his shoe soles. A bird needed a lot to eat, because of its metabolism, the number of seeds and insects it had to eat to stay alive and keep scratching away at the insects living *on* it, in its feathers and on its skin. Everything eating. The thought began to exert an unpleasant spell. He couldn't decide whether pink, the pink of rubber bands, was supposed to be the color of pigeons' feet—he could not recall ever seeing it before—or whether this was a rare group of pigeons. All right. He pressed his back against the tree; he was not going to dwell on birds, or their feet, or the life of no arms and of pecking the sidewalk.

He was not going to pay attention to anything and everything, as he had.

He blew on his hands and pressed them over his cold ears. Suddenly a woman walked past the front window. So Lofgren's wife was at home. She was supposed to be a checker at the Safeway, that's what his mother said. He could see that she was small, like his mother, and not screaming at anybody, not holding her head or waving her arms. She merely passed by the window, holding newspapers under her arm. No screams, no tears. She did not see him.

Just after four o'clock by his watch, the door opened. He crouched behind the bin as Mr. Lofgren came out onto the porch. He was taller and bigger in the belly and shoulders than Gabe had been remembering, longer-armed, pulling on his football jacket with the leather sleeves. The air lifted the thin blond hair on top of his head. Like an animal emerging from a burrow, he aimed his big forehead and nose to one side and the other. He bent and picked up two yellow leaves off his doormat and dropped them over the edge of the porch, and then he ran down the steps, shaking out his knees to either side. He opened the trunk, pulled out a car seat and chucked it into the back of the car, and swiped leaves off the windshield with his sleeve. When he got in, the tires spread with his weight. They scraped, angled out, and he drove away down the block.

The car stopped with a thud and went into reverse. He roared back, braking in front of the recycling bin. "Hi there," he said, rolling down the window. "Why don't you get in and I'll give you a ride home. I'm going to pick up Lars. Get in."

Gabe stood frozen.

"Get in."

He had to. When he did, he and Mr. Lofgren faced each other and shook hands. He looked briefly into Mr. Lofgren's big shiny eyes and away. Mr. Lofgren's hand was large, dry, and hot, while his own, he felt, was cold and moist and had not kept pace with his growth.

"So I hear Lars was the name of your brother," he found the voice to say after a block or so, when Mr. Lofgren drove on without speaking.

"Yes it was."

"I didn't know that," he said lamely. *Lars Lofgren*, he said to himself. *Stupid name.*

"Well, we'll be getting to know a good bit about each other," Mr. Lofgren said, driving with one hand. Some moments passed before he looked over at Gabe. "My brother Lars," he said, "stepped on a mine. He was dragging his sergeant, bringing him in. I didn't see it, I was back at the base." He pulled up in front of a small house with a tricycle in the yard.

"That musta been bad," Gabe said. "Both of you out there."

Mr. Lofgren leaned towards him. "That's exactly what your mother would say." He jumped out of the car and on the sidewalk he signaled for Gabe to roll down his window. He came close, breathing on the glass as it went down. "Man, it was the best thing we ever did."

While they were piling the satchels, pack, infant seat, and

blankets into the car, the baby, slung into the car seat sideways, began to cry. "Hey!" Mr. Lofgren said, and closed his hand over the baby's whole face. He rubbed. The crying stopped and the baby's stunned eyes fixed themselves on Mr. Lofgren, who did it again. Slowly the baby smiled. He widened his eyes, and then shut them tightly, waiting. Mr. Lofgren did it again, more roughly, and again, until Gabe felt a stitching in his own scalp and said, "I don't know, does he really like that?"

"Does that grin tell you anything?"

They let themselves into the house with Mr. Lofgren's key. After they dropped the stuff in the hallway the first thing Mr. Lofgren did was grab a bottle out of the refrigerator and crash down into the new chair. He tilted the chair back and jostled the baby into the crook of his arm.

"Don't you have to warm it?" Gabe said.

"Nah, that's a myth." He was jolting the baby up and down as it sucked. "This is her milk, you know. Pumps it every day. It's an incredible thing, a beautiful thing. We bottle-fed all four of ours. What did I know?" Gabe could hear the air bubbles going into the baby's mouth from the nipple. That was not right. He remembered Chris's mother feeding Katie from a bottle, speaking to him, Gabe, for some reason. Saying how you had to do this and that. In Chris's room they made fun of the baby. They must have been four. If they were four, his father was alive, maybe coming to get him at Chris's house.

He sat down in the rocking chair and shut his eyes. The streaming of the bubbles went on and on. Finally he said, "Maybe you oughta burp him."

"Well, why not?" Mr. Lofgren said. "Let's give it a try." He heaved the baby onto his shoulder and thumped him, whereupon milk spewed all over the back of the chair. "Whoa, cleanup crew. Gabe?" The phone rang. Mr. Lofgren rolled out of the chair and scooped up the phone with the hand that had the bottle. "Hey. Whadda you mean who is it? It's me. We're feeding Lars. Gabe. Yeah. Gave him a ride. Yeah. He came to see me." He winked at Gabe. "Well, come on then. Yeah. I can stay. I'll stay for dinner. They're all right. They will. They'll come through all right."

"Who will?" Gabe said rudely when he hung up.

The blond eyebrows drew together in the big dented forehead. Mr. Lofgren said with dignity, "We were discussing my kids. My girls. Not the big ones, they're OK. The little ones."

"I bet they're mad," Gabe said.

"Mad? No. No, I wouldn't say they're mad."

"Well what are they?"

Halfway into the chair Mr. Lofgren gave him a look before he let himself down with the baby. He arranged himself. Then he said, "I'll tell you. What are they? They're forgiving. They're forgiving." He thought for a minute. "That's the way girls are, with their father." Then—Gabe could not believe it was happening—Lofgren's eyes developed a brighter shine and a big flashing tear welled out onto his cheek.

He didn't make a sound, but muscles were pulling in his face and a few tears dripped onto his shirt and onto the baby. Gabe couldn't look. His own face felt large and hot. He was surprised, somewhere else in his mind, that the wind rattling the window and the leaves sailing past it and the sound of the radiator banging on did not crowd in on him as they might have. In the months of his illness these things would have distracted him from any embarrassing situation. In fact they had done away with any such thing as an embarrassing situation.

At length Mr. Lofgren wiped his eyes with his thumb and took a shaky breath. With no preliminaries, the baby had fallen asleep. Gabe didn't want to get up and leave because leaving would suggest he was not in the living room of his own house.

That was another thing, the drug slowed his decisions. He had always been quick to decide. There was still the baby's mess going down the back of the chair. "Guess I'll wipe that up," he said, without doing anything.

Mr. Lofgren said, "Your mother is a wonderful woman."

Gabe remembered a cartoon in which a cow was telling a calf, as another cow jumped over the moon, "Your mother is a remarkable woman." He remembered the calf's stupid, open mouth, its eyelashes. He felt himself grin. Mr. Lofgren frowned, his tears gone. "You think that's funny? I'm not trying to be funny. At school, you boys, you get used to me being funny, I know that." He had fallen into a kind of singsong, leaning forward. Because he coached basketball he sometimes tried to get a black rhythm into his talk, a habit everyone, black and white, made fun of. Harmless fun, because it was Mr. Lofgren. "You boys think highly of me, I know. I know that. I would guess there's some disappointment. Especially you, Gabe. You must be disappointed at what I've done."

"What, having a kid?"

"You think that's all there is to it? You think we just went and had this kid? There's a lot involved here. This is a *life* here."

Maybe a serial killer, Gabe thought.

Mr. Lofgren lumbered to his feet with the sleeping baby and laid it down ceremoniously on the couch. "Listen," he said. "We named him Lars, right? That means something to me. That means he's my responsibility. But I have four more kids. Your mother understands that."

"You mean you're not getting married."

"We're getting married," he said, his big mouth turning down. "I know it, your mother knows it, and my wife knows it." He pointed two fingers at Gabe. "I'll tell you something. My brother Lars didn't get married. Why not? He matured early. He could have gotten married. He almost did, before he went. These were two kids who never broke up in four years of high school. Next thing, he was *dead*. But I'll tell you this, if he had married Ronna—had *he* married *her*, they'd have been married for life. That's the kind of person he was. No fooling around, no giving in. No retreat, baby, no surrender. He would not have disappointed you boys. You see what I'm saying? I'm disappointed in myself."

"Well, don't do it, then."

"That's just what your mother says. 'Go on back to her.' Like *her*, right? With your dad. Faithful to a dead guy. She's like Lars. My brother. Same kind of a person."

"Except *she* hates the military."

"That's right. Yes, she does."

"She hates it."

"You're saying you're surprised she picked me."

In its sleep the baby—put down at an angle, its big head closest to the edge—began to roll over. In the time it took Gabe to open his mouth, the head hung in air, the body finished turning and dropped headfirst onto the rug.

"Oh Jesus!" Mr. Lofgren leapt, colliding with Gabe and almost stepping on the baby. Gabe shoved him out of the way and gathered the baby up. Mr. Lofgren tried to haul it out of his arms and for a minute they scuffled, turning, arm against arm, as if Lofgren were fouling him as he tried to shoot.

The baby could not get breath to cry. When he got his wind he howled. The howling was deep, for a baby, and angry, and Gabe understood that the baby was furious at having no power to alter whatever happened to it. Mr. Lofgren had stopped trying to wrench it away from him and was feeling all over its scalp with his broad hand. "He's not hurt," he kept crooning, as if he could tell with his hand. "He's not hurt. That's all I need to do, is hurt him." Gabe got the baby firmly against his chest and Mr. Lofgren backed away and sank onto the radiator in front of the window instead of the big chair.

Gabe sat down while the baby peeled off one howl after another. He had not held a baby before, but something told him to put it up against his shoulder, although that way the yells funneled directly into his ear. He felt the furious muscles contract all over, struggle against him, and only gradually give way. He kept his hold strong. The baby was not big, as it appeared from its big joggling head, but small, a thing that could be dropped, or stepped on, or thrown out the window. He felt its lip, wet on his neck; he positioned his hand behind the head so his fingers covered the big soft ear that was in the open, to keep out the noise its owner was making.

The baby continued its jerking bawl. Mr. Lofgren sat with his elbows on his knees and his head in his hands. After a while he groaned through his fingers, "Walk around." He remained slumped on the radiator for so long with the light behind him that when he finally came to and jumped up, hearing the key in the door, Gabe saw his image still there on the window.

Mr. Lofgren got to the door and there was a kind of scuffle in the hallway. Gabe could hear his mother's voice, embarrassed, low. "Carl!"

"Hiya!" she said coming in, still in her coat, smoothing herself. She bent over the rocking chair and cupped Gabe's face in her cold hands before she even looked down at the baby, who had gone to sleep again, to his surprise, on his stiffening arm. "How did it go today?"

"Great," he said.

"Lars had a little fall," Mr. Lofgren said, behind her.

"A fall?" She turned slowly. Her lips had gone pale. Gabe saw them look at each other.

So one was not all she ever needed. Or if it was, it was this one. "It wasn't me," Gabe said.

"No, sweetheart. No. What happened?"

Mr. Lofgren said, "He fell off the couch."

Gabe waited but Lofgren said no more. Gabe said, "It wasn't me."

"Did anybody say it was you?" His mother smiled at him, still breathing fast. "He's OK, isn't he? He looks as funny as ever, don't you, Funny? At least he didn't fall off *that*. The Leaning Tower." She and Mr. Lofgren smiled at the big chair in a stupid way.

Then Mr. Lofgren said, as if suddenly remembering, "It was my fault." He left it like that. It sounded as if he were covering up for somebody.

She lifted the baby away from Gabe. "Oh, I hurt. Oh, it's too long to go," she said to Mr. Lofgren, who sank back in the big chair while she undid her buttons. "Hey!" she cried, right away. "Oh, Carl. Oh. Here we go, feel this. A tooth." She pressed the baby's top lip open and made a ticking sound with her fingernail.

Gabe went into the back to his room and took his guitar out of the closet. He sat down on the bed and played a few chords. He had had a hard time getting it in tune. And then the drug affected his fingering. Now he set himself to tune it properly. He couldn't be sure but he thought his tuning ear was off.

After a long time, he heard the baby again and he got up and went back in. The baby sat propped with cushions on the rug, beating the air with his hands and letting out hoarse squawks. In the kitchen his mother was already chopping something and singing. "*Well it's Saturday night, You're all dressed up in blue.*" She stopped and called, "Gabe, can you come in here?" Mr. Lofgren, sitting at the table grading papers, caught his arm as he passed.

"Would you listen to that? Doesn't have a dime, her life's a mess, work is screwed. She's in there singing songs. Right? We're a couple of lucky guys."

He did not like Mr. Lofgren's reference to his mother's nature. Lofgren referred to her in the same way he had spoken of the maturity of his brother, as if it were a property he did not own but had the use of. And "a couple of lucky guys." No, there was no luck he shared with Carl Lofgren. His luck was his own. He wanted to put his hand over Lofgren's face and twist it with all his might.

He could not do that. He felt how what had happened to him had him, now. Maybe for the rest of his life. He could never do anything freaky, now. It would be on him if he did, his own bad luck. Assuming what had happened to him in the summer didn't come back. Assuming he could choose.

Mr. Lofgren seemed to want to talk to him. "You know she tried to get the week off because you were coming home. They wouldn't give it to her."

"Why doesn't she just tell them where to stuff it? Why doesn't she quit?"

"Are you seriously asking that question?"

"Yeah, seriously I seriously am."

Mr. Lofgren put his chin on his arms on the table and closed his eyes. Almost. Gabe saw them move behind the blond eyelashes. It seemed to him that Mr. Lofgren did not absolutely want to, but might be going to make him pay for something. Mr. Lofgren scratched his chin back and forth on his arm, mowing down the long, tangled blond hairs with it. "If she quit," he said finally, "she would have no medical coverage."

"So? She's not sick."

Mr. Lofgren went on stroking his arm with his chin. "No, she's not." His blue eyes were open and he was looking at Gabe. His lips had a darker outline, like the baby's. He did not look like anyone Gabe knew. He looked like somebody who might be looking at you through a keyhole, who would pretend later he had not been there.

"Oh I get it," Gabe said.

CHRIS'S NEW HOUSE was out in the stretch of countryside between Seattle and Tacoma, down past the airport.

All day Gabe had been hearing jets rumble down the long channel of sky to Sea-Tac. Other than that it was quiet, countrified. His mother had driven him down early, before she went to work. He had thought he was spending the night but it turned out, as Chris's mother explained to his mother in the doorway, that Chris had a date and the overnight wouldn't work this time. He threw his duffel bag into the back seat with the baby. "Gabe," his mother said, getting back in the car. It was a question.

"It's all right," he said. "I don't care."

Chris had not said anything all day about a date. As recently as last summer he had never called a girl. Gabe didn't want to bring it up unless Chris did. They listened to Pearl Jam half the day, so Chris could pick out the chords. He didn't play his acoustic any more, he had a Strat, now, with a big amp.

Before she left for her appointment with his teacher Chris's mother came down to the basement every half hour or so to check on them. Once Katie looked in, without greeting Gabe. She kept her eyes on him, though, while Chris was telling her to leave. She had changed. Even though she was eleven and supposed to be in love with her horse she had on lipstick and threw her hip against the doorframe. Without really grinning she seemed to be going over something funny in her mind. "Quit staring!" Chris told her, and she gave him the finger.

"Come on upstairs, Katie." Chris's mother came down with root beer and popcorn. She told them what was in the refrigerator for lunch. Once she looked in when they were lying on their backs on the floor lip-synching. That time she said, "Christopher." Once she gave Gabe a thumbs-up sign. "You are looking so *good*," she said. "Now, Gabe, you make sure Chris keeps track of Katie."

"*'I'm still alive,'*" they sang with the CD. "*'Son, she said. Have I got a little story for you.'*"

"So how come you didn't bring your guitar?" Chris said.

"Oh, my guitar. I told my mom to sell it."

"And she did? She *sold* it?"

"Well, I don't know. I didn't really look for it. I've only been home a day. It might be around somewhere."

"No, man, I don't think your mom would sell your guitar. I've got two guys out here I'm playing with. Got a great bass, a kid that can sing. And a kid just down the road who plays drums, but he's not so hot."

"So you shoulda told me to bring my guitar."

"You always brought it, how was I supposed to know? Come on, let's go out."

Now it was late afternoon, cloudy. A wind caught them on the hill behind the house as they climbed a gate. The hillside had been in shade all day and there was still frost on the grass. The soles of his shoes made prints on the frost. Chris wanted to show him a horse. Not Katie's horse—another horse occupying the same field, a draft horse that was supposed to impress him. "It'll come right over," Chris said. "Unlike Katie's horse. They're going to sell that fucker. She can't even catch it."

"So why'd you move out here? I thought you guys changed your mind."

"Oh, my dad was like, '*They got a metal detector!*' At school. Stuff was going on. A kid got locked in his locker, and nobody knew and he was in there for—"

"Wait, forget it."

"In PE, somebody had a gun. He turned it in to Lofgren. I guess you didn't get news. Did you have TV?"

"We had TV. We didn't get *Seattle* news, dickhead. Of which my mom says there never is any."

"Just quoting your mom, huh."

"Yeah. Yeah, you don't like it?" With one hand he grabbed Chris by the throat. Chris's eyes went wild when he did this.

He let go, fast. "Hey, man." He made his hand into a mike. "Like, '*My mama said . . . na na na na . . . said I told you never, I told you never never never never . . . nyaaahhh!*'"

Chris laughed loudly and socked him on the arm as they resumed walking. The grass crunched. "There!" Chris said, pointing.

The horse had risen over the far hill and was plodding downhill towards them. It did not look as big as all that. But as it drew nearer Gabe saw that it was big. It was a mottled gray color, with a light-colored tail that blew to the side like a skirt. It got close enough for him to see tufts of hair in its ears and hear it blowing its breath out in sighs. It swung its head to one side in a way that suggested it was not deliberately arriving at the place where they were. Then it came on, picking up each hoof like a bucket of rock but putting it down tenderly, like a bare foot.

"He's a Percheron. He's old." The horse's flat, pursy nose and hanging lip did have an old, preoccupied, crafty look.

The horse began dipping its heavy head and throwing it back up in a belligerent way. "You can pet him. Here, I brought him an apple. That's what he likes." The horse lowered its head, reaching with its upper lip after the apple.

Gabe put his hand on the forehead. It felt like a canvas bag full of pipes. With two fingers he felt right into the interior of the indentation above the eye, that pumped in and out as the horse chewed. He felt the bones clashing inside. The eye rolled.

It looked out with no curiosity, just a stupid, but not entirely stupid, patience. When the eye rolled again he removed his fingers.

Close under the jaw the hair was stiff, and then too there were long, fine hairs soft as cobweb coming off the great bone fenders of the jaw, between which he could have fitted his own head if he stood right against the neck.

"This is a big horse."

"He's big. I told you. And this isn't even the biggest breed. Man, I can't see a horse any bigger than this."

"This is an elephant."

"A mammoth."

Gabe could feel the approach of excitement. It was coming on the heels of his relief that the horse actually was huge. His reaction had not disappointed Chris, with whom things seemed normal, finally.

"I'd say this horse is from another planet," he said in a deep radio voice that caused the horse to turn its head sideways and look at him out of the back of its eye.

"Watch out," Chris said. "There's his teeth! Look at those mothers. He looks like he's gonna take a bite outa you."

The horse had dropped its jaw open as if it were yawning, but it was not yawning; it had stiffened its tongue and elevated its lip, exposing pink gum and shockingly long yellow buckteeth with gaps between them that made Gabe laugh. "Does he bite?" But he didn't move out of the way, and the horse angled its head in under his arm. It bit him. It actually bit him. It pressed the big teeth in, low in his side. The teeth went in only so far, just a pressure really, his jacket and flesh being compressed. But it hurt. It was an uncomfortable squeezing of his side and it hurt.

"Hey! Hey man! Did that hurt? Did he *bite* you?"

"Yeah. Sorta." Gabe just stood there, feeling around inside his jacket, even though the horse could be getting ready to bite him again.

"He never did *that* before," Chris said.

The horse propped its hoof and stood with them as if nothing had happened, blowing its breath on the frosty air, dull and patient. It shifted its weight ponderously, in a satisfied way. But then the eye rolled again in Gabe's direction and he knew that it was not stupid, it knew it had bitten him. It was old, old in experience of humans. It had picked him and not Chris.

"He didn't hurt me," he said. He looked into the horse's near eye. If Chris had not been there he would have spoken to it. *You bit me. OK. All right. Tell me why you bit me.*

A jet rumbled above the clouds, coming lower, grinding on the air. He turned to Chris and saw him tying the hood of his sweatshirt, and shook off the feeling that Chris was somewhere else, not in the same field where he and the horse were standing. If you placed a feeling right away, you were its master.

Chris said something to him, and when he looked again, seconds later it seemed, Chris had started across the field to the fence. He heard Chris yelling for him but he put off answering and looked up, turning in a circle as he listened for the plane's engines. A wind was scattering the clouds. The horse eased back the pink edges of its nostrils and blew on him.

He ducked under its neck and stood on the other side, putting the plane behind him. The horse lowered its head and shook it from side to side like somebody shaking a gallon of paint. The eye rolled. "Gonna do it again? Hey, you think I care? Nah. I'm forgiving." He got hold of the head by both jaws. "Go right ahead. Do it."

He had broken into a sweat under his jacket and the air had found his damp skin. With the chill on his skin he felt good. He felt prepared.

It was nothing to him if a horse bit him, it was nothing to him if a horse was to pick him up in its jaws. He could forgive a horse. He already had. He could forgive anybody and anything.

You could still hear the turbines of the plane. Now the horse chose not to bite him, not even to object as he held onto the head and peered into the dark, opaque eye. It was possible the plane, a quarter-inch thing, would cross the eye with its load of invisible passengers. If it did, and the passengers were lucky, he would see it. When they landed, not a one of them would know what had returned them to Earth.

She Had Coarsened

• • •

THERE WAS A man who was blindfolded, turned three times, and set loose in the world. The same thing was done to me, in a country thousands of miles away, and in my case words were whispered that would send me to that man.

We met. It was an arduous love, unlucky, unfair, long-lasting. I had always known the love of my life would be this way.

"NO, NO, SHE met him after she was married." Who were they talking about, my mother and my Aunt Maggie? I didn't know, and I have no way of knowing now. "That was the unfortunate part. But that was that. He was the love of her life."

"I think you're right."

"He was the one."

It was someone we knew or someone none of us had ever met, it was someone in Hollywood or someone from town, it was a relative, it was a stranger. Someone who traveled through the talk as balanced and wavering as one of Maggie's smoke rings and then blended with other smoke rings.

Names did not have to be spoken: the pause, the guarded look took their place. How little they cared that they were embedding in two little girls the idea of doom, a fortunate doom. My sister and I ate our Cream of Wheat and listened soberly: nine and ten, girls old enough to linger at the breakfast table after the men went up to shave, young enough to slip our aunt's rings off her relaxed, lotioned hands as she talked, and try them on.

The love of her life! The man after whom the gates clanged shut.

Later I would come upon novels in which people lived out these phrases, but even as a child I knew them for the landmarks they were. "She had coarsened." Distinct on the page as a snail in the lettuce. It didn't matter if I saw it only once, in school, somewhere in Turgenev or Maupassant, or any one of those writers who looked with worldly, sad benevolence on the century before ours. In those days a sentence easily took the place of a book. Usually the sentences that did this had to do with women and shame: the obloquy that could fall on a woman in the passing of a breath as the narrator revealed the gray straps of her camisole, her veined hands, her sudden volubility, her extinguished fire. The heartbreak for a reader, when the heroine failed to remain true to sorrow and ended in some blind, maternal contentment. No way back, after you coarsened.

"Of course her life was in a shambles," my mother went on crisply. "She couldn't look back, once he wrote for her to come. She had to go."

My mother and Aunt Maggie sipped coffee, sighed. My aunt gracefully lit her one Pall Mall of the day, and their mood affected all of us, including the men who came down smelling of Aqua Velva and resigned to a weekend of talk. "Her life was in a shambles, you say?" my father said, winking at his brother-in-law. Maggie half closed her eyes and turned her cigarette against the rim of the ashtray, filing the ash delicately, sadly.

Uncle Ted was her second husband, a tall, quick-thinking, athletic man of forty with many schemes, I see now, for consolidating the property of others under his own hand. Now he would be called a developer, but I don't recall hearing the word then, when what he did for a living was spoken of with a little smile as though it were a helpless mischief. Uncle Ted was handsome, however, and if it had been suggested to him that he was a poor substitute for his wife's first husband, at most his hand would have hovered an extra second over a contract before his exuberant "Ted Brown" raced onto the line.

Oddly enough the dead one in the case, Uncle Randall, had been even more successful than Ted. Aunt Maggie took care not to let material want spoil her loves. But Randall was redeemed and recovered for legend by illness and politeness. From his name flew a pennant: THE POLITEST MAN IN VIRGINIA. It was said that when someone had uttered a crass inebriated suggestion to Maggie on the lawn, Randall had strolled forward in one of his cream-colored summer suits and said, "Now, your people, sir, must be wondering where you've gotten to," instead of "What was that you said?" Or worse, nothing at all, ignoring the offense. As men were increasingly doing, Maggie said with a faraway smile, even then, even in the South. I could picture the kind of man who had come up grinning to Aunt Maggie, even put a hand on her pretty shoulder, somebody too much of a cutup for his own good, like Ted Brown.

"Randall's lovely manners," my mother would prompt.

"Ah, Randall," Maggie would sigh, lifting her eyes to the ceiling where the boards creaked as Ted Brown roved about the bedroom getting dressed, and the soft languor that settled over us at the breakfast table seemed to say that men who were gracious had an ascendancy over men who were not. Even years after they were gone, the gracious ones, their heads rose above the ones bobbing and maneuvering below, and looked around collectedly like statues, blind and just.

But he suffered, this polite man. This was what gave his manners their shine. Randall. He had a disease that wasted him in a year and pinched away his nervous system. I don't remember ever seeing him. He died before he was thirty, in the days of Aunt Maggie's flowered sundresses that tied at the back of the neck.

"Of course she never got over it."

JACK AND I were buying olives in a Greek grocery store. I had known him a year. His internship was almost over, a year he had put in on call every other night in the hospital and the rest of the time trying to exorcise the ghost of the love of my life.

Jack! After the foreign syllables of my unforgotten lover's name. Where did he get the name Jack? Jack, a doctor! A doctor from the Midwest. No one else I knew in Chicago was from the Midwest. A Jewish doctor, from a prosperous and assimilated family who without any conversion or renunciation had nevertheless shed all the bother of being Jewish, and had further camouflaged their sons by sending them to a military academy where they attended chapel and learned to play polo. Jack played football there, and again in college, where he lived happily in a fraternity and graduated summa cum laude. On to medical school and into his internship, his hair—hair was nothing, feet were stirring the dust of the moon—long enough to touch the wide shoulders from his football days. He was going to be a surgeon and he was going to work for the day when the country would be ready to accept socialized medicine.

That was when I met him, the spring of his internship, when he was tired to the core, tired even of fun. In the middle of the night in the emergency room he was feeling the seriousness of life, and he wanted a serious life with me.

I could not consider such a man, so unscathed, so unsuspicious and liberal, so optimistic. My heart had been sealed with a black wax, censed with a bitter myrrh. The man I had known from the first to be the love of my life had shriveled my benign past with the cold wind still blowing out of his lost country.

Escape, exile. The stories of this man had been glimpses, rather than any consecutive account, of the dirt compounds and hungry boredom and incomprehensible negotiations his family had lived through during and after the war. He had fed these scraps to me—in place of my own historyless American diet—as a sacred food, bursts of outraged reminiscence washed down with so much alcohol that most of what met my eyes in those years had a brooding, tilted, provisional look to it, and Chicago, where we lived, exists in memory like huge stage props thrown into storage. In time I allowed myself to think that the ordeal of living within his mood, within the dark worry and ecstatic remorse of his exile, had made me his equal.

But of course it had not. The country of his birth had been seized and swallowed in a war. His family had fled. He had been a Displaced Person for years, finally arriving with his exhausted parents in the coal-mining hills of Pennsylvania, bitterly wary at ten as he climbed the school steps with vitamin-toughened Americans who knew the language the teacher was speaking. At twenty he got married to a nurse who saw and liked a skinny, serious kid in an air force uniform. Their quick failure settled his conviction that there was to be no happiness in this country. He got out of the service and into college, where, suddenly, he was not out of place but foreign. He was "older." There he began to come into his own, gathering in the women, girls most of us, barefoot on our campuses in the first faint cat-smile of the Sixties. The wedding ring, which he would not take off until the divorce was final, entered my consciousness one day in a seminar. I was eighteen.

His hand on the table was not American: a hand, as I saw it, from Europe. A square hand, foreign. The hand of someone only half a dozen years older than we were, but a man, not a boy.

Suddenly, when he was getting ready to leave for graduate school in Chicago, he asked if I would go with him.

Friends warned me. By then anyone could see that although he was surely my fated love, it was unlikely that I was his. But of all those he had gathered in—and his open arms had been the subject of talk—I was the one he wanted in Chicago. There is no way to know why this should have been so. *Wanted* is the wrong word. I'm not sure what the word would be. He was willing to have a thing but he was careful not to want or expect or safeguard it.

For a shocking length of time I didn't know there were women, wherever he was, who knew this willingness of his, who knew that if they called and asked him to come, he would come. That he would call another woman waiting somewhere—in this period, myself—and say, "I won't be home."

I see how long ago the years of these phone calls were when I remember that a popular magazine of the time did a feature on couples who lived together. In those days that made for a human interest story. They were chic, fearless couples who stood pampas grass in clay jars against walls with unframed paintings hanging on them. They didn't want frames on their pictures; they sat on pillows; they didn't want couches or houses or families. But I was not living in a half-furnished apartment with him out of fearlessness. It was living streets away from him that I was afraid of, while his touchy remoteness, his casual secrecy, gradually freed him from the life I did not even know I was planning for us.

We lived above a tavern on the South Side, but we drove all over the city to go drinking and arguing in bars. Usually I ended up in tears in the bar and in the car driving home. Crying on the stairs at night. Crying in the daytime on a South Side beach, where nobody stared, even though we were white. The crying made us disappear. Crying on the El on the way to my job, once I got a job. Because he didn't know, and he was unable to know, whether I should stay or not. Maybe so. But maybe not. But meanwhile the women beckoned, a new kind of audacious women, like the ones in the magazine article, all of them photographers or dancers it seemed to me, women with satchels I glimpsed and sullen curses I heard, because before they let him go they were going to come with him right to the curb below our window, holding on to him, no one could stop them, women having about them some promise irresistible to a man so melancholy—I knew it was irresistible, just as I knew I didn't have it—of recklessness and bitchiness and oblivious demand.

But it would never work with those women either. Something had gone wrong. The war.

The war. The war had ended twenty years before. "Don't speak if you know nothing!" he told me, his face turning ugly. Because I did not understand his country, or anything about a country such as his, an Eden of larch trees and peaceful rivers and ancient cities, one risen from the ashes thirteen times, and conservatories of music—a country that could be *consumed* in war. Nor did I understand anything about him, a man in the mold of his birthplace. And not just him but the whole forlorn, wrongly dressed, belligerent company, in cities like Chicago, of the permanently displaced. I had grown up in Virginia; I had studied literature, not history. I knew about the wars in novels. I did remember Khrushchev banging with his shoe. This was years after Khrushchev had vanished, and to this abhorrer of every emanation from the Soviet Union I said, "I liked him."

In no time there was another war, of course. He was loyal. The United States of America did not err in its choices. If such a country were to hate, it would not do so in error. If such a country went to war, it would be to liberate the captive.

First the Germans and then the Americans had liberated his family. He had memories of candy bars: something to unwrap, unspeakably glorious, after potatoes. So he always bought candy bars. He had memories of his parents in tears, pleading with someone. Others might forget but he remembered: rescue. Rescue somehow not completed.

And I, I could not complete it? He laughed. This went on for years. Finally he decided, of course, to leave me.

I COULD NOT get over it. I did not want to get over it. And so in the Greek grocery I was looking at Jack, the intern, and telling myself, *Nothing's gone wrong for him. His father is a doctor, his son will be a doctor. Of course he loves life. Why not? How has it ever hurt him? Look how he buys retsina, and tastes the glowing, wrinkled black olives set out on the little plate on the counter. Of course he has eaten olives in Greece, he has eaten the delicacies of the world, hiking and engaging people in conversation and staying in their houses as often as in hotels, welcomed and served, nowhere offered any impediment, any defeat.*

That was my litany. But while I was repeating to myself these things so familiar and provable, the proprietor was wrapping up our olives and staring at Jack. He was a giant bald man with black eyebrows that must have once matched his hair. He had on a bib apron that almost reached the floor. For some reason he couldn't take his eyes off Jack. Jack was a handsome man, but the Greek was not noticing his good looks. Suddenly he came out from behind the counter. He grabbed Jack by the shoulders. "See there!" he said excitedly, seizing Jack's chin and turning it up to the ceiling. "See there!" There was a row of framed photographs on the topmost shelf, above the gallon cans of olive oil.

"My father!" cried the man, pointing to a mustached man in uniform, in a brownish picture.

"That's your dad?" said Jack good-naturedly.

"My father. Killed in '41. Crete. April of '41. Eh? Eh?"

"What was his outfit?" said Jack.

The man rolled out an answer in Greek and grinned at Jack cagily. "Not Greek?" he said after a pause while the three or four other people shopping in the store all smiled at us.

"No, sir, I'm not," Jack said regretfully. He still used the *sirs* they had taught him at the military academy.

"Yugoslav?"

"No. No . . ." said Jack with a sigh and a look at me. "Jewish." He sounded surprised himself, but firm, that first moment of turning his back on his family's precautions and becoming Jewish.

"Ah," said the man, jostling me and moving in to look closely at the pores of Jack's face. "My father," he said again and gestured at the picture. "You are the same man! You see?" he said to the other customers and to me. Some of them craned their necks at the picture and saw a resemblance. The Greek hauled out his stepladder and climbed up and took the picture off the shelf. He came down and handed it to Jack, who studied it while the man stood rubbing his hands together. He had tears in his eyes. To his wife, who had come to the doorway of the little room behind the refrigerator and stood drying her hands, he said something in Greek. He pointed upward. With a quick look and a shake of her head the woman folded the towel. But the Greek had made his judgment; he stepped up to Jack and gave him a bear hug. Over Jack's shoulder hung his big face, eyes shut and tears running into the mustache. "Just like my father!" he said to the spectators with a tearful laugh.

Jack wrapped his arms around the man's back and returned

the hug. He did not pass it off, he neither moved nor smiled as the Greek let go of him and stepped back, keeping his fingers with their longish nails on the sleeves of Jack's coat. There was a stillness in the store while the respect and honor due the soldier in the picture was offered to Jack.

Then the two of them shook hands, and the man wiped his eyes and went back behind the counter to ring up our retsina on the huge cash register. "Brass!" he said, tapping the etched flank of the machine with his nail. "Antique. Found it on Jackson a block over. Old Greek had it, didn't speak any English, sold it for nothing. The antique stores, they all want it! Old but as you see . . ." His big fingers caressed the register. His voice died away as he surveyed his long counter with its drawers of pasta and trays of herbs in bundles tied with string. Then, speaking straight into Jack's eyes, he said, "I had this one ever since I had the store, twenty-four years. You see this store? I got this store with my uncle Giorgos in '45." He ran his fingers through the silky lentils. At last he took his eyes off Jack and turned to the other customers, as the past, with his father in it, receded.

We left the store. I took Jack's hand. I was thinking about the war, how belatedly I had understood anything about it. If I understood at all.

I was wondering how it was I spent so little time thinking about or writing to my family, whom I had left such a short time ago to follow the man who had done the harm to me. *But what if he was harmed by me too?* I suddenly thought. *By my selfish American tears and my stupidity? My not knowing what a war was?* How crude were the uses to which I had put my own courage: lying to get a prescription for sleeping pills, for example, to leave on the table where it might jerk back to life his boyhood fear that he could not perfectly understand anyone in this country, or know how far we might go.

I thought of my father. He had given me so many humble warnings, whenever I flew home from Chicago with circles under my eyes and made grim, tearful, late-night phone calls and then turned around and flew back. Without pretending to firsthand knowledge, having missed being sent overseas in the war himself, and without ever censuring the man I was suffering over, in fact protecting him, trying to turn me out of his path, a girl deliberately raised in ignorance of life! Maybe my father regretted my ignorance, thought it was not too late for me to be made to see how the little rivers of private life might join up with or dwindle off from the huge river of war. But I couldn't see.

I thought of my father as he must have been at my age, when the war was coming and young men all over the world didn't know whether they would live or die, and as he had been on those Saturdays with my aunt and uncle, when we were children. Hidden from my sight, although he stood in the same kitchen where I sat with my sister, my mother, and my aunt at the table, wrapped in the scent of shaving lotion, which would drift like his ghost across hotel lobbies in later years, to find me. Hidden from me, because my concentration was on what awaited the female. The fateful events, the loves and cruel sorrows that would attend her.

I thought of my father aging without any attention from me or my sister, who was just like me, far away on quests of her own, while something in both of us had coarsened, had hardened towards our families and our pasts, in order for us to spend our full energy, our remembering and planning, on men we loved. I thought of the face of the Greek in the store as he stared so hopelessly at Jack. No getting through. No getting back to the time before that war. No restoring his father, or reversing the exile of my lover and his parents, or showing mercy to those people as handsome and fated for accomplishment as Jack, who saw, from inside, the doors of boxcars slide shut.

This was approximately when I decided the theme of *War and Peace* was not the coarsening of Natasha, was not even love. First I decided that the books I had thought were about love were about time, and death, and then, that I did not have any idea what they were about, because my lover had been right, I knew nothing.

IN THE YEARS after Uncle Randall died, Aunt Maggie did not so much coarsen as become the woman we all knew, who looked with wide, daydreaming eyes on everything as if to say, "What is this to me?" She always glanced at my sister and me wonderingly if we spoke, as if we had come up from under the table. She woke to our voices reluctantly, blinking, to let us know she herself had come up out of memory, out of the embrace of that great life-sullying misfortune, Randall's death. When we came running into a room she looked past us with a faint smile, for some witness to this scene of normality—happy children, activity—in which she couldn't hope to participate. But talk was something else: she would talk all day, as long as the subject was the perfection of certain lives, the lives in which women and occasionally men—if they were men honed and modeled and made unforgettable like Randall—stepped up to and met their fate, swallowed the communion of pain.

When Maggie died in her old age, my mother said matter-of-factly, "Nobody will remember the same things I do, now." My father was alive then, but his memory was gone. I saw in my sister's attentiveness, her careful stirring of his coffee, that she too had waited too long to make up for her unconcern, her single-minded pursuits. We were there with all the family, both of us with our children, around the kitchen table after Maggie's funeral.

"Would you say you remember things the way Maggie did, the way she said they were?" Jack asked my mother, with the interest he always showed in our family's history, despite its being so narrow and individual.

"Oh, well, yes, some things, dear. Some people."

Jack said, "The way she talked they were all so . . . complete." It was safety, they lived in safety, I could have told him. For he was probing for something to explain people so free of any wish to change themselves, people so unscarred by what was going on in the world at the same time they were watching for a fate of which they had no fear.

"Oh yes. But some of that was Maggie." We all looked, as one, at the table where the ashtray for Maggie's cigarette would have been.

"But that first husband? Uncle Randall? He was really such a prince?" said my husband Jack.

"He was indeed," my mother said. "But you know Maggie was untrue to him. Did you know that? With Ted Brown." She paused and sighed, turning her own wedding band. "Of course, Ted was the love of her life."

Mance Lipscomb

• • •

MY HUSBAND DRAGS my arm under the pillow he has over his head. "Poor Joe, poor Joe." He is mumbling into the mattress, keeping my hand against his cheek.

All I say is, "Oh, I don't know. Maybe there's a young thing out there for Joe." We have drunk so much bad wine at Joe and Kate's house that we can't get to sleep. We toss around and finally turn on the TV and watch a program on the naked mole rat. "They look cozy," Cy says, as the teeming pile of babies clambers and suckles in their burrow. It appears each mother can smell her own. We can't be sure, we have the sound off, but it appears the fathers grow long teeth and enlarge the burrow.

Earlier it had been a clear night with a moon, but it got chilly after dark. Kate kept going inside to get sweaters for us, a fringed red shawl for herself that I had never seen before, and finally an old sleeping bag. "Move in close," she said as she draped it over our shoulders on the picnic bench. We were out in back on the deck. Cy stuck his arm through a hole in the moldy lining and Kate said, "Looks like Joe got the good sleeping bag."

She displayed each wine bottle in a dishtowel before she screwed the top off. "I can bring the tape deck out. That's all that's left. With this wine we need something funky to listen to, but all I have is what we had before CDs. Joe—"

"Joe took all the good blues," Cy growled at her.

Kate and Joe have both suffered financially in the divorce, each taking only half of everything. That doesn't bother Kate. She always made fun, anyway, of people like their next-door neighbors the Rileys, a handsome younger couple who take courses in wine and Italian cooking and planning a remodel. The Rileys have been redoing their house ever since they moved in; every time they paint a room Kate gleefully reports the colors. "Papyrus and . . . urn!"

"Urn?"

"Urn is dun."

"And how are the Rileys and the fair Riley-ette?" Cy will say. That is the little daughter as pretty as the mother. For some rea-son this couple, the Rileys, whom he knows only to wave to, stirs up a little flame in Cy. Kate knows it. She agrees it's the wife. "Oh, the Rileys are exceptionally well!" she will sing out. "They've found the granite for the counters!"

Kate's counters, where you can see them through the frying pans and stuck spoons and propped-open books, are the cracked linoleum put in in the '20s; she and Joe never painted or re-arranged or altered anything in their house. They were lazy; once their kids were in college they liked sleeping all weekend. Our best friends. Two big, unhurried people, alike in their habits. As lecturers they were fond of the slide projector, both of them popular, all their fifteen years in the History Department with Cy, as givers of easy tests.

Joe always smiled and shrugged if Kate got started on the Rileys, or sometimes he allowed himself to grunt, "Now, Katie." Joe has a mild stutter, for which he is known on campus. Stu-dents can be heard "doing" Joe: "Some will blame the entirety of the World— *War* on the— on the kaiser's— uh, uh— *withered arm!*" It's a kind of tribute. Joe is always at the top of the student polls, with Kate, despite her sharp tongue, only a little farther down, while my husband Cy is more demanding, sought out by a smaller, fiercer group of students.

The street winds up a hill that puts the Rileys' deck a level above Kate and Joe's. Occasionally through the sparse laurel hedge we see handsome legs: Riley's muscular in tennis shorts; Mrs. Riley's very long, dreamily crossing and uncrossing, ending in big smooth sandaled feet with polished toenails. Seen full-length she is tall, thin, and swayingly top-heavy, with blond hair pulled back from her moody delicate face in a French braid— exactly the kind of woman who can bring my husband low.

Like Constance. She even looks a little like Constance, though Constance was even taller; Kate put her at six feet. Constance the music student. She was the most serious of all of Cy's attachments, the one who most aroused his sympathies.

Cy doesn't know Mrs. Riley's name but I do. It's Kristen. A name suited to a woman of that distant, graceful type. I am not that type at all. Once it seemed to me a secret advantage I had in our life together, that I was not Cy's type. That was during my twenties, when I was braced in all things by his eyes following me around the room.

Kristen Riley's husband's name is Roy but he doesn't look like a Roy Riley, he looks like a Marc or a Philip. He is a torts lawyer and he hits her. He has left bruises on her, sometimes just thumbprints on the upper arm, sometimes large blots of dead brown blood hidden under slacks and scarves. Once he knocked her out. After that he strove harder to get himself under control, and the strain told on him so that occasionally he wet the bed.

It was before their little girl was born, I was told, that Roy Riley did these things. I don't know about since.

He wants everything just so, and so does she. They both grew up poor; that's why they work so hard on the house and on making sure there are beautiful things around them at all times. He had a father who beat him and of course that put something into him, some seed, a meanness that hardly ever shows itself, that can't be gotten out.

It may be that I am the only person in this city who knows these things, or knows them not from waking up in the damp, woeful proof of them in the sheets but from being told by Kristen Riley.

"I'M LONELY. COULDN'T you have invited Joe?" Cy complained to Kate as he poured. Joe is so mysteriously *gone*.

"That day may come," Kate said evenly. "It was time, Cy," she told him in a soothing voice. "It was just over. It had been for . . . oh, a long while. We have to get used to it."

"Who has to?" Cy pondered, shaking his head. He is a white-haired man with a heavy mustache and a drooping eyelid that he has had since he was a little boy playing baseball. He was the catcher. He got it, and a deaf ear, when the bat knocked his mask off. Being teased about his eye as a child gave him a weaker case of what the stutter gave Joe, a sensitivity, a reluctance to wound, so that as soon as someone, a woman in particular, awakens emotion in him she has a key to the same storeroom of attentive pity that I do, as his wife.

"It makes me mad," Cy said. "Joe is my best friend."

Kate lowered her eyes. We know she is interested in someone. "Uh-huh. We'll be hearing a lot more about that," Cy predicted sourly in the car on the way over, and the authority was his, certainly he knew the churned-up and trampled earth around forsaking all others.

The phone rang. Kate jumped out of the deck chair on the first ring and was gone for a long time. When she came back, flushed, she arranged herself and the red shawl rather lengthily, emptied her glass and said, "Cyrus, listen to me. I care about Joe. Of course I do. Do you honestly think I can just put the Hundred-Years-Marriage out of my mind?"

"She jokes. She jests. Over the *bones*. Let me just tell you." Cy put his head down between his shoulders, tipping his glass at Kate. "I see Joe every day." Wine spilled on the picnic table and he began a slow, aggrieved circling of his finger in it, letting himself appear drunk, even getting drunk, in order to say what he had to say.

Kate looked at me and mouthed, *Mance Lipscomb*. She waited for Cy to summon his hardy example. She knew and I knew that he was going to make use of the words of this old Texas bluesman to *defend marriage*.

Mance Lipscomb was the kind of man Cy would have liked to be. Years ago we walked over to the campus blues festival with Kate and Joe to see a film about him. In fact everyone at the festival wished, that evening in the auditorium, to be as this man was. Mance Lipscomb said some pure, doting things on camera about his marriage to his wife. An angelic keenness got into his sunken, thin-skinned face as he picked his guitar, if angels can be sly as well as pure. You expected to see a sort of fairy godmother of a wife to match him, a little thing ready with a tickle or a pinch. Instead his wife was big and close-mouthed; she ate dinner with the plate on her lap and looked away from the camera. For a grudge, she hadn't sat at the same table to eat with Mance Lipscomb in fifty years.

"Love makes you take things." That's what he said to the cameraman. He smiled, and the four of us turned in our folding chairs in the dark and smiled at each other as warmly, sardonically, and wisely as friends our age could smile, a deep, four-note chord of smiles.

Thus what Cyrus was going to say now, he had said before. "Does anybody remember Mance Lipscomb?"

Also in the film was a man living down the road from the Lipscombs whose wife had shot his leg off. He beat her up one time too many. He recovered after she made for him in the field and shot him down, but he lost the leg. Mance Lipscomb said it improved his character. *That* man's wife had the little, impish, fairy godmother face.

"The truth," Cy began, finding his place, "the truth is—"

Kate raised her chin so that the doubling smoothed out, and cried, "Oh, Cy! Have mercy! Truth is not necessarily what we're after."

She was not to be jarred out of her firmness, that purpose that can be seen in her now, along with the eye shadow glinting in the creases of her lids and the half dozen silver bracelets slipping out from under her sleeve. She is noticeably thinner, though she has not given in entirely to whatever it is that awaits her when the telephone rings; she hasn't dyed her hair or left off wearing clogs.

We were drinking our wine under the tree that comes up through a hole in the cedar deck. The deck was built around it, a pretty little tree with three or four slim trunks that fan into an umbrella of leaves. The hole was spacious but one of the trunks leaned as it grew, and a board dug its way into the bark and made a gall there. The tree goes on growing, putting out its pleasantly bitter-scented white blossoms late in spring and dropping them into the salad bowl in the summer.

"It isn't the— house, it's the— tree," Joe said one night when we were there, after the news was out. "Who gets custody of the— the tree?"

This divorce is passing through its stations without any scourging or denying; it is a split marked by little considerations and favors, reciprocal offers, rueful jokes. Joe is just keeping up his end, but in Kate there really is a maddening lazy blandness, as if she is taking some drug that keeps her just below a normal reactive state.

I have failed, with Kate, as she did not fail with me. The whole thing seemed to happen in a matter of weeks. Their daughter called me from school. "What *is* this? I've tried to talk to Dad but he can't *speak*. What is going *on*?"

Say you don't know, I told myself. "I don't know," I said.

CY HAS FINALLY gone to sleep. He lets go of my arm and draws his legs up as high as they will go, claiming the eternal sweetness of the sleeping male. I don't think a woman sleeping has this sweetness. Sometimes the position he lies in causes me a bristling sensation such as I imagine a guard dog patrolling a factory would have, and I know that if a landslide were rushing down on our bed I would have to throw myself onto him to keep him alive. In the past I used to imagine others who might feel this same way about him. All of us, awake at night, breathing the same air as it traveled the city. I used to wobble at the edge of the board that leads to the silent, rigid dripping of night tears, but I didn't dive off because if I cried hard enough to get any relief I would get the hiccups and wake him.

At other times I thought of mashing the white hairs into his scalp with a baseball bat. "That's just marriage," Kate used to say, whenever I mentioned either feeling. Another thing she said no more than a year ago, when we were all gossiping about other people's divorces, was, "Oh, it's the same thing as going out and deliberately losing your *dog*. Let's just *not*. All right, everybody?"

I don't like these Laodicean divorces. I like divorces with flagrant adultery, arson of treasures, vampire lawyers, pills, psychiatrists, cars driven into ditches, screams in the night. I like them to stop just short of the actual proceedings, with imploring speeches, and family members rushing onstage with impossible demands or blind pardons at the last minute.

We had the kind of children who participate, all of them. Our daughters flew home from school on their own earnings and lectured Cy. Both are feminists, but they did not put all the blame on him. They agreed that I was neurotically possessive, unfair, unrealistic, hopelessly undisciplined in my own way.

As far as they knew, Constance, while a rude surprise because she had been their friend in high school, was the only one.

In high school Constance was a *wunderkind*. Five or six years before Cy saw her again on the campus when she played with the symphony. She had won a contest. When she came tipping out in the clunky shoes they wore, and bowed beside the piano before playing her concerto, which was long and dramatic and caused the platinum hair to leap off her shoulders once or twice like running water out of a spoon, Cy murmured, "That kid's even taller than she was last year." So he had already noticed her, when she was our daughters' friend, little more than a six-foot child.

When they found out, both daughters flew home to take Constance out to a lunch that went on for five hours. "Constance is coming unglued," they said when they came back to the house. "She gets out her plastic gizmo with the compartments for the days of the week. She shakes it. It's got so many pills you could keep the beat with it. Dad doesn't have any idea. She's nuts. Look, someone like that can't take it, she's not like you."

They had deprogrammed Constance, they said, and indeed the affair came to an end. "Concertina." That was Kate's name for her: a sisterly attempt to undercut the gloomy radiance, the magnitude of Constance.

Our son was fourteen at the time and he said, "Go ahead and get a divorce, I was going to kill myself anyway." It might have been then that Cy's plans, if he had them, crumbled. He had installed our son, the last-born, in a vacancy he had inside. It was an echoing garage, left empty when Cy's own father drove away in the Depression and never came back. Without forethought on his own part, or any misstep along the way, our son Ben took the huge, gaping place of Cy's father—and maybe that of the mother too, giddy with her solitary cocktails. Cy, unable to rest from promising comfort to women all his life, found his own solace in Ben.

Look here, I'd be glad to tell Mance Lipscomb if he were alive, love doesn't just make you take things. It makes you deal them out. If I could threaten to take Ben away from Cy, and if Cy didn't know I would never do that, then it's no surprise that neither of us ever knew for certain *what* would happen to us, until it happened. I might sound as if I saw it all coming but I never did, and what would have been the good of prediction, if I had? What's the good of figuring everything out? What's the good, really, of consciousness? If we are wrapped in blankets of ignorance with only the tiniest peepholes, it is probably a beneficial adaptation. Who knows the damage reason would do.

It was not so long after that that we sailed unexpectedly out of the Bermuda Triangle where we had been circling all those years. Just like that. I said so anyway. I told Kate we seemed almost to be in the clear.

Stop it! Stop talking! I kept wanting to shout at Kate in her new incarnation. Stop laughing! Don't you remember what happened to *us*? Was it worse than that?

In the future there will be no such thing as wedlock. People will be milling around, trotting off to mate, busy with their projects.

But oh, someone will invent it. On the tranquil surface some dark bubble will appear, with an oily rainbow on it, and enlarge, and gently burst, and spread. Some silly pair will attract follow-ers, imitators. They'll go off, form a colony. Children will be named, kept close, infected with the habits of the parents. Rules for what they have devised will be drawn up. I think Ben read a story in high school in which that happened with war.

I COULD HAVE told Kate another story I know. It's the story of an old friend of mine, my best friend, in fact, for many years. Kate is an old friend too, but as happens in cities—just as Kate has never talked, except across the painters' ladders, to her next-door neighbor Kristen—my two friends didn't know each other. Kate would have remembered her if I had mentioned her, but I didn't do it. Kate is a historian but she likes to look ahead; she and I have the reckoning and plotting, the complaining and hop-ing relationship, rather than the regretting, reminiscing one.

This friend was the one Cy called the country girl, though she didn't grow up in the country but in a sizeable town in West Vir-ginia by the name of Classic.

Lynnette. Cy liked Lynnette. He gave her compliments and he teased her about being from Classic, but that dark challenge of his never got into his voice. There was something too simple and immune about Lynnette, something too narrowed down and squinting and little-girl inquisitive to appeal to him. She was a lid-lifter in the kitchen, a waiter-in-line for whatever book you were reading. "Where'd you get the *i*-dea"—she put the accent on the first syllable—"to put horseradish in?" "What's this? Should I read this?" On her own bookshelves, besides a ratty doll of her mother's with cloth arms, china hands, and a cracked china head, and the stacks of material for her sewing, all Lynnette had were six or eight paperbacks and a high school poetry anthology. Once she knew you she would break into "Abou Ben Adhem" at the dinner table, or "I Had a Mother Who Read to Me." Teachers in

Classic had made them memorize, and Lynnette knew the whole
of "The Arab's Farewell to His Horse." With a wineglass in hand
she was a teller, in detail, of whatever dream she had had the
night before, and she would come back to it, expecting you to
remember the details, once she knew what that particular dream
had explained or foretold.

Cy listened to the dreams, passed over the ambitions. In the
female, he drew back from anything smacking of organized progress. Not in his students: those he dutifully encouraged and rec-
ommended, taking care to leave them alone. For Cy was not just
any campus Don Juan. He was not, and is not, a self-absorbed
man, I know that if I think about it. Anyone can see it, in his
eyes alight with interest. It is true that one of those eyes has its
own message, seductively weary, all preliminaries out of the way.
But he is a man who can be reduced to shamed tears, who wages
war, every day, against himself. He went and got counseling but
the counselor sent him away when she had an intimate dream
about him. She drew the line at such a client, with his gift for
listening to women, his liking for them. Her dream ended with
his offering her a watermelon. "You are a man with whom I would
want children," she said when she terminated his sessions.

We were in the kitchen when he told me this, looking out the
window at our neighbors loading their van to go skiing. They are
a couple our age, with no children, always playing, like brother
and sister. Cy rubbed behind his bad ear. "Oh God," he said, and
I knew he meant was he, Cy, to be someone like this jovial neighbor of ours with his sister-wife? Were there indeed to be no more
of the sudden passions for him, always startling, unfamiliar in
their demands, invigorating, redeeming? A danger that must be
kept at bay in a marriage such as ours, out of whose soil such
irregular geysers shoot, of ardor and shame and disbelieving rage,
and—this one so familiar it is a comfort in itself—a demand on

both sides for the other's attention, every bit as much as for lofty things like forgiveness.

All the while I offered him wrongs in exchange for his, different in nature but substantial in themselves. For one thing I said unspeakable things about him, which got repeated. That isn't loyalty to one's husband as, say, my parents would have understood it. I would have said I did it out of loyalty to *us*, a double creature of some kind, an "it," with its own exigencies. "Don't flatter yourself," Kate said. "You're an oven of jealousy and spite."

"Jealousy prolongs the course of love. Proust said so."

MY FRIEND LYNNETTE was a writer. That is, she wanted to be a writer, a novelist. She was always taking leave from work for writing workshops, and corresponding with the people she got to know there. I met her when she came to fill in for the secretary who was having a baby, at the magazine where I was a copy editor.

If Lynnette read a book she had borrowed she said, "Well, that sure wasn't anything I would have figured. I liked it though," as if I had given her horseradish to eat, and she set the book aside as having no bearing on her own undertaking and never referred to it again.

Lynnette had married young, the day before her high school graduation, in fact.

"Oh, God, you got up after your wedding night and you went to graduation?"

"Yep. It was a Saturday. We drove back in from the motel down the road. We had been there before, believe me! I remember we passed the 4-H fairgrounds coming in. Travis said to me, 'Did you know three years ago I had the Reserve Champion cow?' I said, 'Nope. Can't say I knew that.' We thought that was so funny. Not my father. No sir! Mama went and hid the .22."

At that time Lynnette's father was a fairly respectable figure in Classic, with his own hardware store, far from his ingrown feuding clan's place up one of the hollers. He picked fights, though. But no matter what wrangles he got into in town, her mother chose the path of allegiance, refusing, in the firm polite country style, to utter a word about her husband when well-meaning neighbors gave her an opening.

"Of course you know what *he* thought when we called up from the Justice of the Peace. But you know what it is when somebody always backs you—my *mama* never thought I was pregnant. She knew I never would be. She dreamed it. She never told, but my aunt did." Her mother had stood by her too, sneaking her own sewing machine to Lynnette as a wedding present. Now this old treadle Singer stood in the window of Lynnette's apartment, covered like an altar with a cross-stitched tablecloth that had been her mother's too; the shade had to be pulled down to keep the colored thread from fading.

Lynnette was an only child and she had that lack of doubt, that oddly inoffensive sense of the importance of what she did, that only children sometimes have, or mothers' favorites. I could see the mother she described, piecing out the skirts for the cheerleading squad when Lynnette made head cheerleader.

One day in the first year Lynnette and Travis were married, the phone rang. For some reason she didn't want to answer it. It hardly ever rang. It was on the kitchen floor—she and Travis had no furniture except a kitchen table with two chairs, a bed and the sewing machine—and she went over and sat down on the floor against the wall before she picked up the receiver. It was her father. Her mother had dropped dead. "I was *sick*." Lynnette doubled over, telling me this, holding herself in her crossed arms. "Losing her. After I went and *left* her! I still hate myself. The only comfort I can get is I know how happy she was for me and Travis. She never did have the *i*-dea my dad had, that we'd get over it if they just could pry us apart. Oh, I miss her every day." She sighed. "But that with Travis, that was the one time I ever was in love. I'd say the same went for him. I don't know, though. He might have a wife by this time. Might have to. He could set some records, if you know what I mean."

It wasn't that Travis, who could have gone to college on a football scholarship if he had wanted to, turned out a failure. He succeeded. When they came out to Seattle he made money almost without meaning to. Eventually he bought out the little business where his experience with tractors had gotten him a job as a forklift operator.

Not until after he was gone did Lynnette even reveal she was at work on a novel, of which Travis was the subject. Actually the subject was teenage love, physical love, from which Lynnette's writing style had boiled off everything physical, leaving as a residue the aftermath, in which a stilted girl and boy lay back and talked, in accents bearing no resemblance to Lynnette's, in motels and cars and woods and in gyms under the bleachers, in a landscape bare of any hill or mine or highway or bird or weather, in a year bearing nary a fingerprint of the time she was talking about, the very end of the 1950s. No trance of arousal in those woods, let alone poison ivy or ticks or even trees. No bitter postponement, no luxury of hidden flesh exposed, no shaming demand, insatiable and mutual, such as I knew, from our talks, she remembered. I knew before she said a word about it. Heat: that was what she had left out. I knew about that. Lust. Delirious lust, yet lust generous and mindful as it would not be again, all plaited and twined with the serious, loyal, future-ensuring intentions of high school couples.

I have never cared for those people who draw a distinction, who claim this is something other than love, in the young.

When I had teenagers I felt it again: the heat, the whole sealed humid bower in faint mirage, rising around my own children as they stood in front of steamy mirrors getting ready to go out. The girls. Their brother did not get involved until he was safely adult; I am afraid we turned him away from it.

Of course Cy and I were not sixteen—though Lynnette let the comparison stand. I was a junior in college; Cy was a graduate student, involved with a faculty wife whose actions he couldn't answer for if she found out about me.

Lynnette and Travis were sixteen, and a year later they had locked the door on their idyll, they were outside it, they were married.

Lynnette said, "Lord, Travis never changed in twenty years! I mean I didn't want him to, really. He agreed in the end. The signs were there right along. I would dream I was his mother. Don't you laugh, Cyrus. We had to separate. I was never *myself* until I got by myself, ever." Cy did laugh at the manuscript she gave us—read aloud it had the resistance of potatoes being mashed without any liquid—but he said, "She'll have to keep going until she gets to the end of it." Lynnette was not that many years younger than Cy but he had settled into treating her like another daughter.

By this time she and I were riding to work together, which allowed me to hear the instructional tapes she played in her car. Some flat-voiced man saying, "You can't go wrong writing what you know." Some woman saying, "You find out what you think"—no credit for the quote—"when you see what you say."

"Don't get stuck on revisions." These were writers, in some capacity. Not ones you would find in a bookstore. "Always go right back and begin to revise." Lynnette didn't laugh at the discrepancies. "Always begin with the outline." "Never depend on an outline."

She would be steering with one hand and holding up the other with the cigarette to silence my comments. At that time she wasn't at her best, she was looking frowzy. I have a snapshot of her in the office, flicking ash off a ribbed sweater matched to one of the flowered skirts we wore then. She made hers on the old Singer. Her mother must have reasoned that nothing going on in the room a young couple rented above the Rexall Drug would outlive the need for a sewing machine.

Lynnette was pale and uncombed; she had flyaway blond hair anyway, which she wore too long for anything but a ponytail, and bangs, and bitten fingernails. She was lugging around a rubber-banded pile of paper, the manuscript she could never finish— she had it in an old straw bag lined with gingham that she slapped into the back seat when I got in—and losing her voice from smoking, and having health problems. She had to go in for this test and that test, treadmills and scans, because of the high blood pressure that ran in her family. At the same time she always put a handful of salt in her cooking water, and chunks of sausage in the macaroni and cheese she made when she had us over for dinner.

Then suddenly, when she was still going to school and writing at night, when she was almost supporting herself at the magazine, Lynnette gave up on her novel and switched to art. And it turned out that she was an artist. She had been an artist all along.

"There's a closetful of sorry-looking paintings back home, oil paintings," she said, modest as she had never been about her novel, "if my daddy didn't chuck 'em."

She signed up for a printmaking course, where she learned how to add photographs and newsprint to her drawings, and to print them on fabric. Soon the back seat of her car was a jumble of taffeta and corduroy, pieces of quilt and dishtowels and rags. Parades, soup kitchens, Laundromats, ambulances, jail windows would gradually show themselves in the pattern of florals and plaids. Close-ups of faces, Dumpsters, guns, exercise equipment. Her pieces had that crowded, freakish comedy you saw in a great deal of art then, sweetened a little by her own impulses.

"Who would have thought it?" Cy would say, inspecting what she had spread out on our table.

A woman was framing them for her, in exchange for sewing. Lynnette did alterations. Gradually, at first seemingly by chance, she was selling her work. She had shows; she was mentioned in the newspaper. "Little tapestries of urban decay," the caption said. "Well, it's like the images are buried in the texture of the fabric," she was quoted as saying. "I just sort of lift them out." Somebody read that out loud in the office, and she stood up and bowed. "Hey, that stuff took me a lot of writing workshops." When a private school hired her to teach eighth-grade art, we knew she was going to leave the magazine and she did, making a tearful speech at her farewell party. She cut her hair, and began the running that she continued for the rest of her life, and she met men. The men were secondary, to her.

Cy must have known that about Lynnette. He must have known something was not there in her, it had been lost with her marriage, the way she had had just the one doll, her mother's doll, and then gone on, left it behind. It might have been the same thing that made her an artist after all.

She hung her first show in a hallway behind a café. By her third she had signed with a gallery, and a critic from the East Coast happened to be in town and mentioned her opening in print when he got back home.

Lynnette was not blasé. "Feel this! I can hardly breathe!" she said to me at the opening, placing my hand on her chest. "I feel like I ought to drop something on the path so I can find my way back when they're through with me."

"Back to what?" Cy said, in that way men sometimes have of inadvertently revealing that they view female life as a kind of fog in which only the most concrete acts can be made out. Black statues of ceremony or childbirth or ordeal. Icebergs of daring sin.

As he got older her husband Travis had found his pleasures in watching football, squirrel hunting in the fall, coaching other people's kids in soccer, and taking his employees out to a weekly, all-you-can-eat buffet. He did make quite a bit of money, and apparently he was free with it in the settlement, even though there were no children. Travis sold his company and went back to West Virginia. He had come out anyway thinking of the Northwest as a place to raise sons: cabins and bears and whitewater rivers.

"Travis thought this would be more like Alaska," Lynnette explained. "When we said Washington State I guess we were thinking of Alaska. Or maybe Montana. I mean the backcountry. We both were, actually. What did we know? We were eighteen."

The only time I met Travis was just before he left town. He was backing out of the hall closet. "Hot dog!" he said, holding up a whistle on a cord. He put out a big hand; the impression was of bulky sunburned fairness and the kind of unseeing patience that people's children sometimes turn on you when they are introduced. He had ruddy skin, the color of apple cider. "Don't worry none about it," I heard Lynnette call from the porch when she ran out after him. Her old way of talking came back in times of crisis. Something of hers had gotten packed by mistake, in the U-Haul at the curb.

"Well, that's him," she said, coming in with reddened eyes. "So hey. Good-lookin', huh?" As if he were a child she had just sent off to school.

"Where'd he get a tan like that in Seattle? Poor thing, he had his sweatshirt on inside out."

"He does that," she said gruffly. "That's not because of me."

YEARS PASSED. LYNNETTE was sitting on a bench at six o'clock in the morning. She had driven out before work to run the three miles around the little circular lake in the middle of the city, as she did every day. A windstorm had come through in the early morning hours, leaving twigs and branches strewn on the ground, but now everything was windless and quiet, and fog had dropped over the lake.

She described the morning to me: the heavy November fog enclosing everything, so thick that although ducks and coots swam into view, they were not *on* anything. Each of them was towing a long scalloped train of ripples behind it in the water-sky.

The serenity was unearthly.

The trees near enough to be seen stood out on the fog like runny letters. On the nearest one a heavy lower limb, snapped partly off in the storm, dangled from tree to ground forming an *h*, the broken small *h*. Lynnette was accustomed to regarding anything like that as a sign. She began listing to herself words beginning with *H*. *Horrible, hectic, harangue. Heat, hurt, hex.* Later, in the school library, she dragged out the big dictionary and leafed through the *H* section. *Hack, hang. Hideous, hubris.*

"H," she told me solemnly on the phone, "is negative. Because that puff of air, *huh, huh!*—that little hawking thing—is for something we want to get rid of."

"What about *help*? What about *hold, home, hope*?" I said. "What about *hedonism*? *Hospital*?"

"Shut up, smarty-pants," she said. "I know, I know—*head, heart, hands, health*. That's 4-H. Bet you didn't know that."

The gouge where the limb had been attached to the tree made her think of the words *partial birth* in the news. But the fact was that those images had been used up; she would not sift through them for her own work. What she was interested in at the moment was shape, as the framed, printed card on the wall said at her last show: the shape of urban event.

While she was studying the gouge in the tree, an elderly woman in a hooded sweatshirt stumbled out of the fog. She seemed to be getting herself untied from something rather than going strictly forward; the effort cost her little grunts each time her feet struck the ground.

"There's a lot of that," Lynnette thought idly. "I wonder if I look like that." At that moment she was sitting down because dimly, among the reeds close to shore a way back, she believed she had seen a duck murder another duck. When she caught sight of what was going on she had already slowed down, a little winded—she was getting over a bad, lengthy flu—and she ran in place watching it happen.

"Did you see that? I'm sure I just saw a duck *drown* another duck," she called to a young man with sculpted calves, running hard, in shorts despite the cold. When I think of this man I always see the husband of Kate's neighbor. Roy Riley. Lynnette caught up to run alongside him. "It never did come back up! I thought they were mating but the duck just *stomped* the other one under. Kept biting it on the head! Do ducks have teeth?"

"Marauding duck," the man said, not even glancing at Lynnette, having a radar, she realized mid-stride, for her age and her thick waist. He sped up, and shifted away from her on the path.

"I'm not after you, dude," she called, speeding up herself and leaving his pumping calves behind with ease.

The next thing she did, to her mild embarrassment, was trip on a branch on the path. She didn't fall; she caught herself and veered off in front of him to the ladies' room. She never had to pee when she ran, but she stood in the unlit cement alcove for a minute or two. After that she ran the long uphill curve. The line of trees at the top, where the bench was, took shape in the fog. She wasn't feeling right; she broke the rhythm of her run a second time and flopped down on the bench to get her breath.

The fog was unusually thick but now there was just enough sun coming up, working behind it, to put color into it here and there, a shell pink, a faint, downy yellow.

"There was something about it. I thought, *I'll kick myself if I don't just sit down for one minute and* look." So she did; she leaned back on the bench and closed her eyes.

When she opened them a boy was standing over her, holding a red kayak on his head. "Hey," he said, "sorry to bother you." He shrugged a backpack down his arm onto the bench. "I'm going out in it. The fog. It's something, isn't it? Mind if I leave this here?"

"Go ahead, I'll be here. Guess I look like I'm down for the count," she said, pushing back her hair. Then, lest he think her too friendly, she said abruptly, "Sure, leave it."

"You don't have to watch it. This early in the morning I just leave my stuff," he said. "Are you all right?"

"I'm fine. I'm resting."

He smiled at her. *Well, he must be from somewhere far away,* she thought, *to smile like that.* He lowered the kayak into the water and got in, and prodded the bank with his oar. Lynnette said *oar* but it would have been a paddle.

Suddenly she got an unpleasant idea. "How will you see to get back, if you go out on the lake?" she called. Lynnette was not accustomed to worries of this kind, but he was young. He was a boy. She thought of us, she said, of Cyrus and me, because of our son.

"I'll stay out until it burns off. It'll burn off in an hour. Hey, don't worry. There's nothing in the pack, no drugs or anything," he added with a grin, twirling the paddle over his head. "No bomb." It was the year the bomb went off in the basement of the Trade Center. "It's bread. For the ducks."

"I thought of telling him about how bread-paste in the craw starves a duck," she told me. "I almost told him about the duck murdering the other duck. I didn't though, I caught myself. I thought, *Lately I'm so full of this creepy information. Why? Why am I?* It's getting into my work. And he's young. He doesn't need to hear it. Is that how mothers feel?"

When he had vanished onto the lake she leaned back again, and stayed so quiet that after a while a squirrel crept up onto the bench with her and began to poke at the boy's pack. It spun itself this way and that on the zipped pocket, from which it must have been getting the smell of bread. It got a claw into the zipper at one point, and hopped and pulled to get free, working the zipper down a tantalizing half inch as it did so. All the while its tail, not fluffy as the tails of squirrels looked from a distance, but spiked with thin hair with a little shoelace of skin inside it, switched ardently. It did not seem to know Lynnette was there.

As a girl in her father's store, sitting on the floor behind the counter hearing the chugs of the adding machine and nails being swept into bags, Lynnette said, she had gone in and out of a pleasant, canceled-out feeling like the one she had now. Finally the squirrel gave up and crouched on the pack, an expression so fixed and thwarted in its black eyes that pity for it swept over her, an intimation of its hurrying, single-minded life, a life that suddenly seemed to her such an ordeal that she was thankful the squirrel had no clear notion of it, connected as it was to whatever necessity among the gliding ducks had led one of them to murder another. She thought of Travis and his squirrel hunting. No necessity there. How he, a man who wouldn't hurt a flea, had gotten up on cold mornings like this one when he lived here and driven into the river valley to shoot squirrels. How this had made him feel at home somehow. Home. Now the squirrel was digging furiously again at the pack, while she sat so still in her absorption that it never looked her way. She might have been a coat dropped on the bench, until the blast of a foghorn startled the animal and it raced off.

The long blast did not come from the little lake, of course; it came from the downtown waterfront, several miles away. Twice it sounded, rolling out over the city in a deep bellow. Lynnette waited; she had heard the foghorn a hundred times before but she could not remember if there were a prescribed number of blasts. She could make out the squirrel's tiny savage scratches all over the nylon of the pack. *This*, she said to herself. *This . . . what? I'm tired of the city*, she thought, without any particular antagonism. *I'm tired of people. I want . . .*

For a long time no one ran by, and she gave in to a deep lassitude. Her eyes grew so heavy she came close to falling asleep in the quiet.

Then she came to and had a kind of hallucination. She saw, she said, the direction her art would take. She saw it in some detail.

She had been gazing at the colors in the fog, columns of them, deeper than the hints of sun. They were peeling off the bank or out of the water right in front of where she was sitting. They had the tense wavering of snakes charmed out of a basket, though it might have been only the fog that was moving.

She sat looking at them in a state of concentration. Her mind was exceptionally alive. The squirrel, not thwarted at all, had come back and resumed its assault on the backpack. She turned her eyes to it and when she looked back that was the end of it, the colors, some prism effect in the water-laden air, were gone, there was not even a hint of them where the fog was curling off the reeds.

She didn't care, she had seen them, and seeing them she had made more than one decision. She didn't care any longer about the runner who had not given her a glance, or about anything she had been worrying about or planning.

She stretched. Streetlights across the lake were beginning to show amber in the fog. Standing up she put her arms out and sucked in deep breaths of chilly air. She still didn't feel like running but she thought lightheartedly, *I'll walk the rest of the way.*

THAT NIGHT LYNNETTE dreamed the phone rang. This is the part she didn't tell me. It stopped after a couple of rings but a while later, in the slow registration of dreams, she decided to get up and answer it. She went and stood looking into her closet, with the feeling—something required of her that was beyond her, some untappable energy—that we agreed viewing our clothes on hangers often provoked in us, when something stronger came over her, some cold foreboding.

She took hold of the folding door to rest her head against it. When she reopened her eyes she saw someone lying on the floor of the closet. She looked for a long time—her dreaming mind reset itself several times—before she saw that it was Travis.

He was curled on his side among the shoes. He had on an old sweater of her mother's with the neck-tag showing. His back was to her, and the soles of his feet in socks with worn heels.

"Travis," she whispered without moving. "Nobody told me you died."

She put her hand out and touched the thigh, which she was able to do somehow without bending over. She would not have been able to bend over, hindered by that bulk of unease that was in her chest.

She ran her cold palm slantwise across the wale of the corduroy to a three-cornered tear she had repaired with iron-on tape on the inside of the pants.

Out of the ridges of the corduroy a grief came up into her such as she had never known in her waking life. At the same time the blunt edge of something heavy sank into place against her chest. The next minute, against her wishes and to her shock, whatever had hold of the heavy thing had levered it into her by some means without breaking the skin, and jammed it steadily forward. A sweat of trying to heave it out drenched her as it paused and sawed a little way back.

"I think I can hold it right where it is," she said to Travis, but she was cold, she couldn't keep warm and hold it at the same time, or breathe and hold it.

IT WAS THE mailman who noticed the mail and the newspapers piling up. He had a thick envelope from a travel agency and he didn't want to leave it. He started to go on down the sidewalk but something stopped him. Lynnette's car was parked in front of the duplex. He knocked on the other door and a woman opened it. She worked at home; usually if Lynnette was going away this woman would take in the mail and water the plants for her. So she had been wondering. No noises from next door. She tried to make a phone call to Lynnette for the mailman, and then she called the police.

A patrol car arrived; a policewoman got out and knocked and tried the door, and without any to-do lifted up her leg and kicked it in, just as they do on TV. After a while she came back out onto the porch and told the mailman and the neighbor, who were waiting together. "No sign she ever woke up. You can tell when it's quick." The neighbor began calling the names in Lynnette's address book.

Why should I tell Kate this? She heard the outlines of it from me anyway at the time. Heart attack in youth. Comparative youth. Misfortune of a stranger. I'm the only link between them.

AND HOW WOULD anyone know what was dreamed?

And if there is a dream, why not a deep dream of peace, like the one Abou Ben Adhem awoke from?

If Lynnette had ever brought her novel to a conclusion, which Cy always said she'd have to before she could throw it away— though he was wrong, she threw it away anyway—probably it would have ended with a tearful reunion or a marriage. Remembering Travis always comforted her. But if this is nothing like what happened to her on her last night on Earth, it doesn't matter to me. It comforts me. Truth is not necessarily what we're after.

It was in the early afternoon of the day Lynnette died that she called me. She was at school but couldn't work. Finally she slammed the door of the art room on her students and shut herself in the teachers' lounge to call me. "Were you up in time to see the beautiful *fog*? Oh, it's set me off. I'm on the move!" She told me about the tree in the shape of an *h*, and the boy with the kayak, and the duck. She told me about the resolve that had flooded her, when she stood up with a series of paintings firmly in her mind.

Not only that, she was about to make her first trip home in thirty years. She had gone out at lunchtime and made a plane reservation, and bought paints and brushes. Because there were colors, dark burned yellows, maple reds, thin poplar greens, colors present to her since that morning—"Don't laugh, it was the most heavenly thing"—in the very words *West Virginia.*

And she was going to look people up. Teachers, if they were still alive, and the sponsor of the cheerleaders, and the clerk in her father's store who had let her doodle up and down the adding machine tape. She was going to pay her respects to people she had never written to and barely thought of in thirty years, who had never written to her either or even sent a Christmas card, and probably wouldn't have any notion of who it was saying hello. A few her age might recall Travis Miller the quarterback. On the other hand Travis might be living right there in their midst, in Classic. Why not? Of course she would ask for news of him, there and in the next town where they had lived above the Rexall.

Much would be changed. A huge outlet mall had gone in. She was going to see what it had left of the Methodist church at the edge of town and the steep ground behind it where the cemetery was. Her mother's grave was there.

She was going to paint. These new paintings would not proceed from anything she had been doing in her prints. They would be static, all their energy held in reserve. It was not that she repudiated the work she had done. But she was finished with fabric, with collage, with making plates, with printing altogether, with *playing*. She had *seen*. "I think they have to be *landscapes*."

It was the most heavenly thing.

DON'T GET HUNG up on something-or-other. I forget what the warning was.

This is four or five years earlier. We were sitting in Lynnette's car while she finished her cigarette and the tail end of one of her tapes, before we got out to start to walk and she reasoned with me, as she always did, illogically, comfortingly, telling me a dream of hers in which Cy had figured, laying out the signs that pointed to reconciliation.

Don't get hung up on . . . The writer on the tape, to judge by her voice, was a young woman hardly older than my daughters. When I said that, Lynnette replied with dignity, "This woman has written several novels."

We were going to walk around the lake to talk about a desperate situation involving Cy. I had to decide. In a book he was reading I had found a snapshot of a tall, beautiful, unstable friend of our daughters'. There was no doubt about this delicate, hungry face; the picture was inscribed to him on the back. The shocking words of love were not written in cursive but heavily printed, as if with malice. You could tell the person who wrote them was not in good control of herself. The letters, in the slant-tip pen she must have used for musical notation, had run a little where they had been touched.

I had burned up this picture, along with some of our own photographs, albums of them, in the fireplace. The fire got out of hand and oily smoke rolled out and blackened the fireplace wall and the ceiling. They were vinyl albums and they had those self-sealing plastic sheets over the pictures, which made it necessary for me and our son Ben to move to Kate and Joe's for a few days while the chemicals that broke down were fanned out the open windows and the room was repainted. Cy went to a hotel. All day and all night Ben, who was fourteen, was lying in Kate and Joe's messy living room on the floor behind the couch, with his earphones in and his hands pressed between his knees. He would not go to school. Sometimes at night I heard sounds, floors creaking, books falling off the stack at the foot of the stairs, and I knew from the uneven beat of one voice coming up through the floor of their daughter's room where I was staying that Joe had gotten out of bed and gone down to see about Ben.

Cy called in the daytime but I didn't go to the phone. Kate's voice, floating in to me, went on for a long time in the kitchen. It's too late, this time. Almost. It's almost too late. He can't come back to us as he was, not this time. That's what Kate had to argue.

When Kate went to give her lecture I sat out on the deck under the tree.

Days went by like this, and on one of them I looked up to see the beautiful next-door neighbor. She was climbing over the railing of her own deck. She pushed through the hedge and slid on her heels and her rump down through the ivy on the bank. She walked over to me, brushing off her long thighs in their ironed jeans.

"I'm making some tea," she said in a high, whispery voice, oddly old-fashioned, like a voice I ought to have known. I do remember: Jackie Kennedy doing the White House tour. "It's 'Evening in Missoula' tea," she said. "I thought I would bring it over. I came to tell you so you'd open the front door, because I can't bring it down the bank. I heard you."

I did not know anyone would be home during the day. I should have, though; I should have known this particular woman would not leave the house, she would be in there holding the wand over whatever room was being changed into something else.

I was just sitting there under the tree with my head in my arms on the picnic table but I might have been making noise. I had stopped my monotonous crying for the time being because I had given myself a sinus headache. Maybe I had been banging my head.

"My name is Kristen," she said when I let her in the front door with her painted tray and her beautiful Italian mugs.

"I'm Sheila. This is my son Ben," I said.

"I know," she said.

Ben didn't take off his earphones, but from the floor his half-closed eyes followed Kristen. Yes, beauty strikes the little cold flint of life, there is no denying that.

The last thing most people would do is interfere in someone's private grief. And here was a person dedicated to the exactly right thing, a person none of us had said more than hello to after the day the moving van pulled up and Kate went over with coffee and sat on a box marked GOURMET MAGAZINE.

Kristen Riley did not apologize. "I've seen you on this deck so many times," she said by way of explanation. "Drink some tea. You'll feel better. It's a man, isn't it. Your husband. I've seen him."

"He's seen you too," I said through my hiccups.

We went out the back door onto the deck and she poured the tea into the Italian mugs, which had pomegranates and long-tailed, fanciful, tufted birds on them. She had slices of lemon and a little crock of sparkling Demerara sugar, with a ceramic spoon.

We talked all afternoon. I told her the story of my life and she told me the story of hers. We began with that day and worked back.

We got all the way back to our home towns and our parents and our sisters and brothers and the people they had married. We dwelt for a long time on our high school boyfriends, and on what it meant that we had chosen those particular ones. Her husband could not be exposed to the story of any boyfriend prior to himself, so many of these stories had lain dormant in her for years. Once married, she was not a person who made new friends. Talk had its ramifications.

Roy Riley did not like talk between women. He grilled her when she came back from shopping for clothes, in case she had stood there in her underwear with her bruises showing and confessed to some salesgirl, "My husband almost tore my arm out of the socket."

And the house took up all of her time.

We talked about her high school days in Florida. Her husband was from the same area, a swampy part of the state, out in the middle of nowhere. She told about a friend who drove into the swamp when his girlfriend broke up with him, and I told about the pills my roommate took in college when her boyfriend called to say he was getting married. We picked up the fruits of love and pressed their skins: abortions and silent warts that turned to tumors, and in vitro fertilizations and adoptions that went awry and the bisexual triangle marriage of a woman she knew, whose husband's lover finally shot her, which led us into crimes of passion, and pleas of insanity and diminished capacity. We stranded men and women we had known or heard of on a sea of custody kidnappings and restraining orders and breakdowns leading to charges of shoplifting and DUI, with infuriated children stealing cars, and voyeurs in the guestroom, and physical jeopardy: floods and mudslides and the San Francisco earthquake. The stories rolled from us: the man she knew who crawled in under the collapsed freeway to look for his ex-wife, the couple I knew who died in their tent in an avalanche. The more we told the hungrier we got. We barely took turns; if one of us paused the other leapt in with a guess, as to the most awful, the most cruelly inevitable detail. We tossed them out faster and faster like bones with the meat still on them. I began to make them up. Kristen's was a purer nature and she kept, I think, to the factual.

She told of a sorority sister of hers (they had sororities in high school, in that part of Florida) who broke down after being levitated at a slumber party, and had to be taken to an institute where she underwent shock treatments for years. The truth was that she had been sleeping with the boy who was her parents' foster child, who lived in the house as her brother. She was fourteen at the time. It wasn't sex at all, it was love: some years later she got out and married him, in a church wedding put on by his birth mother, whom he had searched for and found. In the interim her own family had made a strange choice: they had sued the family of the girl who held the slumber party where the levitation took place.

We talked as if there had been a great deal of choosing done by us and by everyone else in our stories, and little of it regretted, despite the absurd details we laughed about until we choked on our tea.

I didn't want to come to a stop but finally I told her I had to, my friend from work would be coming for me any minute. I said my friend was taking time off that she couldn't afford, to drive me over to the lake and walk with me. She didn't want me to pick her up at work because I had had several little accidents in the car. I said that for some reason I listened to this friend's advice when the subject was love, though she was divorced herself and had written a book, more or less, that was no good.

That reminded Kristen of her cousin, who had entered a contest for a part in an opera but had not won. The cousin's first baby had lived two days. She had been born with an undeveloped twin inside her body. *Fetus in fetu* was the Latin for it. The cruel wonder of this, indeed of everything, set us off again.

Now Kristen was pregnant herself. She said that shyly, pausing at the front door and balancing the tea tray on one hand while she stroked her flat stomach. Then her whole face drew down. She got the pale-eyed stare of a wolf. She said if he was ever rough with a child of hers, she would kill him.

Sometimes when Kristen Riley is on her deck we have smiled at each other through the leaves, but as for friendship, that was it, that was the talk we had. It was the only one. She was not free to repeat it, and I had decided to say no more.

I told Lynnette a little of Kristen's story in the car. To keep names out of it I said I had just hung up from talking to a friend long distance. That had the ring of a lie, and made Lynnette think it was my own situation that I was trying to trick her into commenting on. "Is that so? Hmm. Physical violence is the last thing I would have expected of *Cy*," she said shrewdly. When we got that straightened out Lynnette said her mother had had at least two friends in Classic who had married men like that and who would die before they let anybody see them in a bathing suit. "That was a thing with some of those boys," she said. "You got laid off, you slapped her around a little, let off steam." She eyed me sharply. "*Travis* was as gentle as a lamb."

"Well, don't let him do it, that's all!" That's what Lynnette said, stubbing out her cigarette in the car ashtray as the tape went into its final admonitions. "Get rid of superfluous information. Don't get hung up on . . ." I wish I could remember what that one was, that impediment. We'd been talking loudly over the woman's voice, which no longer commanded Lynnette's full attention.

"Don't let him." She repeated it as we walked. "You don't have to let him go."

How did Lynnette know this? She didn't seem to know much of anything—this was the year before she threw out the novel and embarked on her real art—and yet I listened to her. *You don't have to let him go.*

"And never hinge a story on a dream."

THAT WAS A resolution I didn't keep: not to go on about Cy. To be, instead, the way Lynnette's mother had been with her father. To do whatever I might have to do but not to complain. Because at the time I didn't see how I could take it back if I did complain. Later I changed my mind, or maybe the firm hand of conviction just opened and dropped me. It was nothing anyway but an old half-tormenting idea that there had to be a thread in life that never broke. Right then I didn't see how I could keep saying, "Oh, that. It was nothing in the long run. It blew over," even if that was how it might seem to me on some future day.

Tom Thumb Wedding

• • •

IT MUST HAVE been not too long after the war—we still say
"the war," even now—that we went to the Tom Thumb wedding in which my sister Gaby was the groom.

These little pageants began in another war, the Civil War,
when the whole country burst out in "fairy weddings" after the
Lincolns received the real Tom Thumb and his bride Lavinia at
the White House. In the 1940s, mock weddings of children had
a revival; they seem to have raised money for the churches and
schools that sponsored them. Perhaps they made for a distracting occasion in wartime.

The Vietnam War does not appear to have triggered them, but
today if you look around you can find reports of them again here
and there. It may be they skipped a generation, to revive in our
new series of wars.

The wedding in which Gaby—the tallest in her kindergarten
class—was the groom was held in someone's garden, and in the
pictures my younger sister Lizzie and I are small enough to sit on
the same chair, our faces pious and sullen. Two and four, we're
shoving each other with our shoulders. I think I remember the

garden, or have arranged it since in my mind with trellises, and sweet peas crawling along the borders, and a gazebo under a load of wisteria. The gazebo is in the pictures. I know I remember the bride, with her trembling nosegay, and the collapse of the folding chair Lizzie and I were sitting on, at the end when everybody stood up. No one took a picture of that, as they would today.

Gaby has the pictures they did take, in a scrapbook with the old black photo corners peeling off. No real groom would have on the outfit they had found and starched for her, consisting of a white shirt, white duck pants, a tie of unknown color (the pictures are black-and-white), and a black flower that must be a red carnation.

There she stands at the gazebo facing the portly, displeased boy in a minister's collar, with her straight back and her straight eyebrows, her sad face with features still childishly small on someone of that height—though she is not sad, she says when we look at these pictures, and why do people say that? "It's because I'm too tall," she says. "It's because you're sweet," I tell her. "Sweet and sad, same thing," says our sister Lizzie, who is a feminist. Was, she says. The word has been usurped. Words, she tells us as the editor she is, have fates just like people. Words stand there in their ignorance for a while like telephone poles when the wires have been tied up and sunk underground, until somebody comes and topples them, the poles, and throws them into those heaps you see from the train window.

In the next picture a ring bearer has arrived. Now bridesmaids, Gaby still patient in her place of honor. A kind of humble honor, belonging to grooms before the arrival of the bride who is the whole point of the thing.

And there she is: the bride, the one they have dressed in exact miniature and sent down the paper runner to enchant us. In her trailing dress she passes between the rows of chairs on the arm of a little boy pretending with glasses on to be her father. She is tiny. She must have been chosen for that and for her hair, which I remember as golden—Lizzie says so too—falling down over the many buttons of her dress like ribbon just curled on the scissor blade. Through the veil we can just see her pink lipstick and tiny chin. In lace gloves, the only thing too big for her, she carries those shaking flowers. Lizzie and I stop pushing each other to gaze at her. She is like something that is almost ours to snatch up and comb and button and smooth—and yes, if we had to, throw against the wall.

One of the bridesmaids was Susan, who would be Gaby's own bridesmaid fifteen years later.

No one worried about confusing Gaby sexually or traumatizing her by making her the groom. It does not seem to have mattered that there were plenty of boys in the kindergarten class and Gaby had been chosen in their stead. And she didn't find being the groom any more confusing than being the horse. When you play horse—and we all did that, little girls, except for an occasional visitor too prissy to snort and canter and whip her own legs—you are horse and rider. Sometimes, in those days, you were sheriff and outlaw. Certainly you were never the *woman*.

We thought back on that time when we got together, all three of us and Susan, who was part of the family. For years after she moved away, Susan came back on the train to stay with us, remaining Gaby's best friend. Back from the North the first time, though, she refused to play horse, and we said she had turned into a Northerner. When Lizzie and I moved away in our turn, Gaby thought the same thing about us.

I flew in from San Diego the night before Susan and Lizzie came down on the train from New York, talking all the way because they both worked for publishers but in the city they had a hard time running into each other. Susan had the most to tell because her husband Trey had moved out. She was divorcing him. If he came back one more time to pick something up she was going to push him down the elevator shaft. "Where's Wes?" she said as soon as she came in. "I want to cry on his shoulder and smack him at the same time. Because he's a man."

"Wait a while, he'll be home, you can smack him then," Gaby said.

Susan's husband Trey had found himself a girl of thirty-two. "You would never guess, with Trey," she said, "but he's as bad as Binney Ward."

"Binney Ward!" said Gaby. "What a thought." It was Gaby's conviction that Trey had only lost his head, and would come home. When she said this Lizzie looked at me and snorted, but it was exactly what we would have expected from Gaby. And indeed the next year Trey did come home; he had the doorman announce him like a stranger to be let in or sent away, and ten floors up, Susan opened the door.

The four of us fell onto the flowered couch and Gaby's soft armchairs and talked all afternoon about the past—the Tom Thumb wedding and our own, old boyfriends and teachers and certain contested report cards that could have been written by witches, so uncannily had they predicted what would actually happen to us—with an occasional note from the present coming in like those tests of the emergency broadcast system in the middle of a song.

Gaby and Wes lived a mile from where we had grown up.

Wes owned a store in town and off and on he had served as the mayor while they raised five children. They had lost the first one, a boy, and after that Gaby kept going, as if she could get him back. They still had the one born late, when they were in their forties, at home with them. Janna. Janna was fourteen. She had not come home for dinner; she was at a sleepover at her friend's house.

We had just taken up the subject of Janna when Wes came home, and then after dinner when he had left us to ourselves— making his getaway, he said, before Susan could smack him any more—we started in again.

"I don't know what to do," Gaby said. "What to do with her." We had never heard Gaby say that about a child of hers, or speak disparagingly of anyone else's, or indeed concentrate any of her attention on what the younger generation might be contributing to the general insidious sadness of the world as represented in the papers and on TV. Each of her six children she had regarded with a little bit of the wonder of the blind man who saw, and saw trees walking. She stayed away from the news if she could, and even her books she chose carefully; she liked books about animals. She didn't read anything timely, nothing published by Lizzie's company or Susan's—and she didn't tell people her e-mail address for fear they would circulate pictures of people or animals that somebody had done harm to.

Did Wes know what the trouble was, the latest trouble? "Oh a man can't. Not this part. Not a father. Lizzie, you may *never*—"

"Oh, Gaby." Lizzie didn't have any kids of her own, or even a husband, but she liked children much the same way she liked men—she always had men around her and she could surprise you with her knowledge of their habits. Despite her sharp tongue she had a friendly view of them, men and children; she doubted their dark powers. "Just because I joke around with Wes," she said, "just because, let's face it, Gaby, I *tell jokes* to *men,* doesn't mean I'd be *crude.* Not that I'm saying this is crude."

"Oh, I'm sorry, honey," Gaby said. "I'm not thinking. Oh, I had a secret I told people, that this child was the sweetest one of all. I know you can't pick one. But this one—she cried when another child cried! Remember how she tried to give her cousins her toys? She—her brothers adored her. She sang in her sleep."

"And she's so pretty," Susan said with her fine irrelevance.

"Some days she doesn't have a word to say to either one of us. And the language, when she does. It would break your heart to see Wes try with her. And now she's going to fail the eighth grade. I can't believe this is the same child."

Janna. She had renamed herself; her real name was Jean. Our mother was romantic, and had given us the names Gabriele, Christina, and Eliza, with the result that we had all taken nicknames and seen to it that our kids got one syllable each. When our mother died we felt sorry; we remembered her wistful printing of our full names on birthday cards. What would our mother, with her memories of cotillion, have thought of this grandchild? Cotillion. Another of those telephone poles of Lizzie's.

That summer Wes was supervising a group of high school kids who were learning upholstery for shop credit. They came in after summer school and worked until dinnertime. They were all boys.

Janna too went right over after summer school—she had failed algebra—and spent time in the store attracting the attention of whoever was still there tacking a sofa arm or sweeping up. She didn't have a boyfriend. That wasn't the problem, having or not having a boyfriend.

The principal had sent out a letter about drugs in the school saying the eighth grade, Janna's class, was ground zero. But even that wasn't the problem.

It was the year of rumored blowjobs. That is, girls all over the country were said to be giving them right and left. Girls in middle school, high school. Maybe even grade school. They were said to feel that this was nothing.

"What's something, then?" Gaby said. She didn't say so, but we got the feeling somebody had caught or reported Janna in this regard.

"Well, they've seen a lot since 9/11. It has to have left some mark. They're hurting," Susan began.

"Hmm, 9/11 . . . blowjobs," said Lizzie. "Good solution."

"But look at them, the kids Janna's age." Susan's own two were married and she said all the time that she wasn't going to worry about them any more. "What do they have to look forward to?"

"Everything," Gaby said.

"It's not like she died," Lizzie said. "What exactly are you afraid of?"

"What do you mean, what?"

"Oh, for Christ's sake, Lizzie, she's afraid her child's life will be ruined," Susan said with an operatic sweep of her arm that knocked her coffee cup off the table and broke it.

It was after midnight and we were on the back porch, listening to the peepers. Back home my husband had had to go out and buy me a CD, *Symphony of Nature*, because some evenings on the West Coast I got so desperate for the sound of peepers, and the sight of Gaby's porch, that I was ready to drive to the airport without even a suitcase.

"And actually I don't think it's really true, what you're saying," Susan added.

"It is, though," Gaby said.

"They just line up at parties? I'd need some proof. I don't want to say my girls weren't just as . . . I'd be the last to say *anything* did not happen. I've learned. But Gaby, I think you read this, like we all did. Everybody was talking about this for a while. This and anal sex. How kids—"

"No. I didn't read it."

We had the scrapbook out there with us, and I thought I would bring us back to the Tom Thumb pictures. I went and got a candle out of the sideboard so we could see in the dark.

"But look at Mary Pat, wasn't she the prettiest thing," Gaby said, trying to recover herself.

"Oh dear," Susan said from down on the floor where she was still picking up pieces of her cup. "You know what happened to Mary Pat."

No, we didn't know. Lizzie and I didn't. Gaby didn't either, it turned out.

"Last winter. I know I told you, Gaby."

"No," said Gaby.

"Oh, Lord. Well, you know how she was. You remember she married Binney right out of high school. Then in the '70s she married Tom Armitage. And his kids walked all over her."

"And she didn't have any," said Gaby. "Poor thing, poor thing. Don't tell me. I don't want to know. And then . . . then she moved. After she married somebody we didn't know. She moved to Detroit."

"Right, she lived in Detroit. Can you imagine?"

Lizzie said, "Imagine."

"No, I mean this was Mary Pat Halley. That sweet girl," said Susan, slowing down to match Gaby's sobriety. "I mean she was still just like she is in that picture. Just looking for the right one. Don't you remember how she was in high school, Chrissie?

Lizzie?" Susan had moved back, by the time we were in high school. "You-all weren't that far behind us."

We didn't remember. High school. That made us all think of the real subject, Janna and the blowjobs.

Susan said, "I know I wouldn't have picked her to be the one to do what she did."

"Don't say it," said Gaby.

"She did. She did it with a rope. There she was, hanging from the *landing*. And he came in the front door. The last husband."

"Last one I *guess*," said Lizzie.

Susan ignored her. "You know Gaby, this was the one had money and they went and lived in Detroit."

"Detroit," said Gaby. She had stood up and gone to the screen, where she stood listening for something through the sound of the peepers. "But at least that was the one worshipped her." That was the kind of thing you still heard said around there, that somebody worshipped somebody else. It meant an age difference, normally. Some gulf that could be seen across, possibly in both directions, with respect or wonder. "Though they said he was a good bit younger," Gaby added with tears in her voice, laying her forehead on the screen. "You know, I always thought something might happen to Mary Pat. Ever since our wedding." She turned around. "I mean it, Susie. Remember them pinning my flower and telling me, Come, come and get Mary Pat over it, she's having a crying fit. It was when they were buttoning up that dress on her."

"It was real to her," said Susan, without Gaby's sympathy.

"And somebody had the idea the lightest little smack would help her get over it but Mrs. Halley said, 'You touch her and I'll scream.' Remember that?"

No one else remembered.

"Shh," said Gaby. "Somebody's on the front porch." We heard the door open. Gaby listened. "That's Janna," she said. The fright had left her voice. She stood up with a tired, helpless eagerness. "Well, I know she did say they were all going to the sleepover. But here she is." There was a long silence and then the kitchen light went on and Janna stood in the doorway. Her hair was all over the place and her eye makeup had smeared onto her cheekbones. Her eyes were wide with the effort to focus. "Honey?" said Gaby.

"I'm home. Hi, Aunt Lizzie. Hi, Aunt Chrissie," Janna said, as if I hadn't seen her that morning. She thought for a second. "Susan, hey. When did you get here?"

"Hi, honey," we said together.

"What's the matter?" she said.

Nobody said, We thought you were at a sleepover. We all tried not to stare at her beautiful smudged child's face. She looked like someone who had crawled free of some snare and dragged herself miles.

"What's this?" she said, coming over unsteadily to the open scrapbook. "Oh my god." She sank against the table. "These are those pictures. Oh my god. You're looking at these. Mom was the groom." She bent over the pictures. "Mom. You were so cute."

We tried not to look at each other in the candlelight, or at her, in our relief. She had come out onto the porch. She was talking to us. Surely life had not altered as much as we had been saying.

"Those fat little babes. On the same chair. My aunties," she said. "Whoa. Those dresses."

"Watch your hair," Gaby said before she could stop herself, as Janna's pale hair fell forward over the candle. A string of notes burst from somewhere, muffled and exultant. Janna began a struggle with a tiny bag. Finally she pried the phone out, and still propped against the table she tried to read the screen. She drew a long sobbing breath as she read, leaning over the flame so it lit her face from below in the dire way women learn to avoid, lest some banshee hidden away in us make her appearance. "But how did you stand it," she said, yanking the hair back and shielding the phone as she glared, "any of you? Living in those days?"

Beloved, You Looked into Space

. . .

O UR FATHER MARRIED a woman who took an ax to a bear. She did it to save her first husband. The bear that charged him was blond at the neck and had enough bulk there that she saw it as a grizzly, a thin one. Later she knew it to have been a black bear, with half a paw shot off and a slug in its shoulder. A hunter told the papers there had been word of a problem bear in the area. The couple had no way of knowing that; they were staying in a remote cabin and although the husband was a hunter himself, he had no gun because they were there to fish and take it easy. So our father said later.

The wife was a little distance upriver casting her own line when the bear grappled him down. Twice she heard a growl she thought was a plane overhead fading in and out. That was before he made a sound. He was trying to get under the water. When he came up he screamed for her to get away. Of course a bear goes into water, and it swatted him back to the rocks where it could straddle him.

They were fishing catch and release, late in the winter season, really the spring melt, when bears are lean and ranging for food.

Grizzly: anger. Black bear: hunger. Something to keep in mind about bears, our father said. He was a veterinarian, but bears were a new interest. His warnings were for my sister Shelley, the one who hiked and camped alone. Shelley had worked for the Forest Service and knew more about wildlife than he did, and by this time she had her own veterinary practice, so she could have expressed an opinion, but she didn't. The subject was his now.

Earlier the husband and wife had been taking turns splitting wood for the stove. *The ax.* She ran uphill and skidded back. The first blow she struck was a true one, splitting the ear and causing the bear to drag its head off her husband, turn a blood-filled eye on her, and stand up. The head swung, a paw swiped her arm and knocked her down. But the bear dropped back to her husband. Unaware she was hurt she pulled herself onto her knees, her eyes level with what was going on. She felt for the ax, got to her feet. Like a batter, she swung it into the neck.

"I mean that next swing picked her up off the ground," our father said. It was he who was compelled to repeat the details, from the time he met her until the time we did, at their wedding. "I think I'm the first person to hear it," he said proudly. "From her."

Gerda. She was a small woman, he said. But she was a rock climber, with arms on her. Scars—although she was not one to spend time in front of a mirror—made her cover them up in long sleeves. I could picture her, short, windburned, one of those sturdy, gray-headed, big-wristed women you used to see looping cord or portaging kayaks on the ramps of the old REI, with a look in her eye like Mother Jones, or like Ripley in the cargo-loader in *Aliens*. And what in that look would make a man, and not just any man but our peaceable father, savior of animals, decide in one week to marry her when he had mourned another woman for decades?

Our mother's sister Karen had met her. Ordinarily Karen would have gone into detail, but she had agreed that she would not. "I promised. Your father made me promise. You'll meet her."

"But not until the wedding." Gerda was in the Midwest settling things. "Come on, Karen. Tell."

"Let your father describe her. He wants to."

This was something new. Our father didn't describe people. Persuaded to speak of our mother, even long after her death, he had never put so many sentences together. "In that situation, most people would be lucky to get an ax blade through the guard hairs in the coat. Thick as rope, at the neck." He was eager to confirm these things. "I mean man or woman. Just wouldn't hit true, nine times out of ten. This girl cut clear down through the strap muscles, just short of the carotid."

For the bear was tracked and shot, examined and photographed. The old embedded slug, missing toes, abscessed teeth, ax wounds—these reached the Seattle papers.

It was three years afterward that Gerda Hagen and our father met, saw each other every day for a week, and decided to get married. To the best of my knowledge our father had gone out with two women in the twenty-three years since our mother died. "I tried," Karen always said. "I had friends waiting in line. Kathleen made me promise her." Karen smiled across the table at Shelley because it was Shelley who remembered the personality of our mother, the powers of tolerance she had displayed, for almost everything that had come to pass.

And Gerda—Gerda had never gone out with anyone but Bob, the boy she married at eighteen. "It's true," Karen said. We were in a restaurant, talking over the situation. "So these two, somehow . . ." Karen had her wallet photos out, flipped to the picture of her sister. "Two virgins," she said to the face.

• • •

ALL THROUGH GRADE school, we got off the bus at Karen's house. We called her Karen, though our uncle was Uncle Cal. Karen didn't like the word *aunt* because she didn't think it expressed her relationship with us. "I know you're not my daughters," she said. "I know that. But I have my feelings and I don't like the word *aunt* and for that matter I don't like *niece*. *Niece*. It's the sound. *Penis*. There's another one, same sound. That *niceness*. *Phallus* is a different thing."

"Stop right there," said Uncle Cal.

"Well, *geese* and *piece*. And *p-e-a-c-e*," said Shelley, who was the smart one. It was said in the family that she had read the newspaper at three. Our mother had taught her. In the second grade she was reading our father's home copy of *The Anatomy of the Cat*.

Karen worked half days; at home she took care of her sons and of us, and fought the nuclear industry. She talked on the phone as she stuffed envelopes and assembled casseroles and cleaned as far as the telephone cord would go. Or Shelley would set up the board and beat her at Scrabble while she talked. It was the height of the antinuclear movement. Nuclear fuel rods stood in a hot pool just across the Sound from us; a couple of states away, underground silos hid Minuteman missiles in the wheat fields. In our minds Karen had some kind of official standing that required her to call people up and warn them. Or her next-door neighbor Lois would come over and the two of them would take turns calling people who already knew the danger, to strategize. With Lois there the talk usually worked its way around from missiles to alarming or disgraceful stories in the newspaper: freeway crashes killing whole families, and cuts in food stamps, and kids found chained in basements.

It was Lois who introduced our father to Gerda. Lois had known Gerda and her husband Bob for years and years; she had known them when they were holding hands in the corridors of Garfield High School. It was no surprise to hear that at the time of the bear attack, Lois had spent hours in our aunt's kitchen going over the details. When Gerda came back into town, Lois invited Karen over to meet her. Inside of an hour Karen had it arranged that Lois and Gerda would come over for dinner and so of course would our father. Just a casserole, Karen said. And really nothing would please Cal more than seeing his brother-in-law John and his neighbor Lois that very night. And Lois's friend of course. Gerda.

"Now don't you girls step on a spider," Lois told us more than once in the early days, waving her cigarette at Karen's frog poster. "Not in this house." The frog presided over the kitchen, crouched in a spiral of print that read SENTIENT BEINGS ARE NUMBERLESS; I VOW TO SAVE THEM. I remember Karen explaining *sentient* to Shelley. It meant that a frog took an interest in its kind. It meant spiders had fears. Hiding, waiting for food to draw near, driven by thirst down porcelain inclines, they feared us. The last thing they wanted, before their intense lives of waiting shriveled to gray lint in the basement, was to run into one of us. To this day I don't think Shelley and I see a spider without wondering whether it has had enough to eat and drink. And the poster didn't sound like a rule but it was one, a Buddhist rule. Karen explained Buddhism. I tried to listen the way Shelley did, but Karen's explanations took time and you were supposed to ask questions. Questions did not come to me the way they did to Shelley. What about bacteria? Sentient or not? What about the ones you cremated along with a person? Our mother had been sick, there must have been a lot of bacteria. No, bacteria were not at fault in our mother's case.

The cremation occupied Shelley's mind for a long time. She

wanted to see where they cremated the dogs and cats at the clinic, but our father wouldn't take her. She took the encyclopedia to her room and made her own study of the subject of fire on flesh. Because what if the person being cremated was sentient? How did anyone know what went on when you were dead?

"She set fire to herself!" Karen told Lois on the phone. "I did not," Shelley said. "I didn't catch on fire, did I, Jenny?" But she had not let me in the room when she rolled up her sleeve, struck a match and held it to the skin of her elbow long enough to raise a blister that opened and reopened in the ensuing weeks, being on a moving joint.

After that she went to see a therapist, an old woman from Karen's meetings and marches. In the therapist's bathroom, where Shelley once went to throw up, there was a cartoon of a naked woman on horseback. The woman carried a flag with a broken bomb on it. Shelley told me about it. Hearing us, Karen explained that the woman on the horse was Lady Godiva, who, being in fact an early activist, had ridden naked through a town in order to make her husband lift a tax on his people. "How come?" Shelley said. "Why would that make him?"

For once Karen had no explanation. Shelley got the encyclopedia and reported that it was a legend. "Shelley honey, lighten up," said Lois. "Somebody did something like that or there wouldn't be a legend."

When Lois was told a bad enough story from the newspaper, she crossed herself. I noticed that; I liked to see the little shake of the torso she gave once she had brushed off some threat. Nobody in our family had a religion except Karen, with her one rule, but we were allowed to have one if we wanted to, and I prayed to everything, from the stars to the giant statue of a dairy cow on the trip to Carnation Farms. I prayed to our fish circling the bowl with its gracious trailing fin, and occasionally to the point of light on the old TV when you turned it off. On camping trips I prayed to the tent flap, arched like a church window when the flashlight shone on it from outside. I prayed to all possible candidates for messenger to or from our mother. For what did I pray? A prayer was not so much a specific petition as a mental drone, unsought and surprising in its arrival, a fit of abjection with a luxury to it, a drama attaching to oneself, however invisible it might be to others. *Tell her to come back. Just once to see Shelley.*

ANY NUMBER OF women at home with their kids answered the phone in the dark afternoons of Seattle. So a lot of us heard the things talked about in Karen's kitchen in the '80s, and I wonder how many think about them the way Shelley and I do when we see kids get off a school bus in the rain. In our minds nuclear war existed in a kind of Magic 8-Ball, coming to the surface along with the numberless sentient beings, the ozone hole, Scrabble words scattered by the phone cord. Stevie Wonder on the stereo singing "Higher Ground," or, when Shelley started piano lessons, Glenn Gould playing and humming an infinity of ascending and descending notes that never quite turned into a song but made Shelley roll her head and goggle her eyes and sing them in a way we agreed was the right match.

She was seven. I was four. I wished to become Shelley, reading words and music, knowing how to find out what people meant, when to argue, when to be unafraid, when to grow cold and far-away. But without tears: Shelley wouldn't cry the way I did, even when she hurt herself. She remembered everything, as I did not. I did not connect a repeating vague bleakness in certain rooms and at bedtime with any condition of my own. I thought I would always have to look for a sign and ask, *Are we sad?*

Rain streaked the windows; our father, stooped and silent,

was somewhere sewing up a dog; our mother's body had gone up in flames; warheads could melt the flesh off your bones—yet Karen laughed, she cooked, she followed her rule. Why? Why protect the spider?

What about the things the spider had to trap and eat alive or it would starve?

"Hoo, you got her there!" Lois crowed.

"Shelley, we can't save everything we want to."

At the end of the day when our father came to pick us up, Karen would open the oven to let out the smell of her casserole so he would stay for dinner. "Oh, John, just let the girls finish their game," she would plead. Or, "Shelley's almost finished her homework. And Jenny's so cozy. She's under the table in the fort. Shh, I think she's asleep."

I liked to think our mother would have been the same way, had Karen been the one who died.

Uncle Cal liked to tell people he had spent years in a commune with four hungry guys and two sisters with feathers in their hair, who painted their toenails and played the guitar and knew how to cook. "Those two," he said. "They would make enough food for ten people and you better go out and find ten or it hurt their feelings. So they could feed 'em *to-fu*."

Karen said Cal was the reason for the women's movement. She said the place was not a commune but just a big student house with rooms rented out and a shared kitchen.

They each had a day to cook the meals, but our mother Kathleen had been the best, Karen and Uncle Cal agreed. She was the youngest, but she could put a big meal together in twenty minutes and every so often she broke loose and cooked *meat*. They argued about who in the house had eaten it openly and who in secret.

I could picture somebody at a skillet, spatula in hand. Meat sizzling. Her feet were bare, her back was to me, the blond hair hanging down. *What did she look like?* Pictures of her had turned into something lined up on the bookcase with the goldfish bowl and the cat anatomy book. In the big, framed one, our father's favorite, she stood in the snow on her cross-country skis, waving a gloved hand. But the hair was pushed up under a wool hat and a blot of glare took out the eyes behind the glasses.

Once when I was lying in the upstairs hall dangling my Slinky through the banisters, into my ear on the floorboards came her voice calling up the stairs: "John?" When I told Shelley, she said the sound was not a voice, and if a voice, not our mother's. But she got down and put her ear on the spot.

When I was four it is said that I would demand the commune story. "Talk about meat!" I saw them all laughing and I couldn't figure out why the person who had singled herself out, the best and fastest cook—why the one who had known they all wanted meat was the one who died.

Also, at that age I couldn't figure out where our father was, in the house story. I didn't have the concept of marriage getting started in a specific place and time, with separate lives leading into it, and some choice involved. At the same time, I knew there were weddings. When the obligation was laid on the bride and groom I wasn't sure.

Even today I find myself thinking something of the sort, about Karen and Cal and others. People their age. Nobody our age. Maybe this is what everybody feels about the previous generation, and it isn't that something has changed.

Straight out of the commune they had their kids, so that by the time Shelley and I were in the house, our cousins were in high school. No one would have expected Dylan and Ricky to sit down at the kitchen table in the afternoon and talk about bombs and kidnappings and hikers lost in whiteouts. And at home, although he would hear us out on the news of ill-treated dogs who partially ate the baby when some infernal relative left them alone with it, our father gave no sign that these things held even enough interest to make somebody want to dispute them.

In time Shelley too no longer sat and listened. "Oh, dear, I've done it again," Karen would say when Shelley backed away from the table. I could tell she worried about Shelley, whose report card said that while she read at a tenth-grade level in the second grade, she took no part in the majority of activities and picked her hangnails until they bled. We knew some of this to be true, but Karen said, "This makes me mad." She called the teacher. "I'm her *aunt*," Karen said, making a face at the word for our benefit. She held the phone away from her ear so we could hear the pitch of the teacher's high explaining voice. "Well, I wondered," Karen answered her. "I wondered if you were familiar with that."

The day came when we both had an interest to take us out of reach of the phone cord. Our cousins gave us their old Donkey Kong, one of the early versions that froze on the screen and had to be shaken and blown on until you spat, which Shelley played so much she could see the little geometric gorilla running up ladders in her sleep.

"In a dream," she told me, "you play a whole lot better. I can get him to do stuff. I can get him up a ladder"—her eyes narrowed over the control pad—"that *keeps going*." Her mouth stayed open with the lips bound over the teeth, which was a sign that she wouldn't stop when it was time to feed the dogs—that was our job after school, because although he lived mostly at Karen's now, one of them, Ben, was our dog—and she wouldn't stop to read me *Wonder Woman* in the fort under the table, where we would have spent every afternoon if the choice had been mine. There I had sworn that once, at the edge of the blanket that hid us as she read, two bare feet had come to stand, with toenails the color in the bottle of polish that still sat on a mirror tray in our bathroom at home.

"They did not."

"They did so. I saw."

Then I felt bad, because while I had not made up the voice in the floorboards, I had made up the feet, and into Shelley's eyes as she tried to force some proof of the vision came the blank look I hated. The day was over. Now she wouldn't do anything except advance through the levels of Donkey Kong until our father came from the clinic to take us home, where she could go to sleep and follow the ladder up to wherever it went.

"He's not supposed to get away," I reminded her. By this time I too was in school, finally I knew something. "Mario's supposed to catch him." There was a hammer in the game that I could hardly ever pick up, though Shelley could, every time. Mario was supposed to use it to save the girl from Donkey Kong.

"This ladder just keeps on going," Shelley said. "I'm going to see."

Even awake she was good enough that our cousins, coming and going with their quick feints as if to sock us, their grins, their loud soccer cleats, would stop to watch her play. Up the ladder the gorilla went, clasping the girl. When they were watching, Shelley played so fast that our dog Ben would look up and whine, and I would have to get up off the rug and hook her sweaty hair behind her ears.

SHELLEY GAVE UP the advantage of having learned to read at three, and quit high school. For a while she groomed trails in a couple of state parks and then she got a job with the Highway Department, driving a survey van. Then suddenly she was so thin she had to hold up her jeans with a belt, and talkative, always scratching her head and revising some plan. On weekends she helped out at our father's clinic. She was good with the dogs in particular, but she had developed a theory that people should not own them. An animal should not have to live indoors with people, doing their will. Where should it go? my father asked gently, the way he talked to owners when they were distraught. She didn't know where it should go. Because the wild dog had been changed by us, so that it was no longer safe without us. "You're putting too much energy into this, honey," said Karen, who had taught us to think about these very things. She tried to hold Shelley's hands to keep her from scratching her head, where you could see scabs in the part.

Then Shelley was going to learn to play the drums. She drove all the way to Portland to buy a set of drums you could get anywhere, and soon after that she fell prey to something.

We got a call from her survey team. The guy on the phone said they were in an emergency room in the suburbs and Shelley was with a nurse, describing for the third time the scrambling legs and thumping tail of a dog they had found run over beside the road. It was not as if this was the first dog they had come upon on the state highways. In the background I could hear Shelley's voice raised over another, quieter voice. "It wouldn't be a bad idea for you to get over here," her co-worker said.

After that she gave up talking and spent six months curled up in a facility where I went with my father and Karen to see her whenever they would let us.

A label might have contained what was wrong with her within two borders, and made it clear that others had had the same thing happen, but nobody provided one. As it was, the thing wrong seemed unlimited, and hers alone. A private effort, a tiring, unnecessary pioneering, fiendish in a quiet way, like hiding while people searched for you, or going to bed to dream about a ladder.

And then, as the doctors had said she would, she got better. She woke up, left the low, quiet building, went for her GED, and applied to college because she had to do that before she could go to vet school. And she did learn to play the drums, and played in a serious band made up of surveyors, the ones who had taken her to the emergency room.

Once she was out, she got back the energy she had had for doing a thing without stopping. Only now she was practical; she was going to get her hands on the severed paws and the crushed spines.

I was more like my mother—or like the woman Karen told me had been my mother, who although she had wanted, with Karen, to consider the worst that can happen, had never for a minute wanted to be on intimate terms with it. "You girls are both like her, in your ways," Karen said. "She felt things. She was not at peace. But who says we're supposed to be, in this life?"

If we were not, still Karen liked to go over the past at enough length that it lost the force of secrets and misery and diffused itself in words, like the words that spiraled protectively around the frog. "Your father was an awful mess. I didn't know what he might do. A poor old guy had just been in the paper, driving off the floating bridge into the lake. You don't remember."

I was always saying I didn't. I said those days were a blank, but I did have a couple of memories. One was of Shelley at the bathroom keyhole. "Go away," she said in a harsh whisper.

"I can look too."

"He's in there. Go play."

"I don't have to."

"He's crying."

He must have heard us and backed up against the wall by the toilet because when she let me look I couldn't see him. Finally he came out, rubbing his face with a towel as if he had been in there washing.

FOR OUR FATHER'S wedding, Shelley and her partner Diana flew in from Chicago two days ahead of time. They stayed with me in the apartment I had shared with my boyfriend Eddie before he moved out. My ex-boyfriend. When she got up the first morning Diana sat down at his piano in her silk pajamas and began to play, with a few wrong notes but a flowing style. After a bit you could tell it was "Stairway to Heaven" she was playing. When I laughed, Shelley said, "She taught herself."

"No, no, I was just thinking of that sign in the guitar store, NO "STAIRWAY TO HEAVEN." And backwards, remember Ricky told us, it was satanic? And we didn't know who Satan was?"

"Yeah . . . she just now got the sheet music," Shelley said, scanning the few CDs Eddie had left on the shelves.

Shelley was driving us over the pass because we had Eddie's car and it was a stick shift. I didn't like to drive it in the mountains. The wedding was taking place at a bed-and-breakfast in the Cascades, on the east side. The car was a hatchback with room for three of us, luggage, flowers, presents, a cooler of champagne and the cake. "I'd trust Shelley with it before I'd trust you anyway," Eddie said. In our laughing days, he had laughed at the way I popped the clutch on the hills of Seattle.

Since then he had been rethinking things. My driving wasn't funny any more and maybe I myself wasn't as entertaining as I thought I was. At one time my interests had had a comic flavor, for him. He would tell our friends, "We used to get the *New York Times* but they didn't have enough obituaries."

Eddie taught music and language arts in middle school and at night he played the piano in a bar where I went with my friend Kitty from work. We were both at the paper condensing stuff off the wires into those two-inch-long items Karen used to read to people on the phone. Fillers, they were called.

If we stayed far enough into the evening, Eddie arrived, sat down, put a brandy glass on the piano for tips, and played for two hours without looking up or asking for requests, so hardly anybody put anything in the glass. He did smile to himself, once or twice in a set. The first night we saw him, I thought about him later when I was at home in bed. I thought he was a man who smiled privately, a man whose eyebrows would go up in pained transport during certain passages, like Glenn Gould's. A man with thick black eyelashes.

His hands stayed low over the keys, no flourishes. They looked lazy but the sound was crisp. Up close, when Kitty and I invited him to join us the first time, he looked more like a boy, grinning and making jokes, quoting movies. It turned out he had graduated a year after we did. Still, there on the table were the largejointed hands from the keyboard, lying at rest as the talk went on, as if what came out of his mouth were no concern of theirs. I don't know why I liked to look at them, and to hear his laughchoked voice, when he really wasn't saying anything, only repeating stories and quoting Comedy Central, or why I waited for Kitty to go to the bathroom and leave me alone with him, when what I wanted was an established grown-up, not solemn but on the melancholy side, with a few creases in his forehead, and convictions.

Eddie avoided convictions. He came from a big Catholic family, with priests in it. I said he should be proud, the Catholic bishops had come out against the war. Furthermore he should be glad he was raised with a religion to comfort him. He laughed at that, but every so often he would sneak off early on a Sunday morning to go to Mass. He didn't offer to take me with him. "You'd give me a hard time," he said.

That summer I had been to his brother's wedding, a big Catholic affair with Eddie playing the organ at Mass and making funny toasts at the reception. The brothers took turns dancing with their mother. When she walked out onto the floor on Eddie's arm, taking small steps in her long girdle, I thought, *He is a kind of prince.* That was my last good thought about him for a while, because we had a lot more of the Signature Cocktail and then a fight on the way home, as I'm sure a lot of people do, shut in cars after the odd brevity and letdown of the ceremony and then all the waiting in line and the tense, antique presenting of this person to that one, and the pouring and toasting and clapping, and the mothers with eyes red and smudged because, they said, they were so happy.

Two people agree to lock themselves in together, in defiance of reason and the Dissolutions column, and we celebrate it every time. I said something to that effect. Eddie said his brother's new wife, far from being stupefied, as I had suggested, by the ornate event she herself had planned in every detail, was simply a girl who knew how to be happy. "Is that right?" I said. "How?" He thought it was just another question like the ones I had asked about the Mass. Why did we clap after they kissed? Did people always clap in church? In movies I had never seen such a thing. Why didn't we kneel? Weren't you supposed to kneel, in the Catholic Church? Where were the statues and the candles? Why was marriage a sacrament?

The second phase began when the narrow space of my apartment—a place I had chosen for the tight shelter of its room-and-a-half—had made room for his piano and skis and kayak.

If I woke up at night I would see his two bikes, the front wheel of the city one facing its horns in on us from the balcony like a rained-on, aggrieved animal, and he, awake or asleep, would have moved onto my side of the bed, against my back. In the hot room his body steamed under the layers of covers he had to have.

Then he started taking my glasses off to look at me. I couldn't see him. He said, "I'm sorry, it's your eyes when you take off your glasses."

"Maybe I should get contacts."

"No, no, it's what I like. I like that sweet, bleary look."

"Shall I take off my shoes and get pregnant?" That's what I said, instead of saying I liked his eyes too, the black eyelashes that cast an openwork shadow when he played the piano or read under a lamp. I don't know why I did that. I don't know why I said one thing rather than the other, and kept trying to break something down in him, some resolute optimism, which had soothed me in the early weeks.

"OK, I won't do that any more."

"I can't see shit without my glasses."

"Are you trying to see shit?" Then to be nicer or to get away from the table he moved over to the piano and played a few bars of something.

"What's that?"

"Hovhaness. It's called 'Beloved, You Looked into Space.'"

That *beloved* did it for a few days. Then he said something. He said despair was learned. Look at Shelley's problems—surely they had something to do with seeing John, our father, deal with things in the way he had, with his protracted mourning.

"Oh, for God's sake," I said. "*Protracted.* Quit talking to Karen."

If, Eddie said, he had had some struggles himself, he didn't intend to bring anybody down about them. What he wanted at this point was to ride his mountain bike or go hiking on week-ends—by himself if I chose not to enjoy such things—and yes, maintain a good mood. Play music. Get married when the time came. Sure. Have children.

Children. Did he have any idea what that meant? *Children.* How *every minute of life*, children were in your power and you in theirs? How if you were no good at it, how if you disappeared—

"Let's say I wouldn't."

"Wouldn't what?"

"Disappear. Say I luck out and get a full lifespan."

"There's no point. There's no point in arguing this."

"I'm not arguing, Jenny. Anybody see any kids here for me to run out on?" Finally he grinned, not so much at me as out the window at his bikes. He shook his head and said, "I've had some tough roommates, but we always worked it out, we always—"

"Go find them," I said. "Have a beer." His expression didn't change but he kept looking out the window. I said I was sorry, because his face, if I looked at it and forgot what he was saying, had that effect on me. I was sorry and I wasn't. I could see that we had fallen into a routine combat but I wasn't sure which one of us I wanted to win.

When we finally decided he would move out, he came back every week to practice. It was too expensive to move the piano a second time. He came at the end of the school day, when I was still at work, but I could tell when he had been there because the radiators would be hissing. I could turn them down, I could turn them off if I wanted to. No more deadweight comforter on the bed, steamed windows, jokes from movies, trips to look at bigger places because our two incomes made one decent one and a piano could have its own room. No more schoolboy analysis of Shelley and me.

All this was in the second phase. It was in the first phase, right after he had moved in, that I was in Chicago to share with Shelley my good spirits, my change of fortune, my repudiation of doubt, and to meet Diana.

They had just bought a condo. If I had had to guess, I would have said Diana would be messy, but the place was spare and chastely neat. With the mirrors, the tall windows, the trees in pots, it had a sneaky luxury, somewhere between a good hotel and a chapel. It had an air of being held in readiness for something other than just sitting around. Some visit not mine, some visitation. I thought of what Eddie would say about it. He would like it. He had not been raised by Karen; he saw nothing wrong with luxury. "Hey, a vet and a lawyer," he would say. "Why not?"

Right up to the day her law school loans came through, Diana had been poor. That's why she had Norfolk pines in the bay windows and hushed lithographs of winter branches on the walls: in the part of town she came from all they had was tree of heaven, which grew in empty lots and stank. Every year, the school nurse sent notes home saying Diana came to school in shoes that were too small. Karen knew about the trees and the shoes from Shelley. Karen could always get things out of you. Karen said if they opened Diana's closet when they were showing me the place, I should not comment on the shoe racks.

I ran my hands over the slate coffee table and appreciated the view of Lincoln Park, the art, and Diana's law books high up, reachable by teak ladders on wheels. Diana climbed up one to show how convenient it was. I looked over at Shelley. She hadn't changed, she didn't notice where she was. She had given me a tour of the clinic where she worked, a cat clinic not far from their new place. She took a scrawny young cat with twitching ears out of its cage and the whole time we were walking around she carried it, confined in a towel because it was demented. A cat could be demented. It had been weaned too soon and had to be held in a firm grip and given something to suck. We had never had cats at home. What about the dogs by the side of the road?

"Good beer," I said when Diana handed me a bottle. "Ale," she said, and winked at me. "*Blond.*" I looked at the label. She took a long swig from hers. Her hair was the shiny flat blond of a Scrabble tile, though it wasn't clear whether that was a natural color because her groomed eyebrows were dark.

"Hey, don't flirt with Jenny," Shelley said.

Since then Shelley had been home a couple of times, but I hadn't seen Diana again until they came for the wedding. Whenever there was a lull in the talk, she would go over and feel out three or four chords, standing up, in her listening-for-the-muse style—I tried to think of what Eddie would have called it. "We have to get a piano, it's time," she kept saying to Shelley as we sat around.

I was on my guard, but she got the story of our childhood out of me. Shelley said, "You already know all that."

"I just want to get the whole picture. You'd be a good witness, Jenny."

"You mean I'm easily led."

"I mean you answer. Not like Shelley."

"Shelley has dignity," I said. "So—now it's your turn."

But Diana was finished with our talk. She went out and stood on the balcony, where there were no bikes now, and came back stretching and yawning. "God, I just want to go back to bed. I do. I have to. There's no *sun* here. Isn't it supposed to be summer?"

They had my room; Shelley's eyes followed her as she closed the door. Into Shelley's face of stubborn reserve came a flush, a humble, all but witless half smile. She said, "She needs more sleep than some people." What was this? This was love? Was this what came about? This stupid, helpless smile?

We left early the next morning. Diana fell back to sleep as soon as we hit the freeway. She slept until the North Cascades Highway began its climb, when her eyes opened and she sat up and said, "OK, who *is* this woman? Jesus. She killed a bear."

"She didn't kill it," Shelley said. "Fish and Wildlife killed it."

"She tried to. She didn't do what he told her to. He told her to run. I mean, how do you know what you would do?" No one answered her. "So OK then, what would *you* do?"

"No idea," Shelley said. "What about you?"

"Well, I don't know! But Jesus, I don't think so. I mean I identify but I . . . no."

"I heard you were a girl of action," Shelley said.

"Yeah." Diana leaned around to me. "What about you, back there? You look wiped out." She rattled her nails with their arched moons against the compartment with Eddie's CDs. "It's that guy, isn't it. Poor thing." She made a pout of sympathy.

"Him or me?"

"You. What about you, would you do that for him?"

"Nope," I said.

"One person in a thousand would," Shelley said. "Maybe would have the presence of mind. Maybe. See out there? They call these the Alps of America."

Diana didn't look to either side: at a plunge into treetops on one and bare rock cut by a narrow waterfall on the other. After a bit she laughed and shook her finger at Shelley. "You would." She faced around again to me. "She would, wouldn't she. Your sister."

Shelley said, "No way."

"You would. You'd do it for me."

"Sure wish I could say that was true," Shelley said. "Think I'd be under the bed." We both laughed, but not Diana.

"Oh, oh, don't you think she would?" Diana went on in a kind of stern baby talk. "Don't you think so?"

"I just can't really say."

"Come on, you're her sister. You know how she is."

"She's pretty brave."

"She's that kind," said Diana, turning back to Shelley with satisfaction. "Yes you are." She put her feet in their glowing leather boots up on the dashboard. She was going to be too hot in those, on the east side of the mountains.

"You could bust a femur like that," said Shelley. "I took care of the dog from an airbag wreck."

"So it happened to a dog."

"It happened to a kid. The dog was in the back."

"You're always saying what can happen," said Diana. "Anything can happen. Let's just get that out of the way."

Shelley didn't answer and after a while Diana took her feet down and went back to sleep. I thought of putting on *Fred the Cat*. It was one of Eddie's favorite car CDs, another one by his favorite old guy Hovhaness. The dead cat goes up a mountain to heaven. Hovhaness was a celebrator of mountains. Eddie's plan for his own funeral was for somebody to play "Fred the Cat Flies to Heaven." I was in a mood to tell Shelley this and play the CD for her, but while Diana was asleep she drove in silence, over the two passes and down the other side, speeding a little on the curve of the Liberty Bell cirque, where the mountains, with their avalanche chutes and crusts of snow, swing back to show the dusty greens and the cream and tan stone and floating hawks of the valley.

• • •

WHEN HE WAS introduced to Gerda, who had come back to Seattle to pack up the house she had locked three years before, our father was already familiar with the story. Soon after it happened he had heard it from Karen, who had had all those talks with our neighbor Lois. Later, news of it came from wild animal vets in touch with wildlife people who had made a brief plea for the bear to be removed to a farther range. But hurt a second time, the animal was a worse threat than before, and local feeling said it had to be shot.

No reprieve for stopping in mid-attack. People had their theories as to why an animal not mortally wounded, not even gushing blood, leaving only a spray of drops on the river rock, would have quit like that. It was weak from hibernation. It didn't have the use of one arm. Bad teeth. Pain. Fate.

Yet it was not uncommon for that to happen, an animal to obey some impulse of its own, native to it, our father said, with his new willingness to expand on a subject. The same way no two people will do exactly the same thing. No, he had never treated a bear but he had done a lot of reading since meeting Gerda. Often a bear just took off, ran for cover. A bear had been a cub. A bear had racked up experiences. About bears he wouldn't use the words *good* and *bad*. He explained this to me in the no-such-thing way he had explained *satanic* when we were little. No devil. No hell.

Then . . . no heaven?

No. No, probably not.

All this about the bear was between the two of us. I knew he would never say any of it to Gerda. He was willing to admit that she had in fact met the wrong bear, the one most mercilessly wrong. Although if you started to think about it, it might have been the hour of the day putting them all at the river that was wrong, or the hour of another day the fall before, when a hunter had shot the bear in the shoulder and when it rose on its hind legs blown off half its paw, or the hour when the sun warmed and woke the bear in its den. If it had a den. Dad said they didn't always have one. But: time. Time being the villain. Some aspect of time. Some cruel aspect.

"What does that get you?" Eddie would say.

Wait. If everything—and not only living things—carried inside it its particle of time. And if no two particles were in concurrence or accord. They could be, but they didn't have to be. They might be in some violent magnetic opposition. Two of these bits of time might be like nuclear fuel rods, not meant to touch. Needing cooling water between them. But no one, ever, knowing this.

"Then . . . ?" Eddie would say. Every *if* had to have its *then*.

The three-inch claws had mauled Gerda in one stroke, but with her the sinking in of incisors never got started, the grinding done with the molars, according to our father, that turns of itself into something unstoppable. Or seemingly unstoppable. For the bear dropped its head, wagged it, flung off blood, leaned onto one forepaw and then the other, and then, instead of launching itself at Gerda, wheeled around and shuffled away.

Bob was close to death. The husband. He had a little more than an hour left to live.

"He was ready to go," our father said, with the care his voice had when he said it about a dog. "He was that bad hurt."

THE PINES HAD a fire pit, encircled by a little Stonehenge of log benches and stumps. We were welcome to sit in the circle if we wanted to but not to cook in the pit, or on the old iron charcoal grill next to it, because there was a burn ban. Nearby were two picnic tables; the Burneys would bring out the food.

The wedding was a package. The Burneys, who owned The Pines and specialized in weddings, were providing the meals.

We were responsible for the cake. It was one of those rum-filled, heavy, dozen-egg cakes that need an industrial mixer, but not having one I had drunk the rest of the rum and beaten the batter by hand until my arm cramped and I had a relapse and called Eddie, and hung up on his voicemail. He had left the car for me without coming up; I could see it parked a little way down the street. He must have been on his way somewhere himself, to drop if off early like this, confident that I still had my key. Where was he going, not saying a word? Not even flipping a pebble at the window behind which we had been lying mere weeks before with our naked legs entwined.

The next day, the day Shelley and Diana were arriving, my friend Kitty came over with a pastry bag to help me. "Whoa, this thing is *preserved*," she said, sniffing the cake and hoisting the weight of it on the foil-covered board. When it was thickly iced she splashed red food coloring into what was left and stuffed the bag full and fluted a messy border of roses. She licked her fingers and studied her work. "She won't mind. This is a woman who killed a bear."

"She didn't kill it." Because that was part of it, wasn't it? The giant exertion, the muscles afire with effort. A divided effort, to murder and save. The ax thrown down. And then life going on. People in the room with you talking. People offering you a ghostly respect.

I had to admit that I was afraid to meet Gerda, afraid she might be crazy. "I don't think so," Kitty said. "Think of who we're talking about. Who would your father fall for? It would have to be someone special." But I was afraid our father might have said to himself, *Now or never.* He might not have seen, in the time they had spent together, that the word *survivor*, by which we mean one who has more or less made a comeback, might not describe the woman who had lived through this event. *Special, survivor*: more of those words. She could be crazy. Even a normal death could affect your mind indefinitely.

Mrs. Burney had a thin face and slender, careful hands, one of them walking its fingers up the banister beside her as she led the way. Each of her statements had two parts, which she uttered as one, to soften the fact that they were warnings. "This is the bath, watch the hot tap in all the baths." We had already seen my room. Since I was alone I didn't have a cabin, but a room downstairs in the main house just big enough to hold the four-poster heaped with pillows. Mrs. Burney apologized because the dresser was in the closet. I said, "No, this is just right."

Diana winked at me and said to Mrs. Burney, "She lived under the table as a kid."

Mrs. Burney let us look into the bridal suite, where a pink dress hung in a plastic bag. Our father and Gerda had arrived the day before; they were off on a little hike, said Mrs. Burney with an affirming smile. "You people," Diana said to Shelley. I hate hiking but I almost wanted to defend the practice. Work, or aimless play—did not the hike put both to shame? No getting around the fact that the genie of it had touched to life a holy order all over the trails of our state, all over the Northwest. Shelley was in the order. Our father was, on a rare Saturday when he didn't work. Eddie was, I was not. Still, I didn't feel I was in Diana's category.

They had already rehearsed the ceremony, Mrs. Burney said. "Or rather, they went over the vows," she said, glancing at us to see if we were anticeremony. She and her husband were Presbyterians, she said, but she had been ordained a minister of the Universal Life Church. "Oh, you have to be. We came out here in the Sixties and that's what people wanted, and now they want it again." As she closed the door to their room with her soft alertness I wondered what had happened in between. At any rate you could tell that she was used to people occupying the honeymoon suite before the wedding.

Mrs. Burney watched as we lifted the cake, in its splotchy collar of roses, out of the box. "We weren't exactly pastry chefs," I said.

"It's lovely, see if we can slide it back onto the board so it won't—" She made a delicate adjustment with the heels of her hands, and quickly flashed a spatula to remodel the side where the sun had hit the icing in the car.

"My husband had a fall, watch the porch steps."

With one wrist in a splint, holding a beer in his finger and thumb, Mr. Burney sat in front of the TV in a little den off the kitchen. He kept waving to us with splint and beer as we admired Mrs. Burney's elaborate trays for the next day and the pies she had made for the weekend, and unwrapped flowers and greenery and stood them in her vases.

She filled the vases with water and turned politely to her husband, who had received some signal to switch off the TV and join us. He was not a fat man but he had on a too-small polo shirt and he wore his belt low, under the belly. He had a gray, Sixties ponytail and a mustache that dangled at the corners of the theatrical smile he had assumed as he was tilting himself out of the recliner. "Why don't you show them where the tables, oh, careful—" She steadied the vases as he braced himself against the counter.

"Pardon," he said, tipping an imaginary hat.

An afternoon wind had kicked up. Mr. Burney, breathing hard in the heat, sat on a log bench answering Diana's questions about forest fires. You could see how she would go about taking a deposition. Burney was giving up all he knew: lightning strikes, fires that ran underground along tree roots and exploded upward, fires that chased herds and leapt rivers.

"Anything can happen," Shelley said.

"You got it." Mr. Burney threw his arms out, sloshing beer at the trees. As a fire precaution they had been limbed thirty feet up; all around us they stood like huge table legs. Put a wind like this with fire, he said, and sayonara to inn and cabins, not to mention thousands of acres of the national forest that surrounded us where we sat.

The wind, loud in the branches, was bashing the wooden seat of a long-roped swing against the tree trunk. "That'll let up," Mr. Burney said, as it whipped our jeans and swept ashes onto the stone lip of the fire pit. You could see the big trunks of the ponderosas rocking. "That'll let up, no problem," he repeated, as if we might want our money back. "Don't you worry, we'll have that ash out of there. Can't have any smudges on the bridesmaids."

"It's OK, we forgot to bring bridesmaids," said Diana. She went back to her questions and while she ticked them off, swinging her crossed leg and stroking the air with her long fingers, Shelley watched for minutes, chewing on a piece of grass, like somebody using binoculars on an animal as it roamed. Mr. Burney had spent himself. Every so often the hand holding the bottle would tip as if he had gone to sleep, and Diana would have to repeat her question. Finally she said, "So I mean, if all this stuff has to be done, limbing and burn-banning and smoke jumpers and all the rest of it so we'll be safe, why are we out here?"

Shelley said, "Maybe we should leave this Earth."

Mr. Burney pulled one of his gray eyebrows down. "Dear lady," he said to Diana, "this was her parents' place. But," he added, "the kids went for it in a big way, in those days. Get 'em up in the tree house and you wouldn't see 'em for days."

"Tree house?" said Diana.

"Look there. Left of the end cabin. Look up. High." And there it was, a neat structure with a slanted roof, on a platform.

"Holy shit," Diana said. "That's high."

Shelley said, "How about when the tree sways?"

"You hold on. Sure. But we got cables up there, we got shocks. Auto shocks. The problem was snow. First one, the roof fell in. So we made it a lean-to. My son came up with that."

"How did you get it up there? Can people go up?"

"Can if they get a ladder truck in here."

"How did you get up and down?"

"Had us a rope ladder. She said it had to come down. A guest'll get on a ladder every time. We had a groom go up there and call for help. No way would he do what he was told. We had to have our boy go up. The little fella. Coulda walked a sheep through a wolf pack. Went up after the guy and brought him down."

"No kidding. I bet Shelley could get up there. She does that stuff. Don't deny it, you do. Well, I guess I'll have to settle for the swing. Now, save my place." She patted the log by Mr. Burney. "Bet you climbed up and hung the swing too, didn't you."

"That'll swing a mile. Many's a kid jumped out and banged himself up, till she"—he waved his splint at the house—"tells me I have to take that down too. But I never did it."

Then for a few minutes we just sat there in the noise of the wind. "Shelley was just reading me about that sound," Diana called from the swing. "There's a tree book in the cabin."

"Her dad was your serious bookworm," said Mr. Burney. "Like her."

The loudness of the wind, as if a bellowing crowd were massing out of sight, was giving me a feeling that was part exhilaration and part the wish to go indoors. This would be the sound that Eddie talked about, of casual threat. Eddie kept track of sounds. He said an eagle sounded like a mouse, not a kingly bird. A bear foraging sounded like a larger, more appalling pig. As for wind, he saw himself as some sort of apostle of it, though not someone who would let it intimidate him. The birds could vanish, the deer bed down, Eddie would stay out in the wind for the joy of it. I argued with him. I know I was always arguing. Let it have its own joy. Who was he to stand up to wind?

Outdoor people. My theory was—here he would back away with his hands up—no, really, they weren't really outdoors, these hikers and climbers, these mountain bikers with their gripper tires. They made it all a kind of indoors. They went into the elements as if there were a two-way friendship out there. Even Shelley forgot her suspicions and talked about birdcalls and the moon. When what was out there was wind, with its purpose that could not be gauged. Wildfire. No friendship. A bear was out there.

Without our noticing, it had gone completely quiet. Mr. Burney reversed course on the dangers of the place. "Here comes Bob now. I told him, we got the tents, you come out here with the little guys, put 'em in a sleeping bag and see if they don't have a time. We used to be out here with our guys. We had three."

I should have asked where the three were now but I was still thinking, *Bob?* Bob was the husband. The dead husband.

But he meant Bobby, Gerda's son. She had two; Bobby had flown in from the Midwest with his family and Glen from Florida with his. The men—they were boys, really—were coming down the path from the cabins without their wives. Both of them stopped at the rope swing.

In no time Glen was confiding to Diana that he had had to put this part of the country behind him. It was ruined for him, the Northwest. Was it, Diana wanted to know, maybe a little creepy to be back? It was, and he wasn't sure why his mother had picked this particular bed-and-breakfast, when she had never been here either. It was nowhere near the other place but it was *out here*.

"Hey, it's a nice place," Bobby said. "We always camped on the east side. Just look around you. That's why they'd bring us over here. Look at those trees."

"Incredible trees," said Diana, raising her eyes with their suggestion that things around her might be extensions of herself.

Bobby said, "See that thick bark." The bark on the pines had a pattern of segmented creatures swimming over each other to reach the top of the tree. "Smell it. Vanilla. There's nothing like that ponderosa smell."

"Mm, I see what you mean," said Diana. "More like caramel."

"Yeah, we hiked, we camped," Glen resumed. "We rock climbed, we orienteered. You name it. They made us go hunting, for Christ's sake. Our dad—"

"That's the dumbest thing I ever heard," said Bobby, socking his brother on the arm. "We wanted to go hunting."

"I've never camped," Diana said, pumping the swing. "My feeling about camping is that I would passionately hate it."

"Come on, I'm pretty sure you wouldn't," said Bobby. Neither brother seemed to know where to locate Diana in the family. She was swinging with her legs out in front of her. She scuffed her boot heels in the dirt and leaned back with her hair hanging. The brothers on either side, not quite arguing, did not push the swing but slapped at the rope when it passed them.

Shelley spoke up from the bench. "You wouldn't hate camping."

"I really want to crawl into a three-foot space and lie down."

"When you crawl out in the morning, it's just the world and you."

"I need more than that."

We heard loud whoops, and Bobby's two little boys came running down from the cabins, with his wife Cindy behind them, and Becca, short and stocky as a child herself, with a child's dusky tan, carrying her baby in one of those car seats with handles. "They wouldn't go down for their nap," Cindy said tiredly but without irritation. "Maybe that means they'll go to bed early." She was my age or younger, somewhere in her twenties, and Becca, as she herself had told Diana, was only twenty-two. Gerda's sons had both married young, just as she had. I wondered how Cindy summoned her weary patience. I wondered how it would feel to have assembled human beings out of your own cells. The way Becca swung the car seat it could have held the groceries. Eddie would have liked that. It wasn't as if no one had ever made the decision to have kids before. You should just do it. Get on with it, without worrying about the giant entry port you had just carved into yourself and a succession of others, for all the possible griefs.

When I looked into the car seat a blue stare leapt out like a shock from a carpet. "Well!" I said. "Who are you?"

"This is Justin," said Becca solemnly, like a child introducing a doll that you will have to pretend is real. "Justin, this is your aunt-to-be. She can hold you if she wants to, after you eat." As I bent over him the blue eyes narrowed, went out of focus, caressed me powerfully when they refocused, fixing me in some world without excuses or even reasons for what anybody might do. Shall I hold you? I asked the eyes, because it seemed the power was his, he could just as easily pull me into the car seat with him.

Diana came over and looked in. She pulled back in the same dizzy way. "Wow. How old?" she said.

"Four months," said Becca. "Exactly a year and a half ago I gave up smoking so we could have him."

"Worth it, I bet," Diana said.

"It was worth everything you have in this world," Becca said with a dead calm as if she were reading from a brochure. "Turn around," she read on. She meant Glen; he turned and she pulled a folded rubber pad out of his hip pocket, and sighing briskly, spread it on the pine needles. Glen hoisted the baby over onto the pad, knelt, and unsnapped him. A sharp sweet stench went up. After a bit Glen said, "This is cornstarch I'm powdering with," like a cook on TV. "The talcum they used on us, on our generation, was a poison. Went straight to the lung."

I had a vision of legions of us moving slowly, powdered white, poisoned. "And then they wouldn't let us have cigarettes in middle school," Becca mused, with the first sign that she could smile.

"Damn!" said Diana.

Glen said, "Becca, that is not a joke." She had her shirt open, showing a butterfly tattoo above the nursing bra, and she was reaching for the baby but Glen held him back from her for a minute before handing him over. Becca began to nurse him in silence, as if language were being pulled out of her. Glen absorbed a tabulating look from Diana, and sat down.

Suddenly I felt, on us all, the eye of the father. The dead man. Bob. What if Bob could see this scene, with his sons, his grandchildren. What were they doing here? What if he could see what was going to happen. That in the morning someone who had lived a life in which she had loved him enough to die for him was going to stand under the trees and get married. So that love— had it not been a singular thing after all? Was it, with the unthinking power it had let loose, somehow repeatable?

After a while the baby let go and started in with a noise, a tone like a distant vacuum cleaner. "He'll make that sound," Becca said, resuming her recitation. At that, Glen's jaw muscles relaxed and they gave each other that look that has to do with a baby and some secret pageant of which it is the cause and the effect. Soon the little boys were running back and forth making competing piles of the broomlets the wind had sheared off the ponderosas.

"You know, Gerda is a wonderful woman," Cindy said to me, quietly.

The older one, Robbie, stopped with his handfuls of pine needles. "Gerda is Grandma," he warned me solemnly. "She killed a bear."

"You'll see. We all love her to pieces. But you know, Jenny, I hope I can say this to you, she has had a lot happen to her. The guys too. I hope the past won't come up. I hope we won't get into that."

"I don't think we will. I'll be careful. I know what you mean." I had just met Cindy; I didn't think I could ask her if her mother-in-law was crazy.

"And so when is your Aunt Karen going to get here?" Of course while Gerda was closing up the life she had begun in Indianapolis near Bobby and Cindy, instead of the one in Seattle she had been planning to leave behind before she met our father, Karen had gotten to know Cindy. On the phone. "Yeah," Cindy said, "if she couldn't get Gerda she'd call me. One afternoon we talked for an hour. She's something, isn't she. I just love her." I could imagine Cindy's afternoon on the phone with Karen. "And I can't wait to meet your daddy. I know he's such a gentleman."

I had one of those realizations you get when somebody makes a comment in passing, that our father was, indeed, a gentleman. When an owner brought in a matted old beast on its last legs, I know my father had comfort to lend, sometimes for an hour or more, waiting for the person to be ready before giving any sign that the agreed-upon syringe of release and departure lay on a tray in the next room. "He wouldn't have wanted a life where he couldn't run." "This was a cat that couldn't have been subjected to daily needles." And so . . . did that mean he understood someone who had killed an animal? Or not killed it, but fought it with the intent to kill? And did he ask himself these questions, or did he just finally meet somebody after all these years? And who was this woman? Did they all in fact love her, as Cindy said? Or was there something about her blemished, touched with animal breath? I knew about that. Bears ate carrion, their lips slopped, baring the gum, their tongues lolled. They were not proud, lofty animals. The males would kill and eat a cub. "And I love your sister," Cindy added. "Aren't these cabins sweet?"

The cabins were knotty pine, with a sink in the bedroom and a row of faded books on the dresser. Every cabin had its books, and behind Mr. Burney's chair in the den were shelves of them, dim and formal, representing some farther-back life than the paperbacks in the parlor for the guests. A tall pump organ with fern stands on either side of it spoke of that life, into which Mr. Burney seemed to have stumbled from a later time but still not the present.

The cabins had tin showers and wall hooks instead of closets, but in the main house there were tied-back curtains and doilies under the lamps and chocolates on the pillow. "Who would have their honeymoon in a bed and breakfast?" Diana had whispered loudly on the stairs. "I mean, young couples."

As the afternoon wore on, Mr. Burney grew more unsteady on his feet. He had lugged out a cooler of beer, and flung a tablecloth over a stump for the wine bottles. Shelley helped him with a case of soda water and I went in to get the glasses, while he veered off to the swing, where Diana was pushing the little boys and listening to their fathers. Mr. Burney stood by for a while, rocking with the pines, and then he stomped over and yanked the cooler open. "Folks, what are you waiting for? Let's get started here." He made his way back to the swing, and with a formal concentration opened two bottles and presented one to Diana. Glen was explaining something to her, counting his points on his fingers, and without taking her eyes off his face she accepted the beer with a little wave. Mr. Burney raised his splint. "Hear, hear! Drink up! To matrimony!"

Then we all got off the stumps and joined in, except Becca. "She's nursing," Glen reminded Mr. Burney. "Anything she drinks, he drinks."

"Hey, look who we've got here!" cried Burney. And there they were, coming out of the woods, our father and Gerda.

I saw them swinging hands. Then she fell behind him, coming down the log steps at the trailhead. I could see a head of white hair and a hot pink shirt. We all got up off our tree stumps and cheered as they came shyly across the pine needles.

Gerda didn't have an especially forceful grip when she shook your hand. She didn't look like someone who would hunt or climb rocks or even work out. Her hair was a solid glossy white and reached her shoulders, and her wide face had pink young skin just crisscrossed with lines at the eyes, which were blue and childishly clear. I felt them touch me, though. You could see she had been through something.

"Here she is," our father said, his face stretched tight with excitement under his new crew cut. He had a smile like somebody coming deafened out of a rock concert. No one knew who should be introduced first, so with his hand on Gerda's waist he started with us.

All she said was our names, turning to him with a look of confirmation as if the bearer of the name were all she could have hoped. She took Shelley's hand a second time and repeated hers. I felt her hand tremble when she came back to me a second time. "The little one," she said. Her eyes were the blue of her baby grandson's, with some of the same drag on you.

So this was Gerda. "Can't I just hug you?" Diana said, cocking her head. Then we all hugged Gerda and each other, and the sons shook our father's hand and the daughters-in-law hugged him and the first part was over.

In the middle of it all, Karen and Uncle Cal pulled in. Karen ran down from the car calling, "Oh, look at us, late to a wedding." She and Gerda hugged, held each other at arm's length, hugged again. "Oh, this is a happy day. Tomorrow I mean. Oh, you've cut off your hair. But it looks great."

"I thought it was time," Gerda said with a laugh. "You should have seen it," she said to Diana. "I hadn't cut it in three years. I had it in one of those braids." Of course she would pick Diana, whose straight hair swung so neatly at the neck. So Gerda did talk, she laughed. Like all women, she explained a haircut.

Our father had said she was small but she was not small. She filled out the pink shirt and she was taller than I was. Her legs, wide at the thigh in stretch jeans, were almost as long as Diana's. The legs looked as if they belonged to someone who would go shopping and buy herself an expensive bathing suit. Dad could not stop smiling. "So here she is, Jenny," he said again, when I took him into the kitchen to see the cake. Was it all right for the groom to see it? Mrs. Burney thought so.

"She's wonderful," I told him. "How long was her hair before?" What kind of a question was that?

"I don't know," he said, bewildered. He really didn't know.

"Hi baby," she whispered when he came back. Very soft on the *b*'s, as if a tall man with a receding hairline really were a baby. She took his hand. It was then that I saw she was beautiful. It had escaped me until that moment.

I wondered if everybody else had known it right away. Who was seeing her for the first time? Only the three of us, Shelley and Diana and I. Two were her sons, of course, used to her—

though Glen had stood apart, seeming to sulk, and made her come away from the rest of us to take him in her arms.

It wasn't the kind of beauty that effectively discourages the ones who behold it, not the pure or absolute, perfect-jawline kind. Whatever it was, it had spurred Mr. Burney to place himself between her and the group reconfiguring itself around her, in order to make sure she took her seat on the best-sanded bench so she would not get splinters. But she got up again and with no permission from Becca gathered the baby out of the car seat into her arms.

Becca sighed. "This is when you want a cigarette. When you can relax and somebody else has him. Not just anybody," she added, to Glen.

"I don't blame you," said Gerda. The baby's gaze, so electric and yet magically sedated with un-knowledge, roved over us. He closed his eyes as she held him to her face and inhaled against him. Maybe I had wondered how long her hair had been because in fact, I now saw, she looked like a woman who could ride by naked and a cruel tax would be lifted.

"Can we maybe just try to forget cigarettes?" Glen said in a high, despairing voice.

"*She* used to smoke too," Becca said, speaking to Diana. "Gerda. We would sneak off together."

"Oh yeah?" said Diana.

"I guess I've done everything bad," said Gerda. I looked at my father. He looked back from under his eyelids, like a man lying in the pool on his back.

"Like what?" said Diana.

Gerda shook her head and leaned forward with her eyes closed to sip from the glass of wine our father was holding for her.

• • •

"IMAGINE IF THERE were a mousetrap big enough for a person," Karen said. She had found a mousetrap under the bed in their cabin. "Just imagine how you would feel if an iron bar snapped down on you!" So there must have been a mouse in it.

"Karen, you will never change," said Uncle Cal, looking around for somebody in our family who would know that he took pride in this fact. Karen was talking to the four-year-old, Robbie. We had eaten everything including a watermelon and two of Mrs. Burney's coconut custard pies, and we were lurching between the tables stuffing paper plates into trash bags. Except for the two mothers, we were all a little drunk, some more than others. Bobby, for one, had stretched himself out on the pine needles.

"But there would never be a mousetrap that big," said Cindy. She took the smaller boy by the hand.

"Uh-*huh*," said Robbie, walking backwards away from his mother as he sucked custard off his fingers.

"Uh-*huh*," the little one repeated, breaking loose.

"Come on, fellas," said Cindy. "Let's get back on the swing."

"I want to see what kind of a mousetrap," said Robbie.

"I do, I want to see it," said his little brother. "What *is* it?"

"No, you are not going to see a mousetrap."

"I want Grandma."

"She's not going to take you to see the mousetrap."

"Where is she?"

"She's coming back out in a minute."

"I'm going up to Grandma's room. She said I could."

"I'll take them," Diana said, getting up, but Gerda was already coming down the path.

We had finished toasting some time before; we had finished hearing the long story of how our father and Gerda had met at

Karen's table and Cal had known that night not just what Karen and Lois had figured out in the afternoon, that they must meet, but that they would marry. Yes. Cal could have sworn to that before dessert. "It's true he predicts things," Karen said. "He predicted Bobby Kennedy's assassination. But seriously, no, it's almost always good," she said, raising her glass unsteadily to Cal. The sons had made little speeches, Bobby's filled with jokes and Glen's with quotations.

Diana wanted Gerda and Dad to tell what went through their minds at the first sight of each other. "I thought . . . I can't really say what my first thought was," our father said, and blushed, and we all laughed at that. The jokes about the shotgun wedding had petered out gradually as we looked at them.

Gerda said, "I thought, he's *good*. Oh, and of course I thought so many other things. Over the evening. Everything just had to sink in."

He agreed with that.

Mosquitoes had begun to whine. Becca held out her darkly tanned arm and said they never bit her. Glen, with his short-sleeved shirt and pale skin—the skin of his father?—was their chosen prey, and after much slapping had gone to put on another shirt as Mrs. Burney was bringing out dessert. She wore an apron stenciled with MARRIED FOR HER PIES. She had lingered as we cut and ate them, trying to get Mr. Burney to go in with her. He had remained outside the whole time, hauling an archway made of varnished branches from the shed and securing it at the base with rocks and pegs.

"I'm so sorry about the mousetrap," Mrs. Burney said. "Usually there's no need, because there's an owl. Well, we'll be going in. You have your celebration."

"Why don't you sit with us and have some of this lovely wine?" Karen said.

"No, no, we'll leave you with the family."

"Well, just for a minute," said Mr. Burney.

"Tomorrow is a big day," said his wife.

"I'm going to see the mousetrap," said Robbie.

"Three blind mice," said the little one.

Karen looked up. "Did you ever notice they ran *after* the farmer's wife, not away from her? After she cut off their tails with the carving knife?"

"We won't get into that," Cindy said.

"Wait, listen to this, anyway," Diana said. "I want to read something. Shelley found this great book in the cabin."

"They're in all the cabins," Mr. Burney said. "Lifetime supply."

"Just listen to this while I can see to read," Diana said. "'If you have been long away from the sound of the Western Yellow Pine'—that's the ponderosa, Shelley says—'you may, when at last you hear it again, close your eyes and simply listen, with what deep satisfaction you cannot explain, to the whispered plainsong of this elemental congregation.'"

"Ah," said Gerda and Dad together.

"I don't see how you can call that a whisper," said Glen. Drink had rendered him morose. But I was glad to think of the trees as a congregation, instead of pillars weighing tons, swaying overhead.

"*Plainsong*," Bobby corrected his brother from the ground, keeping his eyes shut.

"What do you think?" Diana asked Gerda, closing the book with a flourish.

Gerda said, "I don't know. I don't know how I thought I could live anywhere else but in the Northwest. I don't know about anything. I don't know how anything that happened, happened."

"We do love these trees," said Mrs. Burney dreamily into the silence that gathered as we considered all that had happened.

"We should be like trees," Karen sang out in a boozy voice. "Know who said that? Thoreau said that. Separate individuals. Individualism! He should see us. Look at this war. Look at our trash. Look what we do to the Earth."

After some thought, Gerda said soberly, "The Earth is our mother," as if she had never heard of the Sixties, and all their precepts that were now comedy, and perhaps she had not, married and a mother at eighteen. "All I know," she said, turning to Dad, "is that I met you."

"To matrimony!" Mr. Burney stumbled in Gerda's direction, glancing off the tree trunk as Mrs. Burney leaned forward to catch the bottle from his hand.

"Diana tells me we have two veterinarians," she began, already pouring for Gerda. Gerda knew how to drink. She kept it up with no perceptible effect. Maybe she was like Eddie's brother's bride, who just knew how to be happy. "And one works with cats?" Mrs. Burney pressed on as her husband settled into a squat. "We love cats. But oh, dear, we can't keep one here. We did have a little cat Mitzi. Coyotes . . . And then we've had bears."

"I almost thought Eddie would show up," I said, as the word *bears* hung in the air. "Because he likes Dad so much and he would have loved to meet you, Gerda."

"How would he get here, you have his car," Karen said. "She broke up with Eddie," she added to Gerda.

"I'm sorry to hear that," Gerda said, and the eyes touched me again with their almost musical sorrow and benevolence. I could see how my father might have been hypnotized into thinking there was a heaven after all. "But nothing's written in stone," she added.

"No indeed," said Dad. I noticed Gerda didn't encourage him when he spoke, the way the rest of us did. She had sat down and leaned on him. Some of the toasts had been long, and made him blush and even bend over in a kind of pain at the things being said of him. Every once in a while she had laid her hand on the small of his back, the way he had done with her during the introductions. He smiled. I saw that he had withdrawn even deeper into his happiness than he had into his unhappiness, now broken in on and honorably banished.

Was that smile the proof that nothing up to now had really been meant as we had taken it, Shelley and I? Could we have said to wasteful memory, or in my case lack of memory, "The deal is off," could we have taken a giant floating stride across the chasm of what was only, after all, the disappearance of one person?

"I guess that settles it about the t-e-n-t," Cindy said to Bobby, who had fallen asleep on the ground with his mouth open. "Animals." Bobby sat up and looked around.

"What about animals?" said Robbie. "Where?"

"Oh, we're quite safe here." Mrs. Burney stood up and went over to where Mr. Burney was sitting with his back propped against a tree. "Let's go back, your show is on," she said.

"Guess I better go in," he said. "Better do that. Leave the ladies alone."

"Goodness, Garvin," she said. It was hard to see how he was going to get up, and he didn't. After a minute she made a little steeple of her hands and said, "Well, everybody, just enjoy yourselves. You just—enjoy the evening and the stars." We all looked up, and the sky was spread with stars where none had shown themselves minutes before.

"Wait," said Mr. Burney, putting his elbows to the tree trunk and finding the muscles that would take him to a standing position. But he wasn't leaving. "For it is customary. On the night before the nuptials. That I say a few words." He threw his head back and surveyed the sky, as Mrs. Burney, in a kind of languor, took a backward step and then another. "It is," she said. "He does."

"I know she had you in there for her little talk. And I would hope, I would *hope*, that you listened. Because she knows what she's talking about. That's a fact. But let me tell you—here—" He leaned close to our father, got his balance and said in a stage whisper, "Don't worry!" He clapped our father on the back. "See, *getting along?* Don't sweat that. First place. It's not her you're dealing with, my good friend. It's not him, fair lady. Nope. It's life. You may not know, or like she'll tell me when we get inside, maybe you do know: *life*—is a thing—all to itself." Here Mrs. Burney fished in her apron pocket and handed him a paper napkin. He mopped his neck and flourished the splint. "I won't say—what I could say—about *that*."

Other than me, only his wife and Gerda had their eyes on him; everybody else was looking at the place where the campfire would have been if there had been one. "Just get ahold, oh, you already did it, you're way ahead of me, get that little hand in yours and say, 'Hey! I'm gonna hold on.' Whoever it is on the other end. Some mean stuff is gonna come your way. Even at your stage of the game. So what you do is, you hang on. 'Know what I'm saying?' as our son used to say. That's what you do."

"He means love," said Mrs. Burney.

"Rose, Rose, I said what I mean. Would you say"—he bowed to Gerda—"I said what I mean?"

"I'd say so," said Gerda. "But Rose is right."

"I would not argue. Rose is right. We can agree on that. Some would say that I on the other hand could be wrong. Where, you may ask, did he get his information?" Here I think Mrs. Burney could have stopped him but she spoke not a word. "Experience, that's where. We lost a kid. That, I will not go into. But. Gone." He tried to snap the fingers of the splinted hand. "The best kid, the best of the lot."

"There's no best," said Mrs. Burney without conviction.

"Rose, Rose. So ladies, gentlemen, keep the faith. Drink up. Tomorrow you will attend the nuptial vows of this fine pair."

"Hear, hear," said Diana, knocking back her wine.

"I'M SORRY," I said, "but what is up with her?" Shelley and I were in her cabin, talking in the dark. Diana had been gone for an hour.

"Jen, for God's sake. She does that. She goes out. She runs around." Shelley had her eyes shut to keep the room from spinning. "She's *promiscuous*." She said it the way a mother says of a kid, "He's active."

"But . . ."

"That's the way she is."

"I see, she doesn't mean anything by it."

"Not that. It's just something to know about her."

"All right," I said. Shelley was possessive. This I did remember. For years, in the evenings when we came home from Karen's, she would make our father sit by her on the couch.

"She doesn't lie," Shelley offered.

"What's so great about that?"

"Wait, I better stand up. Better lean." She went over to the wall. "You didn't notice this before?"

"OK," I said when she opened her eyes again, "but it's Gerda she's coming on to. Her—her stepmother-in-law-to-be."

"Yeah."

"Right. But it makes me mad. How can she be a feminist?" I sounded like Karen.

"You're kidding."

"No."

"A feminist? Not interested. No interest. *Nada*."

"I see."

"Look, her father was in jail. Her mother was an orderly in Cook County Hospital. Sold pills, messed herself up."

"I do see."

"So Diana was in foster care, she was in group homes. The rest of the kids in the family are all still doing that stuff. And she's out there doing . . . a lot of what she does is pro bono. She's a good person, Jenny. See, she's just . . ." She slumped against the wall, squinting at nothing.

I wished I could get up and play her "Beloved, You Looked into Space." But this was the way she used to be about the ladder and the gorilla, far from any remedy of mine.

"Oh, God. Those things are streaming. Those holes." She meant the knotty pine. "Whoa. They're going sideways. Fast. I hope I'm not going to throw up."

"I don't think you will. How much did you drink anyway?"

"Too much for the drug." She would always have to take something. I knew that, but I would forget. "Did everybody go to bed?"

"Not the Burneys, not Karen. They're in the parlor. Karen and Mrs. Burney are still at it. Stories. Burney's passed out in his chair. That was him playing the organ. Could you believe that? Did you hear?"

"Sorta. The high notes carry. That *vox humana.*"

Mr. Burney had sat down at the carved organ—actually Mrs. Burney had prompted him, though warning him about using his thumb, and we had steeled ourselves to listen—and pumped it full of sighs. This was around midnight, some time before Gerda and Diana went out to walk off the wine under the stars. He ran up and down the keyboard into "Come Rain or Come Shine," and threw in a line or two of the lyrics with his stage smile. Then he stopped and asked for requests. Gerda whispered to my father and he nodded. They wanted "Memories Are Made of This."

To my surprise, Mr. Burney was like Eddie: he could play anything, even without the use of his thumb. Of course he was going to croon this particular song in the voice of Dean Martin, but he couldn't completely obscure the organ, which ascended during the "sweet-sweet" passages into a high delicate region of its own. All the music of the Sixties that had belonged to them, people the age of our dad and Gerda—all those songs, and this was what they asked for, as if the time of their own youth had passed beyond use, the time of my mother and Karen cross-legged on the floor with their guitars, singing "It's All Over Now, Baby Blue" and "What Have They Done to the Rain."

Mr. Burney at the organ was like one of those collarless dogs you see in the city, panting and loping on an errand of its own. I wished Eddie could have been there to hear him, slouched over the keyboard and pumping away with his feet. And indeed the next day, with an amp set up on the porch, Mr. Burney would play Mendelssohn just as well as Eddie could have played it, for Gerda walking down the path in her pink dress with a son on either side.

"I don't know where Dad is now, maybe out looking for the bride," I said to Shelley. "Are you going to have a fight?"

"You can't fight with her. She gets enraged and then she cries. She'll cry all night. It clears her head." She gave me the helpless smile.

"Clears her conscience."

"The next day she's OK, normal. Here she comes."

"Shelley?"

"Yeah."

"Hey, don't get any ideas. Don't go up there."

"Where?"

"The tree house. Or anything. Anything to impress her."

Shelley knew how to climb without a harness. But she answered me, "Ha ha."

GERDA PULLED HER husband, who weighed a hundred and eighty pounds, out of the shallows of the river where he had rolled. His clothes were soaked and heavy. She could feel a pulse in his neck. She took off her shirt and tried to wrap the open shoulder. One sleeve of the shirt she took off was torn but she thought the blood was his. On the other side of him she found the artery under the dangling arm, crammed her rolled-up vest tight against it. Propping him with a rock under his shoulders she fixed the arm tight to the vest and bound the whole mess to his chest with fishing line. She pulled him a few yards by his collar and then afraid of choking him she ran to the cabin for the sleeping bag, got his legs in and worked it up under his back, picked up the other arm from the rocks and stuffed it in, and pulled the bag up the hill to the car. By stages she got him onto the floor in the back. How that was done she couldn't describe to Diana. Some way. She started the car and drove nine miles to town on a dirt road. How fast? Fast. She knew at a certain point that he had died. A girl on a bike directed her to a clinic, which was closed, and then the girl, who had realized it was a Sunday and followed on her bike, yelled how to get to the doctor's house. She saw the girl glance down at the blood on the car. The girl rode up onto the sidewalk and streaked away. She had the doctor out of his house when Gerda got there, a big old man coming down the steps with the Sunday funnies in his hand. He performed CPR. His wife ran out with his bag and stood with Gerda, who was wearing only a bra with her bloody jeans. The bike girl stood with them. The doctor pretended to do things to stanch the bleeding that had already stopped, and after a short time he got to his feet and began tending to Gerda's arm.

All of this Gerda told Diana because Diana asked.

So of course Diana asked about the bear. The bear's eyes had no whites. They did not seem to be open very wide. The heat coming off the head and neck had a smell—no, there was nothing to compare it to. The broken teeth dripped a foamy red spit. The nose, the nose was the worst, two holes like toilet plungers. Yes, she could remember. She could remember everything. The whole time, she kept talking at the top of her voice to the lump on the ground. Of what? Of love.

Where did a marriage like this begin? This Diana failed to ask. What was the source of it, what made it get underway and continue and become a mighty thing?

At one point, at the car but not in it, he woke up. He was far gone, not in his right mind. It was hard to understand him. He said he wanted something salty. Could she give him something salty.

No one else, Gerda said, no one other than our father, had ever asked her about any of these things. People would tell her they had read it in the paper but that was it. Even her sons didn't ask. People cared, of course they did. But they didn't think she wanted to talk about it and they were right, she didn't. Yet she did. She had to admit it. She wanted to. She didn't want to join a group or anything like that. In a group, her friends told her, she would be safe. That's where it would be safe for her to talk. Both daughters-in-law said that. They said her sons were each attending a group, just dealing secondhand with the whole thing, their father in the jaws of a bear.

It was as if, Gerda said, as if . . . as if, if she were to talk in the wrong place, she would be in danger. Or somebody would. People let her know this without saying so. For a long time she felt as if she were up in a plane, at the controls, circling and circling. Bob was gone, the one who would have helped her land.

Then she met our father. Land.

And here she was pouring it all out again to Diana. "This isn't like me," she told Diana. It was the wine. It was night, trees, wind. John's wonderful family. No, she didn't cry, she just stood there in the dark with Diana, who had run out of questions. Diana's impulse was to put her arms around Gerda, but one of the things Gerda had said was that for a long time everybody did that when they saw her, everybody. People wanted to, as if for luck. That's when she first laughed, weakly, because Diana, who had done exactly that, said, "You must have felt like you should open a booth."

"That made her laugh." Diana was talking to Shelley, who at a careful walk had crossed the room to the little sink. "And oh my God you should see her arm."

"She showed you."

"Her shoulder and arm. Like a fork went down a cucumber."

Shelley had turned on the tap in the little sink. The pipes gurgled and the tap spat until she turned it off.

"I should go," I said. I wanted to tell Diana to be careful what she said to Shelley. Shelley was not just anybody, a person you could tease and torment.

"Anyway," Diana said, "after what she went through describing the whole thing, it would have been like trying to hug somebody who had just come out of an operation."

"People do that with their dogs," Shelley said.

In the end Gerda said, "But don't worry, I won't do this, you won't have to say, 'Quick, hide, here she comes, don't let her get started.'" They began to laugh, both of them drunk, and laughed and stumbled as they walked back. Gerda asked Diana to forgive her for spilling out the whole thing like that, every bit of it. Diana said she was honored.

Diana said, "Shelley, I just happen to have been the right person for Gerda on this particular night. When she's leaving her old life behind. People tell me things," she added with a look at me.

"They do," Shelley agreed.

"It's not like I pump them."

"No," Shelley said.

I started to say something like maybe it was easier for Gerda to talk now that she had our father, now that the padlock was off the story, but Diana went on. "OK, so how come I bring that out in people?" She was throwing things out of her suitcase into the little rattling drawers, and it was true, tears shone in her eyes. "Maybe because I talk to them. Maybe because I don't just sit there staring into space. It's not like I go looking for these people."

"No evidence for that," said Shelley. Diana stopped unpacking and they faced each other.

"God damn it," Diana said.

"Well, goodnight," I said. "See you in the morning."

"'Night," Shelley said.

I climbed into the tall bed. I wished Eddie were there. I thought about what the chances were that he would find some transportation and get there. The room was hot and I threw off the fat comforter that he would have rolled himself up in, not caring that it was August.

How weak love was, dying of the weight of the covers if you let it. How weak it was at its birth. Eyelashes, hands on a piano. Could these become my father's mourning, Gerda's ax?

The wind had come up again, pine cones were banging on the tin roof and rolling off. I sat and looked out the window, which was so close I could have leaned my head on the glass. I could

see Shelley and Diana's cabin. The light was already out. I could
see the tree house. I had imagined Shelley climbing up there
drunk and desperate. But I was wrong, she had not done that. It
could be Diana had not meant, after all, to dare her to do it. Mr.
and Mrs. Burney were out there. She was winding greenery onto
the arch, he was shoveling ashes into a bucket. She still had on
the apron and it was flying up. She hunched over, and I thought
she was sinking her face in her hands because of his day of
drunken gallantries and the harsh way he had spoken to her,
when she was guilty only of trying to extract a kind of perfection
from the given materials, for our sakes. For the sake of a wedding, of all things. But she was only pushing the hair out of her
eyes and calling some question to him, while he leaned on the
spade a little distance away, facing the trees.

About the Author

VALERIE TRUEBLOOD grew up in Virginia, in then-rural Loudoun County. Before moving to the Northwest, she worked as a caseworker in Chicago and at the Folger Shakespeare Library in Washington, D.C. She has published essays, short stories and poems, as well as articles about nuclear weapons, and has worked for many years in the peace movement. She is a contributing editor to *The American Poetry Review*, and a co-trustee of the Denise Levertov Literary Trust. Her novel *Seven Loves* was selected for Barnes & Noble's Discover Great New Writers program. She lives with her husband Richard Rapport in Seattle and the Methow Valley. They have one son and have been married for thirty-eight years.